Redemption

BY

KC KEAN

Redemption
Featherstone Academy #61
Copyright © 2023 KC Kean

All rights reserved.
No part of this publication may be reproduced or transmitted by any means, electronic, mechanical, photocopying or otherwise, without the prior permission of the copyright owner.

Cover Design: BellaLuna
Editing: Zainab M. - Heart Full of Reads
Proofreader: Sassi's Editing Services
Interior Formatting & Design: Wild Elegance Formatting

Redmption/KC Kean – 1st ed.
ISBN-13 - 978-1-915203-35-9

Redemption isn't an act of service to another, it's a stepping stone on our journey where we become the very best versions of ourselves.

This is to you, on whatever journey you're on.

KC KEAN

I'm like a moth to the flame, and I'm not afraid of getting burned.

— Wren Dietrichson

ONE

Wren

My black leather boots splash in the puddles as I trudge across the pavement, my destination looming ahead. Nerves run through my body, zapping at my spine, even though confidence drips with every sway of my hips. With the oversized parka I have on, it's questionable, but fuck it, I know it's there.

I need every ounce of confidence I can muster after the visitor I had a few nights ago. I should have expected a quick turnaround on what they wanted from me, but I was still surprised by the message I received earlier.

The message that has me trudging through the city a

little after ten at night.

It feels like a lifetime since I've been in New York, even longer since I was last present in Richmond, Virginia. And between the two, the Big Apple sure feels safer.

Not warmer and certainly not drier, but here I am.

Thank God they sell umbrellas at the airport.

The neon light shining bright from across the road is enough to capture my attention. Despite its casual appearance from the outside, it's all luxury inside. High-gloss woodwork throughout, high-end liquor as a minimum, and an even higher level of clientele. All for the love and desire of a sex show.

I've never stepped foot inside, but my research told me everything I needed to know; this place is dripping in money.

Burlesque is my preference over an aristocratic sex club, but it's not my choice to be here. I didn't choose the location. I'm here to serve a purpose, and that's what I'll do, but a nice view is appreciated.

As I lower my umbrella, droplets of rain catch on my newly bleached locks. After a quick shake, I step into the open doorway.

Plush navy carpets soften the stomping of my boots.

With his black suit and white shirt, finished off with a bow tie, the doorman looks like a sophisticated maître d' at an upscale restaurant with a six-month waiting list. He doesn't seem to falter at the fact I bypassed the line of people desperate to get inside; instead, he greets me with a knowing smile teasing his lips.

"Good evening, Miss. How may I be of service?" he asks, lacing his fingers together behind him. I don't miss the widening of his brown eyes, or the way his forehead crinkles with curiosity.

"I'm here to meet someone. There should be a reservation confirmed under the name of Steele... or Featherstone," I add, uncertainty playing in my mind as I all but choke on the one word my entire family has revolved around for so long. Featherstone. A deceptively corrupt school for deceptively corrupt criminals that just so happened to be my home during my stay in Richmond.

My mind attempts to send me back to that fateful night almost six months ago, but I sink my teeth into my cheek, forcing myself to stay in the present.

The doorman swipes through the tablet attached to the podium beside him. He pauses a moment later, returning his gaze to mine. "I have a reservation under Featherstone here, Miss. Would you like to check your coat before you enter?"

With a nod, I hand over my umbrella before removing my coat, treating him to a full view of my revealing outfit underneath.

The doorman doesn't utter a word at my scantily clad figure, likely having seen more on stage than I'm displaying anyway. A black silk skirt that barely covers my ass, the smallest scrap of material for panties underneath, paired with a strappy crop top that resembles a bikini. With all the exposed skin, goosebumps tickle across my flesh, the AC chill making its presence known. With the addition of the black, heeled boots into the mix, I'm definitely going to fit in downstairs, and that's what matters right now.

Moistening my lips, I blink up at the doorman, who keeps his eyes on mine the entire time. He hands me a ticket before leading the way and I release a breath, readying myself for what is to follow. The black double doors leading inside open, a set of stairs stretching downward behind them, and I take my time following him, using the moment of calm to steady my nerves.

The soundproofing muffles the music coming from the other side of the doors at the bottom of the steps, and the doorman smiles at me before he pushes them open.

I'm assaulted with the sound of sultry dance music and dim lighting, but not too dark to be blinding, and I allow a small smile to form on my lips. The setting is... perfect.

The navy carpet continues from upstairs throughout the entire floor. A large glass and mirrored bar takes up the center of the room, seats circling around it, with a few tables and chairs dotted throughout the space. There are even a few secluded booths strategically placed, all of which have views of the exterior of the room.

Where the sins and pleasure play out.

There are at least six setups in place already, but my focus is more on the doorman leading me toward the bar instead of the shows.

It's surprisingly busy for a Thursday night. Tables are quite full, and a few spots at the bar are occupied as well. When I'm led to a seat at the bar, separate from any other patrons, I sigh in relief.

"When the rest of your party arrives, Miss, you'll be escorted to a booth," he informs me, pulling out a seat.

He doesn't wait around, not expecting a tip since the pay in this establishment is beyond the standard living wage. I know because I researched right down to that finer detail on the way over here. The fact that it's operated and run by Featherstone makes it even more intriguing.

As a nineteen year old, I shouldn't have a clue what any of this is, let alone what desires lie behind every door, but I'm a descendant of Featherstone, with a bloodline destined for a place like this.

I was groomed for it.

I was born for it.

I would die for it.

Or I was supposed to, but now, after that night and the mess that followed, I'm not sure what my purpose is anymore. It'll be whatever they tell me it is. More specifically, whatever *she* tells me it is.

After all the decisions I made, she chose to keep me alive, and that was definitely intentional. I have a purpose to serve. I was allowed to hide away for six months, get lost in myself as I figured out my life without my parents, but I wasn't foolish enough to think it would last, so now, it's time to step up as is required of me.

After placing my cell on the pristine black bartop, I cross my legs, getting comfortable in my seat. Mirrors run around the edging at the top and bottom of the bar, as well as behind the bottles of liquor. It almost stands in the center of the room like a disco ball, projecting light across the entire space as the sensual music plays and the sound of moans and groans bounce off every wall.

The bartender signals that he'll be just a second, and I offer a nod in response. Distracted by my phone vibrating on the counter, my eyes immediately drop to it. Quickly unlocking it, I skim through the text.

Luna: Targets confirmed. I'm trusting you, Wren, and we both know I shouldn't. I have men on the ground if your safety becomes an issue. Don't make me regret giving you this chance.

I had a feeling she would have eyes on me, waiting until I was seated and in place before reaching out. She shouldn't trust me. Well, not the version of me I was six months ago.

I was a bitch. I mean, I still am, but I'm not… heartless, driven by evil, and controlled like a puppet like I once was. No, now I have no fucking clue who I am. Gone is the caramel hair, stone-faced expression, and the desire to slaughter anyone and everyone in my path. In its place is the platinum blonde I'm slowly becoming accustomed to, a forced smile that gets a little less fake every day, and only cravings of a sexual nature thrums through my veins. The murderous kind is on the back burner.

I'm attempting to piece some form of life together, and this is where it begins.

With a quick response, I confirm my understanding before situating the phone back to its place. I'm here to do a job. The better I focus, the quicker I can get the fuck out of here.

The drinks menu is within arm's reach, so while I wait for the bartender to appear, I peruse the list of cocktails. Sitting in a Featherstone establishment, under a Featherstone reservation, no one is going to question my age, so I'm making the most of it. But all the cocktails sound far too sweet and cutesy. I need something strong and sharp to relax the nerves warring within me.

When I sense a presence approaching on the other side of the bar, I look up to see the smile of the blond-haired bartender. He has a dimple to the right of his mouth, soft, full lips, and piercing blue eyes. Any girl's wet dream, but he's far too delicate for me. I like a man with a hint of mystery in his eyes, who radiates power in his every stride, and gives off a complete *fuck you* vibe. This guy has none of that.

"Good evening," he murmurs, placing a yellow and red cocktail before me, topped off with a little umbrella and neon green mixer. My brows scrunch at the choice of drink, and I wait for him to continue. "A gift from some patrons," he adds in explanation, but the wrinkles on my forehead only deepen.

"Do I get to know where these patrons are, and why they'd assume *this* is what I would opt to drink?" I ask, disbelief evident in my tone as I raise an eyebrow at him.

"Feisty. I like it," he retorts. *I'm sure you do.* It's with great effort that I don't roll my eyes at him. "I'm not saying they're sitting in the booth directly behind you, staring this way to see what you do, but I'm also not *not* saying that, if you know what I mean." He finishes with a wink.

Wow. Just wow. Can this guy stop talking already?

I rake my teeth over my bottom lip, forcing every snarky response down like a hard pill before I finally respond. "I understand. And the drink? Am I supposed to just accept something I don't want?" I tap my finger on the bartop, watching as he peeks at my breasts before finding my gaze again.

"You can switch it for whatever you like," he advises,

running his fingers through his hair, and a smile spreads across my face.

"Perfect, I will take a shot of Sambuca and a bottle of water, please. Actually, make that two shots," I order, spying the bottle behind him in one of the stands. It was always available at the parties on campus at Featherstone Academy, and I haven't had it in forever.

He takes the cocktail away, fixing my order, and I sense eyes burning into my back, assessing my every move. I don't want to turn and look at them, not yet, but my gut knows it's exactly who I've been sent here for.

A moment later, the bartender returns with two shots and a bottle of water, and I offer a tight smile in thanks.

Focus on what you're here to do, Wren. It's exactly what you've trained for your entire life.

With that thought in mind, I down one shot, letting the liquor burn my throat, shortly followed by the other. A satisfied smile stretches across my face as I grab the bottle of water. Rising to my feet, I turn on my heels with purpose.

My eyes flash as I catch a glimpse of my admirers. Yup, it's them. Every single one of them.

I have their attention without even trying, and that

makes the sultry glint in my eyes brighter as my sensual grin widens.

Tonight, they're mine.

TWO

Matteo

"I don't give a fuck what they're saying, Vito, it's bullshit, and a move I won't take lightly," I snap, my hands clenching with anger. My brother nods in agreement, likely as pissed as I am, while my youngest brother, Enzo, shakes his head, wiping a hand down his face as he contemplates the situation.

Enzo may be the youngest, but he's also the brains.

I'm the eldest, with the ability to think fast, manipulate others to get what I want, and a venomous attitude toward anyone who tries to cross us. While Vito, the middle brother, prefers violence and talking with his fists—or blade, or any weapon necessary, really.

"Don't you think that seems too convenient, like someone's setting this up? Setting *us* up?" Enzo asks, undoing the top button of his shirt as he relaxes back into his seat in the booth. The luxury leather molds around his body as he gets comfortable—nothing but the highest quality for a Featherstone establishment.

What a fucking joke.

There are a lot of answers we've yet to uncover and far too many questions popping up every day, but we didn't travel all the way to New York from Italy for nothing. Although, while sitting at the table with my brothers instead of the Russians we were supposed to meet, I can't help but agree with my brother's thoughts. Unless Enzo is onto something.

"How?" Vito grunts, clearly on the same train of thought as I am. His shirt is already unbuttoned at the neck, his blazer slung over the chair placed at the opening of the booth we're seated in. His pristine white shirt almost shines with the lighting, which only serves to illuminate the scarring on his hands and neck.

"Why would the Russians call a meeting at a Featherstone property to begin with? Only to not show up when they were also promised so much by Totem?" Enzo asks, quirking a brow at me.

I tap my fingers on the table, mulling over his words. "I assumed it would be because they had some insider information, just like you two did," I murmur, appreciating the low volume of the ambient music so I can still hear myself think.

We've been eager for insider information for some time. Especially after Totem, a man feared even by name, wound up dead at Featherstone Academy, a school whose student body is strictly limited to criminal bloodlines. He had promised many people many things, all for it to disappear, along with his body as it rots in an unmarked grave.

"I know what you mean, brother, I just…" Enzo trails off, his jaw gaping open as he looks across the room toward the entrance, making me frown. He doesn't get distracted, not as easily as Vito and me, so what the hell could—

"Holy fuck." The words slip from my mouth like a prayer, my eyes glued to the wonder that is being led through the room.

It's like she's walking in slow motion—the sway of her hips, the flick of her hair, fuck, the swell of her breasts…

She's like a siren as she's being guided toward the bar.

We've been seated in the exclusive sex club for almost an hour, unwavering and uncaring of anything happening around us. On the stage across from us, a show plays out with a woman choking on some guy's cock while another fucks her from behind, all while he's also being fucked by a third man. They look like they're having the time of their lives, but it all melds into the background.

Not her though.

Definitely not her.

My cock stands at half-mast already, begging me to get over the issue with the Russians so I can relish in the feeling of myself under her, but this situation has been out of hand for long enough. We're now in the States, and we have to focus on resolving these issues while we're here.

"Is it my birthday? Because it looks like there's a present for me to unwrap," Vito murmurs, brushing his fingers over his lips with interest flicking in his eyes.

Fuck.

All three of us are like moths to a flame for the random beauty that just walked in. I don't blame them. She's dressed the part for the location, after all.

Is she hoping to indulge tonight? Experience pleasure

like never before?

Shit.

Falling victim to her body is far too easy, especially when she's wearing a strappy top that leaves little to the imagination. That black fabric against her pale skin makes my lips dry, the cut-out detail revealing the curve of her hips and teasing at what I can only imagine are the pinkest nipples on earth.

"Well, since the Russians aren't here yet, we may as well have some fun," Vito comments when neither Enzo or I respond, and I scoff, halting him as he moves to rise to his feet.

"I'd say she's caught everyone's attention, wouldn't you?" I state, refusing to lose out to my brother so soon.

Enzo chuckles, strumming his fingers on the table top as he glances toward me, his eyes lighting up as he realizes where my head is at. "Is our drinking game in order?" he asks, glancing at Vito for confirmation, who groans, not pleased at having competition, but always eager for some fun to break up the madness that is our life. Running the De Luca family isn't for everyone, but hell, the mafia life is in our blood, our souls, and it's our livelihood.

"It seems we need something, or *someone*, to distract

us from going on a rampage in New York right now. I'm in," Vito says, raising his hand and calling a waiter over.

"Good evening, gentlemen. How may I help you?" the waiter asks as he approaches, and a grin spreads over my lips. But before I can speak, Vito takes the reins.

"We'll take three beers, and your most popular cocktail for the lady in black at the bar," he orders, pointing to the vixen who has captured our attention. The waiter nods, not saying another word as he places our order on the tablet in his hands and walks away without a backward glance.

"I assume that means you're taking the cocktail section?" Enzo asks, eyes wide with excitement as he glances at me. "I'll take spirits with a mixer," he adds, laying claim to the next big category, and I groan, annoyed that I hinted at the game, only to be the last to select.

"Fuck, that leaves Matteo with what… beer?" Vito says with a scoff.

"Whatever, let's just watch," I grumble.

The aim of the game is to send a drink to someone we're all interested in. They can switch it out if necessary, choose whatever they want, and if it's within the category we selected, we get to make our move. It's as simple as that. I mean, there have been occasions where they've opted for a different brother, and we respect their decision, but fuck, it's fun to leave some things to fate.

Three beers are placed down in front of us, but none of us pay the waiter any mind, all of us focused on the woman who has captured our attention.

The bartender places a sweet-looking cocktail down before her, and I hate that her back is to us so we can't properly see what's happening, but hope pools in my stomach when the waiter takes the cocktail away moments later. Vito groans as Enzo chuckles. I do nothing, completely enraptured with her every move.

It feels like an eternity passes before the waiter returns, shot glasses in one hand and a bottle of water in the other.

What. The. Fuck?

"What the fuck do we do now?" Vito asks, but I pay him no mind as the bartender peers over at us. My breath falters in my chest, a response playing on my lips, but her next move has a smile spreading across my face and my thighs parting to accommodate my cock as it pulses with need.

"It seems that doesn't matter, because she's heading our way."

THREE

Wren

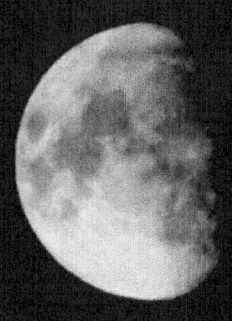

Of course they're fucking attractive. I shouldn't have expected anything less, but shit, with the dimly lit room, low music, and the moans and groans that swirl around me, it only seems to amplify how hot they are.

Squaring my shoulders, head held high, I aim my gaze in their direction. There are three of them. Three men who are undoubtedly related, with an air of arrogance emanating from them.

The man to the right looks to be the youngest, with mousy-blond hair that frames his face tucked behind his ear, making him look like a model. His grin is enticing, playful, and infectious as his brown eyes sparkle with a hint of mischief, observing my every move. He rubs his finger over his chin, his perfectly manicured hand making me wonder how skilled he is with them.

My eyes drift to the man in the middle, his brown eyes matching the guy's beside him, only they seem more calculated and mysterious. His jet-black hair is swept back off his face, except for a loose tendril that flicks down to his eyebrow. He swipes his tongue across his lips, drawing my gaze to the scar running top to bottom along the right side of his mouth.

What would it feel like under my tongue? It makes me bite my cheek to stop myself from pouncing on him.

Forcing myself to stay focused, I slow my steps so I have a chance to appreciate the guy sitting to the left of the booth. With his brown hair cut short and his eyes matching the others beside him, he assesses my every move with hawk-like interest. A shiver runs down my spine. He has 'don't fuck with me' vibes, and it makes my stomach clench. Even with the dark lighting, the scars marring the skin at the collar of his shirt are visible, but they only entice me further.

Three men, definitely related, with the same deep

brown pools for eyes, yet oh-so different.

Shaking my head, I berate myself for getting distracted, especially when I'm here with a job to do, but fuck, it's been far too long for me, and they're hot as hell.

Only two steps away, I let the smirk desperate to tease my lips take form as I come to a stop at the edge of the booth. There's a blazer on the seat before me, and I place my phone and bottle of water on the table before leaning against the chair.

The material has a soft and expensive texture to it, and as I glance at the guy to the left, the only one not wearing a jacket, I make sure to run my finger along the designer fabric, all the while his eyes trail even the smallest move.

"I don't recall ever seeing you here before," the guy to the right says with a grin as I turn to look at him, his eyebrow quirked as he feasts on my exposed body.

"That's because I've never been here before. My friend recommended this place to me while I'm in town," I lie through my teeth. I know for a fact these men have never stepped foot in here before either.

Glancing around the room, taking in the various sexual exploits on display, I rake my teeth over my bottom lip as I turn back to them. "I'm undecided on the vibe so far though," I add, shrugging, as my eyes fall to the guy in the middle.

"Well, you came to the right place if you want a good time, didn't she, brothers?" the mousy-blond replies, shuffling to the end of the booth and rising to his feet beside me. He swings his arm out to the side, offering me to slip into his seat, but I raise my eyebrow.

"I love a good time, but I don't accept drinks and take a seat with just anybody," I say with a smirk, extending my hand in his direction. "I'm Ava."

The name feels natural on my tongue. It's the one I've used since I left Featherstone Academy, and it offers me a new lease of life. No baggage, no bullshit parents, no fucked-up shit that I've done.

A new beginning, or so I'd hoped. That isn't what I got though, but I deserve what I get now.

Those are thoughts for another time. For now, my focus is on them.

"Pleasure to meet you, Ava, I'm Enzo," he responds, shaking my hand firmly yet gently at the same time.

He releases my hand as his brothers around the table rise to their feet.

"Matteo," the guy in the middle states, extending

his hand across the table, his hold lasting a split second longer than necessary as his thumb strokes gently over my knuckles. I shiver at the contact, and the small lilt to the corner of his mouth tells me he felt it. *Motherfucker.*

As soon as he releases my hand, I'm gripped by the third and final brother. His hold is stronger, purposeful, filled with intent as my gaze meets his. "I'm Vito. Ava, please, join us."

His raspy voice washes over me in waves, my body heating under their gazes as I nod in response.

"Thank you." The words are barely more than a whisper as I slip into the seat Enzo offered me.

My body brushes against his, the heat unmistakable as his fingers caress the swell of my ass in passing. I don't utter a word or lean into his touch, too busy trying to contain the fact that goosebumps have pebbled at that spot.

As I take the seat beside Matteo, Enzo drops down beside me, and they spread their thighs, touching mine.

Fuck.

I'm in so much trouble, I can already feel it.

"So, what are you in town for, Ava?" Vito asks, reaching for one of the beers on the table and bringing it to his lips as he waits for my answer.

"I was supposed to catch up with my friend I mentioned, but her flight was canceled, so now I'm here for the next three days. Alone. Unless she can make it out here before my flight home," I explain, overdoing it slightly, something that makes me cringe on the inside but is necessary to the cause.

They nod in sync before Matteo stretches his arm out behind my head, drawing my attention toward him. "It's such a shame that a beautiful young woman like yourself has been left alone in such a big city."

"It's not a new situation for me, I like my own company. Relying on others seems like the perfect way to head straight for disappointment anyway," I reply with a shrug before leaning across the table to grab my water. No one speaks as I take a sip of the cool drink, but I sense the glances that pass between them.

I may be acting under a different name, but what I say is the truth, and they seem to agree.

"More importantly, how familiar are you with an establishment like this?" Enzo asks from my left. I place my bottle on the table, turning in my seat to face him better, which only pushes me closer to Matteo.

Fucking focus, Wren.

"I visited them a few times in college, but it's been a little while," I reply with a smile.

Featherstone Academy counts as a college, right? I was eighteen when I used to attend the parties held by the Byrnes, and fuck did they put on a show—orgy?—whichever way you looked at it, they were as decadent as any sex club.

"And what intrigues you? What draws you in?" Matteo asks, his fingers trailing over the exposed skin at my shoulder, dragging along my collarbone and making the hairs on the back of my neck stand with anticipation.

His lips are close to my ear as he plays with my body so innocently, yet so explosively.

"I love sex, in all shapes and forms. The feel of desire coating your skin, heat building in your core, curiosity inching you closer. It's electric. And all from one body touching another, or multiple. Everyone is searching for the same end goal. No politics, no opinions or judgment. Just pure, raw need." The words slip from my mouth like a prayer, and I could swear one or more of them groan, but I couldn't pinpoint who, my own words turning me on as I think about them.

"So tell me, do we have to draw straws between the

three of us to get closer to you, to explore *that* side of life with you?" Enzo asks, inching closer as he tucks his fingers under my chin, forcing my gaze to meet his.

"Just one?" I ask, beaming at him, tilting my head to the side inquisitively. "I prefer men who are prepared to make a decision, Enzo. Right or wrong, that kind of power and decisiveness is ecstasy to see," I purr, watching his pupils widen and his jaw tighten in a mixture of surprise and need. "I thought I signed up for that when I came over here, that's what lured me in, but maybe I was wrong, and maybe this is a mistake," I add, unable to stop myself as my need for them intensifies.

Fuck the job.

Fuck the eyes I know will be watching.

Fuck it all.

With the two shots of Sambuca swimming in my veins, I'm more than happy to let my inhibitions melt away.

"Fuck. That," Matteo growls at my ear, and in the next moment, hands grip my waist from behind half a second before I'm lifted into the air and placed in his lap.

With my back flush against his chest, his lips against the nape of my neck, I freeze for just a moment before relaxing into his hold.

"Challenge accepted, *Bellissima*," Vito murmurs from the other side of Matteo, before grabbing my chin in a firm hold, eyes burning into mine, waiting for me to back out of the challenge I presented. But that's never going to happen.

Ever.

His eyes stare so deeply into mine that it feels like he's committing every spec of my iris to memory before his lips descend on mine.

Firm, demanding, intoxicating.

He dominates me, and I'm more than happy to let him. My hands lift to his neck, but just as one of my fingertips touch the scarring that marks his skin, someone else's hands grab my wrists, pulling me away.

My gut tells me it must be a hard limit for him, but it doesn't stop the power of his mouth against mine, our tongues dancing a rhythm like they've been in sync our whole lives.

With the way my arms are pinned to my chest, I assume it's Matteo who has a hold of them as his own band around me completely, the feel of his stiff cock beneath my ass only making me melt between them even more.

"Do you need us to pause and ask for permission at every point, Ava, or do you want us to just make the decisions—good *or* bad?" Enzo asks, repeating my own words back to me as Vito tears his lips from mine for a moment.

Dazed, I tilt my head in his direction, quirking my brow at him.

The smirk on his face widens as understanding grows between us.

He's offering me another decision and I want him to just take it.

Enzo trails his calloused fingers up my thigh, my skin eliciting once more with goosebumps as he nears my core, but just before he feels my heat, Matteo interrupts.

"Vito, make the booth private. Now," he barks, his voice gruff in my ear as I frown in confusion.

"Isn't the whole point of a sex club to experience everything together?" I ask, my chest heaving with every breath. The appeal of more than one guy has always lured me in, and now is certainly no different. If anything, I need it more than ever.

"When you fall apart, *Stellina*, I want it to be for our eyes only," Matteo mutters against my ear, and I almost explode with the way the language rolls off his tongue so effortlessly. Between him and Vito, I've got no chance of surviving this.

Without further ado, Vito pushes the table out of the space effortlessly before reaching for each end of the booth, and the two privacy walls extend out of each side.

Excitement courses through me as Vito turns to face me.

"Luckily for you, Ava, between the three of us, we're each into our own things, and you're about to experience them all." Enzo drops to his knees before me, his gaze focused on the tiny scrap of material covering my pussy.

My mouth dries in anticipation as Matteo releases his hold around my body before dragging his large hands down my arms, dusting over my skin with precision. His fingers lace with mine as he lifts them up over my head, holding me in position.

The move juts my chest forward, the material covering my breasts doing little to cover my nipples as Vito moves back into his spot beside me again.

"Matteo loves to restrain," Enzo murmurs, his fingers making their way up my thighs as he gestures to the hold his brother has me in, and I gulp. "Vito loves…" He doesn't finish his sentence as the brother in question grabs the string behind my neck and pulls the material, my breasts spilling out before him.

"Pretty pink peaks," Vito mutters, finishing his brother's sentence, before he dives forward, engulfing my nipple with his hot mouth.

Matteo's chest rumbles against my back, a laugh playing on his lips at the way my body immediately bows to his brother's touch.

"And I love... this," Enzo finishes, rounding out the desires for the three of them by slipping my panties to the side and plunging two fingers into my needy cunt, making my hips buck up out of Matteo's lap. "Fuck. Especially when you're bare, *Bella*," he adds with a groan, swirling his fingers deep in my core as he lifts the hem of my skirt higher.

A breeze caresses my clit, my body clenching with pleasure, before Enzo cuts the distance between his mouth and my detonator, raking his teeth over the small bundle of nerves.

"Holy fuck," I hiss, my eyes rolling back in my head as Matteo keeps me pinned against his chest. He may not be touching me like his brothers, but the grip he has on me is only intensifying what Enzo and Vito are doing to me.

"Louder, Ava, I can't hear you." Vito nips at my flesh,

watching for my reaction as I gasp, riding the fine line between pain and pleasure, and loving every moment of it.

"Give me more and I'll happily turn it up a notch," I retort without missing a beat, a fire from my belly igniting like I haven't felt in forever. His eyes darken at my challenge, and it excites me further.

Thank God there's music playing in the room, but fuck, I know people will still be able to hear me. Not that I care right now, not more than chasing the orgasm that's already tingling through my veins.

Enzo's fingers dig into my thighs as he feasts on my core, determined to leave bruises in his wake, while Vito latches on to my nipple once more, but this time, it's so hard I'm sure his teeth touch around my hot bud. A cry rips from my lungs at being unable to hold back my shock at the pain, but I fucking asked for it. As soon as the noise stops at my lips, he laps his tongue over the wounded area, twisting every inch of pain into need burning inside my core.

"Fuck," I whimper, my head falling back onto Matteo's shoulder as I tilt my gaze to look up at him. His eyes are on me as he watches me with a mixture of contentment, confusion, and enjoyment.

Before I can even consider asking him what's going through his head, he brushes his nose against mine and whispers against my lips, "My brothers are going to bring you to the edge, and I'm going to swallow each and every one of your cries of pleasure."

Slack-jawed, I stare at him with a mixture of surprise and excitement before his lips capture mine.

In complete sync, Enzo grips my thigh with one hand, fucking my pussy with his other as his mouth consumes my folds and clit, playing me perfectly. All while Vito snaps his teeth from one breast to the other, quickly following with a stroke of his tongue and spinning my world into near darkness as everything my body feels brings me closer to climax.

Matteo's hands tighten on mine, my knuckles hurting from the grip as he claims my mouth, and when Enzo bites my clit in time with Vito at my nipple, I can't take anymore.

The world goes dark, my body exploding all the way from my toes right to the ends of my hair as my groans and cries of ecstasy are, indeed, swallowed by Matteo. Enzo's tongue drops to my center, lapping up every drop of my release as my hips grind against his face.

None of them relent until they've wrung me dry, my

body limp in Matteo's hold as he slowly lowers our hands. My shoulders groan in protest, but I don't utter a word as my eyes fall to Vito, who sits beside me, swiping his thumb over his bottom lip like he had the most delectable meal of his life.

Enzo's fingers stroke circles on my thigh, drawing my attention toward him as my chest heaves with each breath. I lean forward instinctively, the button of his pants calling me closer, but Matteo reclaims my hand, pressing a soft, delicate kiss at the crook of my neck.

"This was about you, *Stellina*. Maybe next time, we can make it about us," he murmurs in my ear, his brothers nodding as I try to catch my breath.

How the fuck are these men completely selfless in a moment like this? I would expect them to want something from me, make demands, but here they are, hinting at another encounter as I scramble to recover from this one.

This is your chance, Wren. Don't fuck it up.

The internal reminder has me smiling at them appreciatively as I shake my hands out of Matteo's hold and quickly tie the back of my strappy top once more. The three of them watch me but don't utter a word, not even when I rise to my feet and open the privacy board Vito closed.

I sag with relief when I see my phone is still on the table where I left it, and I grab it quickly, pulling the case off to reveal what I have inside. Taking a deep breath, I stand taller and turn to face the three of them once more, their looks filled with curiosity, desire, and apprehension. For what, I don't know, but now isn't the time to ask.

"Maybe next time, it can be about all of us," I offer, taking a step toward Enzo and offering the card in my hand with my name and number on it.

Without missing a beat or waiting for a response, I turn on my heels, my legs still like jelly as I head for the exit. It's only once I'm through the double doors that I unlock my phone and send the message I know they've been waiting for.

Wren: Tracker given.

REDEMPTION

FOUR

Wren

Sweat drips down my spine as I tussle in the sheets, my brain slowly gaining consciousness, but the air conditioning must have turned off in the night because there's no way it was this damn warm when I initially plunged into darkness.

Blinking my eyes open, I frown, glancing around the room as I get my bearings and remember where I am.

New York.

It's taken me nearly six months to settle into falling asleep in Philadelphia, where I've been biding my time until Luna called upon me, so waking up somewhere new again is wreaking havoc on my pounding heart.

The memory of last night washes over me, and I flop back onto my pillow with a sigh. Scrubbing my hands down my face, I hold back everything and anything that might take me back to the club, forcing myself to sit up and get out of the bed.

I don't do well with overanalyzing everything in bed. It's always been a process for the shower, and now is no different. Instead, I focus on taking stock of the room, moving over to the floor-length window to my right, looking down on the city in all its glory.

It's a little after eight in the morning, which explains the heavier-than-usual rush hour traffic. My suite's altitude is so high that everyone looks like ants, unaware of my prying eyes.

I can't help watching people these days, wondering what is going on in their lives, what brought them to this exact place, at this exact moment. Analyzing other people rather than delving deeper into myself is more preferable anyway. Acknowledging that fact alone proves that self-therapy works. I'm healthy and stable. Self-aware, even.

Ha.

Turning back to face the room, I take it in properly.

I barely spent ten minutes in here when I first arrived last night, dumping my suitcase and changing into my revealing outfit in minutes before leaving again. And when I came back, I was so worn out from the orgasm and the attention of the De Luca brothers that I barely wiped my makeup off and got into my pajamas before crashing into a deep sleep.

There are two queen-sized beds, each with bedside tables on either side of them. A small walk-in closet to my right, opposite the beds, and a bathroom near the door. The sheets are a crisp white, the walls a pale gray, and the carpet a rich navy. With the missing cringy colors of red and gold, it's obviously not a Featherstone hotel, and I'm thankful for it.

Pushing my hair back with a sigh, I head for the bathroom, desperate to shower and spend five minutes reliving what happened last night. As I pad across the plush carpet, I hold back the desperate need to throw myself on the bed and literally feel last night at my own touch, but I manage to make it to the bathroom, shutting the door behind me and quickly turning the knob for the shower.

As the water heats, I observe my frame in the full-length wall mirror. My platinum blonde hair barely grazes my collarbone, making it difficult to do anything with, including piling it on top of my head like I'd grown accustomed to.

My arms are leaner and more muscular than they used to be, my exercise and training routine getting me through most days. I'm a far cry from the girl I'd been at Featherstone Academy. I participated in the necessary classes there, like Combat, because I was required to, but now... now I actually enjoy it. The burn, the power, the physical contact. All of it.

Yet another thing I *have* to be grateful to Luna for, or her father, Rafe, I guess. It's his gym I'm allowed to sneak into at night.

Shaking my head, I strip out of my tank top and shorts, discarding them at my feet before slipping into the shower. The bathroom isn't huge, but the white tiles make it less dingy since there are no windows in here.

The moment the water hits my skin, I tilt my head back, my body sagging with relief beneath the power of the spray. I stand stock-still for a few minutes as the water cascades over my body before I finally relent, letting my mind drift to last night.

Matteo. Vito. Enzo.

The De Luca brothers.

The whole reason I'm here, my attempt at fucking redemption, yet they have the ability to get under my skin. Corrupt me.

When Luna explained why I needed to plant a tracker on them, I ran through every scenario I have been taught at the academy. I was literally trained to infiltrate, corrupt, embezzle, everything. You name it, I mastered it.

My whole plan was to blend in at the club, my outfit doing most of the work, and possibly get a chance to flirt with them. I had two trackers on me: one on the sole of my shoe, ready for me to pass on if needed, and the other in the form of a business card with my details on it.

If I'd gotten nowhere last night, I would have tried another approach today. That had been the plan at least. But I didn't factor *them* into it at all.

Not one single bit.

And that was a complete rookie mistake on my end.

No one can prepare you for three hot brothers, each with the same mysterious brown eyes, a roiling storm brewing behind them, yet each of them bringing something different to the table.

Matteo is clearly the oldest, and their leader. It's visible in his eyes when he's looking at you, trying to break down how he can get into your mind and under your skin. I can't imagine it being too different when he meets his enemies. Everything is a puzzle, one of great importance, and something tells me he never loses.

With his cropped hair, scarred neck, and sharp jaw, Vito screams enforcer. If anyone is going to hit flesh with flesh, it's him. He moved with purpose, experience, and determination. Even when he gripped my chin and claimed my mouth, I felt the power behind him, and I fucking loved it.

Enzo. The youngest, the one with the softest eyes, mischievous grin, and calculating brain. He has an ability to knock you off guard, to make you forget who it is you're actually dealing with, and that's a strong fucking trait to begin with. His calm aura hides the mafia monster who lives behind the curtain, one I'm sure has made an appearance or two in his lifetime, but doesn't show up as often as his brothers' monsters.

The De Luca family, all the way from grand old Italy. I know why they're here. Even before Luna caught me up to speed on everything, I knew. They're here for answers. For an explanation as to why they haven't received everything my father promised them. I'm sure they're aware of his death, but that means nothing to men like them. Once something is promised, in their mind, it's theirs already.

Fuck.

The water drenches my hair, and I swipe my hands down my face, clearing the water droplets with the motion.

This is all such a fucking mess. I shouldn't have let things go so far last night, but I was a prisoner to my own body. It was never part of the plan, but a few seconds in their presence and I was a melting pool of desire and need.

It was uncontrollable.

It was passionate.

It was everything I didn't know I needed.

I haven't felt so alive in a long time, not since I put a bullet into my father's body, ridding the world of his evil. But even before then, I was never truly living.

Reaching for the shampoo to wash my hair, I silently contemplate how I can move forward with the plan now. I made things complicated last night, and if Luna's eyes are half as good as I imagine they were in the club, she knows it too. But fuck, I would do it all again in a heartbeat.

The reality is that the presence of these men is unpredictable, and I need to get better control of myself before I fall headfirst into them. Which won't end well for anyone, especially me.

I have to take each day as it comes, work my ass off, and hopefully get the fuck out of here before the shit hits the fan. If I get to have a little fun along the way, then lucky me, but that's all this is. Fun.

With my new mindset firmly in place, I reach for the shower gel and wash my body, the lemony scent filling the space around me as I rinse clean. Switching the water off, I step out of the shower and reach for a gray towel, wrapping it around my body before grabbing a smaller one to pat my hair with.

The mirror is fogged up, steam billowing around me as I open the door and make my way into the bedroom. The instant change in the temperature sends a shiver down my spine, but I still cut the distance to my nightstand, grabbing the controller for the AC and flicking it on high. The noise of the machine kicking into action makes a small smile tilt my lips as my cell chimes beside me.

Luna's name flashes across the screen with an incoming message, but I decide to get dressed and check everything on my laptop before I circle back to it.

I reach for my suitcase sitting just inside the walk-in

closet and lift it onto the bed. There are a pair of yoga pants, a white tank top, and a red-and-black-checkered flannel shirt on top that I choose. Grabbing a white lace bra and panty set along with it, I pick out some thick black socks and zip the case back up.

Dried and dressed in minutes, I relax in comfy clothes that I've found a new appreciation for. Once upon a time, when I'd been ruled by my mother, I wore nothing but skimpy outfits and revealing clothes. Fuck, I'm sure she bought the outfit I wore last night. I was never able to wear what I wanted or express myself in a way that suited me. Everything was about the bigger picture—*their* picture, to be more specific—but now? Now I get to be whoever the fuck I want to be, and this bitch has a new obsession with comfortable clothes.

Reaching for my laptop, I take a seat on my bed, my back pressed against the headboard as I use the pillow as a lap desk. I take a few minutes checking the surveillance camera I installed outside of my room, followed quickly by the tracker for the business card I handed over to Enzo.

It really does look like a thick piece of cardstock, but inside is the thinnest tracking sheet I've ever seen. It's undetectable, not something they're going to notice on them. After what happened last night, it was definitely the safer option between the two devices I had.

It flashes The Ritz-Carlton Central Park's location, and a grin spreads across my face. They kept it. That's a good sign. Or they at least waited until they got back to their hotel to discard it.

A mixture of guilt and pride ripples through me. Pride in the sense that for once in my life, I'm doing what people with actual decent morals do. Well, as far as Featherstones go anyway, which is questionable on its own. But compared to working for my mother, the head of Featherstone Academy, and my father, Totem, the villain in everyone's story, it feels like a breath of fresh air.

Yet, at the same time, I feel some kind of connection to the De Luca brothers. The lie about my name twists in my gut, the fact that we're tracking them weighs heavy on my chest, and I don't know why. Guilt isn't an emotion I'm familiar with, not really, and I have no idea why I feel it after only spending such a short amount of time in their presence.

Fuck.

I can't delve further into that. Not until my next shower at least. For now, I need to see what Luna has to say.

Reaching for my cell, I click on the notification, but before the message appears on my screen, it's interrupted by an incoming call from an unknown number.

Well, it says unknown, but the way my heart skips a beat, I know exactly who it's going to be. Or I've at least narrowed it down to one of three.

Taking a deep breath, I let it ring a few more times before I lift it to my ear and answer. "Hello?"

"*Stellina*, I was worried you weren't going to answer the call and this was some fake number." Matteo's deep voice drips through the line, a hint of teasing in his tone catching me by surprise and making me beam all at once.

My teeth sink into my bottom lip, my thighs clenching together as I attempt to muster a response. "What can I say, Matteo? You left me on the edge of wanting more last night," I say with a smirk playing on my lips as he huffs.

"I believe it was you who left us wanting, *Bellissima*." Vito's statement sends a jolt through my body.

"I offered more, you declined," I state, short and sweet, and I can tell the chuckle that rings in my ears belongs to Enzo before he even speaks.

"*Bella,* we were being gentlemen," he soothes, and this time, it's my turn to huff.

"I don't recall meeting any of those last night. Thank God, because that's not what I'm looking for." My desire for the three of them takes over once more, no matter how hard I try to fight it. Subconsciously, the thoughts and words are just there and my filter has completely disappeared.

Silence greets me for a moment, like there's a private conversation going on between the three of them, before Matteo finally speaks. "I'm glad you said that, Ava, because I was hoping you would be free again tonight." My stomach twists, anticipation and excitement coursing through me as I try not to just scream yes. But before I can respond, Matteo continues, "If you only have two more nights left in the city, we want to be a part of your plans, *Stellina*."

Fuck.

Luna and everything I have going on with Featherstone plays in the back of my mind. The thought that this might be something for them has me balancing between saying yes or no, even though the intoxicating hold they have on me has me desperate to say yes.

"It isn't an offer, *Bella*, it's a demand," Enzo states, a hint of a grin flitting through the phone too. This motherfucker remembers every damn word I said last night. Including the fact I want a man to take the decisions away, and this is him doing just that.

"Give me a time and a place." My voice comes out huskier than usual.

"We will pick you up at seven, just tell us where to be." Vito, this time, and I immediately shake my head like they can see me.

"I like my own company, remember?" I force a smile to my lips, hoping it will convey through the phone. "I'll be wherever you need me to be, but no requirement to collect."

My eyes squeeze shut, worried they may push back and I'll have to relent, but thankfully Matteo hums in response. "At The Ritz-Carlton at Central Park, *Stellina*. Seven p.m. sharp," he barks before the call ends.

Holy fuck.

I know I'm playing with fire, but it seems I'm more than happy to get burned.

FIVE

Vito

My fingers flex at my sides as Matteo ends the call with the woman who has been stuck in my brain ever since we laid eyes on her last night. She was in my thoughts when we left the club, my dreams when I slept. She consumed my soul when I had to find my release in the shower this morning.

There's something about her. I can't pinpoint what it is, but it's alluring, intoxicating, and sinful.

Shit.

I really do need to feel her on my dick, then maybe I can get over it and focus on the task at hand: the Russians.

Grabbing my jacket off the sofa beside me, I slip my arms into the sleeves, looking between my brothers who are getting ready to leave too.

The Ritz is opulent, tasteful, and grand, which is exactly what we like, especially in the large suites they offer, which allows the three of us to be in the same place with our own rooms, with a large living space for us to share in the center.

"Fuuuck, my dick is so hard right now just hearing the sound of her voice. Are you sure we can't reschedule the meeting this morning and focus on our *Bella*, instead?" Enzo squeezes his dick, emphasizing the hardship he's dealing with, and I roll my eyes as Matteo slaps the back of his head.

"This isn't some love story, brother, it's a night of fucking, two at most before she leaves town, nothing more. We must remain focused." Matteo steps away from the seating area, moving for the door without waiting for a response from either of us.

I agree with him, one hundred percent, yet my gut tells me that it's not going to be that simple. Why…? I don't know. But I'm sure we'll find out eventually.

"I'm not saying it is, *brother*, I'm just saying I can still taste her on my tongue and—Ow!" Enzo's teasing words are cut short by Matteo smacking him upside the head once more, and I bite back the chuckle threatening to slip past my lips.

"That's not a conversation for right now. We have a meeting to attend, and I don't relish the idea of my cock being rock hard in my fucking pants the entire time," Matteo grumbles. I hiss, adjusting my half-mast dick.

What is she doing to us?

"Let's go," I grumble before I get too locked on the thought of her. If I don't focus on this damn meeting, I'll be storming back into the bathroom and finding my release once more.

I practically charge for the door, swinging it open with unnecessary force, but my brothers don't utter a word as they follow behind me. I pay no mind to the hallway at all as I punch the button for the elevator, thankful when it pings immediately and the doors slide open.

Stomping inside like a kid who lost his candy, I fold my arms over my chest and glare straight ahead, both Matteo and Enzo giving me a wide berth as they step into the elevator. The ride is passed in a comfortable silence as Enzo presses the button for the ground floor.

No small chit chat, no incessant need to fill a void, and no overwhelming urge to talk about some bullshit none of us actually care for.

The same silence continues as we avoid the main entrance to the hotel and take the back door the manager showed us when we first arrived. We prefer to be as discreet as possible, and one of the reasons we like The Ritz so much is for the simple fact they understand that.

We step outside toward a blacked out SUV, idly waiting for us, and a moment later, one of our men, Torres, slips from the driver seat and rounds the vehicle to open the door for us.

Matteo climbs in first, Enzo hot on his heels as I hold back, meeting Torres's gaze as I tuck my hands into my pants pockets. "Any updates?" I ask, short and blunt, but anyone who works for us has come to expect nothing more than that from me anyway.

"Nothing, sir. Everyone has been accounted for this morning and they've had nothing out of the ordinary to report," he explains. After the Russians didn't show last night, I had every single one of our men planted throughout the city call in. If there was anything going on that we needed to know about, I was hoping they would pick up on it. But in this case, it seems I'll have to ask the cunts outright myself.

I nod before climbing into the SUV with my brothers. They clearly heard the conversation but have nothing additional to add.

Torres takes off through the streets of New York like a mad man, or as mad as the traffic will allow him to be at this time of day.

Since they didn't show last night, it was only fair to reschedule for a time that was on our terms rather than theirs. Even if the early start makes me grouchy in the process. The new location is one of their choosing—a nightclub they own on the other side of Manhattan called Ivan's.

As we pass through the city, I stare blindly out the window, my mind replaying the taste of Ava's plump tits in my mouth, remembering the groans as I sank my teeth into her flesh. Fuck. She liked it, almost as much as me, and I'm beyond ready to see her tonight and do it all again, only this time, with my cock buried deep in her pussy.

I'm immediately pulled from my thoughts the moment I see the neon sign for Ivan's in the distance, any part of the yearning man inside me disappearing as I become the impenetrable, hard shell that is Vito De Luca.

It's a mask I've perfected wearing. One I sometimes forget to slip out of because it's become so natural to me. Matteo is the leader, stoic and calculated; Enzo, the playboy with a cheeky smile and a plan for success; while I'm the brutal, unforgiving scarred motherfucker that no one ever wants to get on the wrong side of, and I like it that way.

"Remember, no rash decisions," Matteo mutters, his face now void of emotion as he adjusts the cuffs of his shirt, twisting the cufflinks so they sit perfectly as Torres opens the door for us.

As I step from the SUV, I stretch my back, rolling my shoulders. The bright green lighting of Ivan's screams trashy to me, and the two doormen standing on either side of the glass entry tell every single person in eyesight that this is a Russian establishment.

We don't guard so obviously as this; neither do the Irish or the entire world that is Featherstone either. Just the Russians, because presence is power to them.

I don't acknowledge either of them as I step inside the building, the reality of the club with all of the lights turned on making it a lot less appealing than I'm sure it looks at night.

There's a dance floor in the center of the room, with a bar to the left, leaving a few tables and booths set up around the space for patrons to relax with their drinks. I ignore all of that, moving for the wrought-iron steps to the right that lead to the VIP area. Reaching the top, I find exactly who we're looking for sitting in the center of the small space at a large round table in the middle, with another bar to the back as well.

I'm surprised to see the two brothers, alongside their cousin, sipping on vodka like it's the perfect start to the day. The menace in their eyes is always clear, and the way they slink back in their seats instantly gets my tension high and war burning through my veins. Which is exactly why Matteo steps around me, taking the lead and approaching the situation much calmer than I would.

"Dmitri, Nikolai, Igor," my brother says in greeting as he approaches the table and takes the center seat on our side, facing directly across from Dmitri. He's the leader of the Volkovs. Nikolai is their equivalent to Enzo, the charmer and smart one, while Igor, their cousin, is as close to me as they'll ever get.

"De Lucas," Dmitri responds, tapping the wooden

table before him as he eyes the three of us, while Enzo and I take our seats. With Matteo to my right and Igor facing me, I can't help but be on high alert. Not that I show it. No. It burns deep within me and never on the surface.

"Where were you last night?" Matteo asks, a quirk to his brow as he stares them down. When a waitress appears, offering each of us a neat glass of clear liquor, I wave my hand dismissively and she takes the hint.

"We were occupied," Igor grunts with a shrug, like that will suffice, and I scoff.

"That's not good enough," I grunt, relaxing back in my seat like this is a casual PTA meeting with a kindergarten teacher instead of the dangerous and bloodied men who sit around the table.

Nikolai scoffs, a grin tilting his lips as he looks at me. "I hear you were busy yourselves, occupied by a pretty blonde."

My heart stills, confusion warring in my chest as I keep my expression blank. What the fuck does that mean? In a flash, my heart rapidly beats in my chest. She was either sent there by them or we've just put her in their line of sight, and either way, I don't fucking like it.

"She was a bit of fun in your absence," Enzo says

with a chuckle, kissing the tips of his fingers like a chef appreciating a fine meal. I only catch it out of the side of my eye though since my gaze is fixed on Dmitri and whatever words are going to spill from his lips next.

"So, you won't mind if I pay her a little visit at the New Yorker Hotel then, hmm?" he pushes, tapping his finger to his lips, and my blood turns ice cold.

She wasn't sent there by them last night, which is a huge relief, but the fact that they know who she is and where she's staying has my mind going into overdrive.

I shouldn't care, it shouldn't be my concern, but I can't stop the burning need to run to her and protect her from this level of danger that we're so used to, yet she's completely unfamiliar with.

Everything I said earlier was a lie. There's no fucking way I'm going to be able to fuck her and run, not when I'm reacting like this to her being on their radar. It's never our concern, *never*, and the bigger picture failed to occur to me. But I refuse to give them even the slightest opportunity to put their hands on what is *mine*.

Enzo laughs, a full belly chuckle, breaking the silence as he swipes at his eyes. "It's cute that you think we even know where she is since we parted ways last night."

That's a fucking lie right there, but thank God he has the ability to bullshit these people right now. The second she walked away from the table, we had two of our men tail her home, all the way to the New Yorker Hotel. Once we knew where she was staying and that she was there safely, we called them away again, but now I'm thinking that was a mistake. Maybe we need to order them back there. Even better, *I'll* go see her with my own two eyes.

Nikolai and Dmitri glance at each other while Igor keeps his gaze fixed on me, and I force a smirk to my lips, silently challenging him to God-knows-what, but to my surprise, he averts his gaze from me.

"Shall we get down to business? I really do have other things to be doing today, especially since we had to make such a last-minute adjustment for this meeting," Matteo states, lacing his fingers together as he places them on the table, and Dmitri nods.

"Of course. I feel it's high time we had a truce, put ourselves on the same page and figure out how we get exactly what Totem promised us," Dmitri grunts in response, lips pursing in disgust. Business we've been wanting to delve into for the past six months, yet I'm still fixated on the fact that they know where Ava is.

Fuck.

Fuck. Fuck. Fuck. Fuck. Fuck.

"He made a lot of promises when he took the reins of Featherstone, but none of that means shit with a bullet in him and no heart beating in his chest. It doesn't mean we don't deserve what he offered," Matteo replies, making all three of the Russians nod in agreement.

I wet my lips, mentally sinking into my chair, nowhere near as present as I'm supposed to be with my mind elsewhere, on *her*.

"Agreed. For us, that only means we have to take Featherstone down and take everything for ourselves. Unless, you want your cut as well?" Dmitri states, and I have to fight to keep my face neutral as I stare him down.

I know what he's hinting at. He wants us to work together, and that doesn't sit right in my gut. Never work with anyone who isn't in the De Luca line. The three of us, and the men we expertly choose, against the world.

I will never side with the Russians, not even in moments like this. I'm more than happy for them to have whatever Totem offered them, but they can't seriously step in here and expect us to fall in line and become their minions.

"That is something I can take into consideration,

Dmitri, but not something I can give you an answer to right away. Especially when there are finer details to discuss," my brother replies with the politically correct response. My answer of a downright 'fuck no' would have started a war before we left the building, and that's exactly why Matteo is the one to take care of the bigger picture. "I'm more than happy to stay and discuss this further with Enzo, but Vito has a package to collect," he adds, curiosity swirling in my stomach as I turn to face him.

He holds his phone out to me, and my eyes scan across the screen rapidly.

Smettila di far rimbalzare la tua cazzo di gamba. Andare. Colleziona Stellina.
Stop bouncing your fucking leg. Go. Collect Stellina.

Shit, I hadn't even realized I'd been doing it.

There's a glint in their eyes, one I don't like, one I know is going to bring more trouble than it's worth.

But right at this moment, my mind and body are focused on Ava. The woman who has the ability to seemingly turn my world upside down without even trying to.

I'm beyond fucked. And I don't even care.

REDEMPTION

SIX

Wren

Inspecting the cleaning job on the gun in my hand, I smile softly, pleased with the perfection. There's something soothing about the process, the intricate attention to detail, as I make sure the Springfield XD is in excellent condition to use.

It's what I used on my father, and the power that gave me makes this weapon my preferred choice. Always.

Placing the gun on the nightstand, I pack away my cleaning kit into the little case it comes in before securing it in my suitcase in the closet.

My stomach rumbles, reminding me that I haven't

eaten a damn thing since yesterday, but after my phone call with the De Luca brothers, responding to Luna's message, and getting lost in the process of gun cleaning, I've been too preoccupied.

Reaching for my phone, I swipe to bring up the room service menu for the hotel, but before I can even click on what's available, a short, shrill alarm sounds from my laptop and everything else is forgotten.

My heart pounds in my chest, my pulse thundering against the backs of my eyes as I grab the gun from beside me, disregarding my phone as the secret security camera footage comes to life on my laptop.

That sound only means one thing: someone's heading my way. I requested a secluded room at the end of the hall on the ninth floor, fully aware it would allow me the ability to have the camera feed set up solely for this room without interference from anyone else.

A huge guy comes into view on the screen before me, and my knuckles tighten around the gun as if my life literally depends on it. It's not until he knocks on the door, the sound making me jolt slightly, that I see his face, and my jaw drops in shock.

As my gaze flits from the screen to the door, to the

fucking gun in my hand, it takes a second for my mind to process what the hell is going on, and then I dive into action.

What the fuck is he doing here?

I place my XD in the top drawer of the nightstand, right next to the Bible, and as I reach for my laptop, another knock rings out from the other side of the door.

"Ava? Open up." Vito's gruff voice sends a shiver down my spine, even in a moment of panic like this, but it doesn't stop me from silencing my laptop before storing it under my bed. I do the same with my phone, not wanting any interruptions that may reveal who I am.

Rising from the bed, I glance around the room, my heart rate still spiked as I swipe my hand down my face, trying to calm the nerves bubbling inside of me. Happy that everything is tucked away, I reach for the television remote, flicking the screen on. Some kind of reality tv show comes on, and as I turn for the door, the knocking starts up again.

Fuck. Why would Vito be here? Maybe I should have kept a hold of the gun? Shit. I don't know.

Before I can overthink it, I reach for the door handle, unlocking the latch and swinging it open to reveal the hot-as-sin man on the other side. The security footage did him no justice.

His cropped brown hair makes him look dark and dangerous, emphasized by the scars that mark his neck, and I'm now noticing them on his hands too. His brown eyes examine every inch of me as I do the same to him, both of us standing frozen in place, sinking deeper into the other.

Shaking my head, I pull myself from the stare-off, silently berating myself for admiring him first and asking questions second. "What are you doing here, Vito? And how the fuck did you know where to find me?" I blurt, confusion and anger fused in my tone, but if it offends him, he doesn't let it show. If anything, the corner of his mouth tugs up, as if I'm entertaining him.

Without a word, he shoulders past me, not hard, more of a brush since there's little space for him to pass, but he shrugs, leaving me to gape after him as he comes to a stop in the center of the room before turning back to face me. "The lady at the front desk told me which room you were in," he states casually, like he hasn't just put a fucking target on her head.

"The lady at the front desk. Are you kidding me? Which

one?" I grumble in response, wanting to make sure I make her pay for this bullshit, but he smirks almost sheepishly, before slowly spinning on the spot to take in my room.

"It's irrelevant."

"No, it's not. There are privacy policies in place that were breached with this shit. You could have been here to murder me and she's just going to give out that information," I hiss, my lips twisting with disappointment. He turns to face me, his eyebrows raised as he swipes his tongue over his bottom lip.

A rugged-as-hell man like this should not be allowed to look so damn tempting when I'm mad. There should be laws to make this shit illegal.

"Maybe I am," he mutters, maintaining the distance between us as he keeps his gaze fixed on mine, and it takes me a moment to understand what he's insinuating.

"Sure. That's cute," I say with a roll of my eyes, batting off his comment like it doesn't twist my gut with uncertainty. "How about we skip the pleasantries and get to the part where you explain what you're doing here. The last time I spoke to you, I was meeting the three of you at The Ritz at seven." I cross my arms over my chest, still standing by the open door. He doesn't utter a word, just continues to move toward me, slow, calculated, like a predator ready to feast on his next meal. "Vito, what are you doing here?" I ask again, frustrated at having to repeat myself, but the closer he gets, the faster my heart races for entirely different reasons.

If he is here to kill me, he'll fucking succeed because apparently, I'm a damn fool for him. His brothers, too.

"That's a complicated question, Ava," he says quietly, coming to a stop in front of me. Toe to toe like this, his body heat surrounds me as he stretches his arm out over my shoulder. I don't understand what he's doing until I hear the sound of the door clicking shut behind me, which is barely audible with the pounding of my pulse in my ears.

So. Fucking. Screwed.

"Then uncomplicate it for me." The anger in my tone melts away with his proximity as my chest heaves with each breath.

He tilts his head from side to side, like he's observing me from every angle until he finally speaks. "What's so alluring about you, *Bellissima*?"

I frown in confusion with the complete change of subject as he lifts his hand to my chin, using two fingers to tilt my head back, giving him full access to peer deep into my eyes and touch my soul. "Stop trying to change the subject," I manage to scramble in response, but my voice is getting weaker, distracted, consumed by him, and the smallest grin on his face says he knows it too.

Vito maintains eye contact with me as he runs his thumb over my jawline, somehow leaning closer to me, our chests brushing as he nudges me backward. I don't stop until my back hits the wall, this brute of a man now consuming every inch of space around me. It would be a lie if I were to say I hate it. But I somehow manage to keep my arms planted at my sides, even though my fingers itch to reach out for him.

"I've missed you," he whispers, his breath fanning across my lips as he tilts his head closer.

"Missed what?" The words slip from my lips before I can stop them, and the glint that flashes across his gaze tells me he knows he's got me exactly where he wants me.

"I've missed watching your skin pebble beneath my touch, *Bellissima*. It's all I've been able to think about." His lips are barely an inch from mine now. "I thought about it when I watched your sweet ass sway as you walked away last night. I thought about it in my fucking dreams as I imagined you in every position and got to know your body more intimately. I thought about it this morning in the shower as I wrapped my hand around my cock and exploded to the taste of your pretty pink tits on my tongue. And I thought about it every second in between as well."

My chest tightens, the need seeping from his words holding me in a vise-like grip as I stand frozen in place. How can his words render me speechless, set me alight, and leave my mind empty of everything but the thought of him? *How?*

A beat passes, followed by another, and another, until my body finally kicks into action, and despite myself and my earlier anger, the words that leave my mouth only confirm what I truly want to happen here.

"Fuck it."

My hands lift to his chest, my fingers wrapping around the lapels of his jacket as I rise up on my tiptoes and crush my mouth to his, or does he crash his mouth to mine? I don't know. All I know is, this better not stop, this better not end, because I need this more than my next fucking breath.

Mouths colliding, tongues sweeping against one another, we completely melt into each other.

He's all I can think about, all I can feel, all I can see, all

I can smell, all I can hear.

Vito's grip on my chin quickly drags down to my throat, making a choked moan burn past my lips as he continues to kiss me. I need more, and I need it right now.

"Please, Vito. Please," I beg, not caring about anything but getting more from him, and he doesn't disappoint.

He tears his lips from mine, taking the smallest step back as I shakily release a long exhale. His gaze drags over me from head to toe, like he's undressing me with his eyes before he does the real thing.

I would be more than happy to take the lead, but I remember his brother stopping me from touching Vito's neck last night, and I really don't want to do anything to spook him right now.

Without a word, he reaches for the collar of my checkered shirt, but before I can shake it off my shoulders, he tears the material in half, right down the back. The torn shirt fabric sliding down my arms effortlessly before he discards it over his shoulder.

Desire courses through me as he grabs the front of my white tee and does the exact same thing. The only sound that can be heard is the cloth shredding in his hands, revealing my lacy white bra underneath, and his eyes darken in response.

"Take off your pants before I do the same to those too," he grunts, his eyes still fixed on my chest, and if I hadn't learned last night that he was a breast man, I would have found that out right now.

Without any further prompt, I quickly step out of my pants, taking my socks and panties with them as he drags his tongue over his bottom lip once more.

"Don't move," he orders, taking a step back to shake off his jacket, placing it on the unused bed in the room before undoing his belt and dropping it beside the discarded material.

Holy. Fuck.

Still clothed in his shirt, pants, and shoes, he moves toward me, his steps filled with promise, determination, and need. He doesn't slow when he approaches me. Instead, he grabs the back of my thighs and lifts me into the air, pressing my back firmly into the door behind me as his gaze fixates on my lace-covered breasts once more.

Using one hand under my thighs to keep me in the air, he brings his other to my chest, running his finger over the lace as he drags the cups down, exposing my nipples while keeping the bra in place.

The way his eyes devour me, I could explode from the passion and confidence it evokes inside of me.

His hand disappears and a moment later I hear the sound of his zipper lowering, and I know he's freeing his cock.

He's unpredictable, unintentionally hot as fuck, and a force to be reckoned with.

My thighs clench, excitement and anticipation getting the better of me as I try to catch my breath, but I'm rendered powerless the second I feel the tip of his cock at my entrance, lost to the man with the deep brown eyes, scarred skin, and intoxicating aura.

He pauses, holding his position as the moisture pools between my legs.

The silence between us is deafening, and I can't take it any longer. "Take me," I plead, my voice barely more than a whisper. In a flash, he thrusts his cock deep into my pussy.

A groan bursts from my lips, his thick cock stretching my core beyond words as my mouth widens and I try to fucking breathe. My head falls back against the door, the pain not registering as he refuses to give me a second to adjust to his size, continuing to thrust into me with calculated strokes. Both of his hands grip each of my thighs, giving him better leverage as ecstasy ricochets through my body.

"Oh, God," I groan, fingertips digging into his muscled arms as I hang on for dear life.

"So fucking hot, *Bellissima*," he grunts, his jaw slack when I peer through my lashes at him. "So fucking sweet," he adds, before leaning forward and capturing my nipples in his mouth.

The painful bite of his teeth makes me cry out, my hips bucking to meet him as my nails dig deeper into the shirt covering his arms.

It's too much and not enough all at once.

His teeth nip, scrape, and bite every inch of my breasts, from the swell to the dip between them and the taut nipples begging for his attention. His thrusts are strong, hard, and unrelenting. I know this man has never been asked to go harder or faster in his life. He knows what he's doing, and he's playing my body perfectly.

Every nerve ending in my body is alight, tingling with pleasure as he slams into me again and again, the door behind me pounding with every plunge.

Any other time, and with anyone else, I would complain

that I'm mostly naked while they remain fully clothed, but I know it's different with him, and it screams power—a turn-on I'm learning I like from the De Luca brothers. A lot.

"Come on my cock, *Bellissima*," he grinds out, his jaw tightening as he lifts from my breast for the briefest of moments, before he sinks his teeth into my nipple, erupting the climax that's been burning at the base of my spine since he lifted me into the air.

I shatter into a million pieces around him, my cries melting into sobs as ecstasy courses through my veins. His movements become jagged, stuttered, before he lets out a deep growl from the pit of his stomach, his mouth releasing my nipple to capture my lips as he comes.

Sweat clings to every inch of me, loose tendrils of hair sticking to my face as I descend from the biggest high of my life. It takes an eternity to relax my hold on his arms, but when I do, he pulls me away from the door, his still-hard cock nestled between my legs as he moves me to my bed, laying me down at the edge.

The glint in his eyes tells me he's not done. That was just round one, and I have no idea if I can survive another, but I'm willing to give it a try.

In a complete daze, I look up at him, arms at my sides as I continue to worry about touching him. That's when his cell rings, the sound coming from his pants pocket. He bites out a curse, instantly searching for the device and bringing it to his ear while his cock remains inside of me.

"What?" he grunts, reaching his other hand forward to stroke his fingertips over my red breasts, clearly admiring his handiwork as his touch soothes the sore skin. "Fuck yeah, no, I agree. Yeah, take her with us, it'll be safer, the employees here are happy to give out a guest's details," he rambles off, my brain still too fogged by my orgasm to fully process what's happening before he puts the phone down.

"What's going on?" I manage to ask, swiping my hair back off my face and groaning in protest when he pulls his dick from my core.

"My brothers are here."

REDEMPTION

SEVEN

Wren

The second Vito drops his phone onto the bed, his demeanor completely changes. The conversation has flipped a switch inside of him, one I'm far too familiar with seeing, feeling, and I know there's an issue. An issue he seems to think may affect me in some way.

Wetting my dry lips, my body still coming down from the earth-shattering orgasm, I push up off the bed. My hair is messy and my bra is still on with my breasts spilling out of the material. All while Vito's cum trails down my thighs.

Excellent.

Ignoring that, I turn to the man pacing the floor before me, scrubbing his hand over his cropped hair. His pants are already fastened, his shirt revealing no marks or damage from my grip earlier, and it's almost like it didn't happen.

"What's going on?" I ask, tucking my hair behind my ear as I stare at him expectantly. Surprisingly, I seem to pull him from wherever he is because he turns to face me immediately.

"Get dressed. They'll be here in a moment and we have to leave." He nods along with what he's saying but doesn't elaborate further.

Hmm. I don't think so.

"Leave for where and why?" I push, folding my arms over my chest like I'm not standing here with my body on display and the remnants of what we just did dripping down my legs.

Vito sighs, inconvenienced by my questioning, but I don't care. I'm not the sweet, naïve Ava I pretended to be yesterday. I've grown up in a far darker world than he knows, and I'm not just going to go blindly with them somewhere. Unless I'm in legitimate danger or at risk of my cover being blown.

The way he shakes his head, waving his hand

dismissively, tells me I'm going to have to learn to bite my tongue for once in my life and get on with it, and it instantly makes my chest tight, my jaw clenching as he speaks. "Get dressed, Ava. We have business to attend to."

I gulp back the angry response burning my tongue, but the way his eyes widen a little, I think he presumes I'm gulping in fear. He doesn't say another word though, happy to leave it like that between us.

Turning my back to him, I head for the bathroom, leaving the door open so I can keep an eye on what he's doing as I clean myself up the best I can without jumping in the shower. The hairs on the back of my neck tingle as my body demands to be on high alert.

One glance in the mirror and it's clear I've been fucked into next year, so I quickly grab a hair tie off the vanity top, sweeping my hair back into a tiny slick ponytail, using hair pins to hold it in place, before I splash some water on my face.

When I re-enter the room, I find Vito by the window, staring down at the city outside, lost in his own little world. Moving straight for the walk-in closet, I discard my bra, opting for a slick black matching set this time as I search through my suitcase for something they may find suitable enough for me to attend *business* with them.

Donning a pair of fitted black pants, a simple black tee, and a matching oversized blazer, I slip my feet into the chunky combat boots I wore the other night at the club. I dress with my eyes fixed on Vito the entire time, but it's like he's switched off from the rest of the world, a numbness washing over him as he prepares for… something. I don't yet know what, but it seems I'm close to finding out.

I straighten my blazer as I move toward my bed, just as a knock pounds against the door. It immediately kicks Vito into action as he spins toward the sound, marching with purpose. "I'll get it," he grunts, barely looking in my direction, and I use it as the distraction I need, opening the nightstand drawer and quickly slipping my Springfield XD into my oversized blazer pocket.

While pocketing the phone, I see a message flash across the screen from Luna. the one word text making me freeze in place.

Luna: Abort.

Fuck.
Fuck. Fuck. Fuck. Fuck. Fuck.

It's too fucking late for that now.

"*Bella,* long time no see," Enzo singsongs, stepping into the room with a burst of energy and Matteo right behind him. I return his smile, quickly swiping the message off the screen as I place my cell into my other pocket.

"It seems the three of you are full of surprises, and it's not even lunchtime yet," I say with a quirk of my brow as he steps into my space, wrapping me in his arms as he presses a soft and sweet kiss on each of my cheeks.

"That just means we've barely started, Ava. The fun is yet to come," he replies with a wink, and I shake my head at him.

"Since your brother doesn't want to clue me in on what's going on, is there any chance you might?" I ask hopefully, but he shrugs.

"What, and miss your reaction to the crazy that is our lives? No fucking way. I'm ninety-nine percent sure Matteo is going to go nuclear, and you and I both know that flex of power will have your sweet little pussy singing in no time," he purrs, stroking his finger down my cheek.

Fuck.

He knows me too well already, and I would agree under different circumstances, but the fact that Luna just messaged me to abort leaves me too wired to think with anything other than my mind right now.

"*Stellina,* come. We have a meeting to attend, and your safety seems to have been compromised with some of our competitors. So, for the time being, I don't wish for you to be out of my sight," Matteo explains, offering me the smallest detail to the bigger picture here.

Releasing a heavy breath, I take in the three men who have veered me off track so drastically. Enzo is as calm and cheerful as ever, Vito zoned out like he's not really present, and Matteo's jaw looks so tight it may snap.

I steel my spine, nodding at them. Against my better judgment and Luna's order, I say, "Lead the way."

Every minute in the SUV accelerates my heart rate. With Matteo beside me and Enzo and Vito sitting across from us, I try to contain the panic, nibbling on the inside of my cheek as the city passes by in a blur.

The SUV is silent as the tension rises. Wherever we're going, they're not happy about it. Even Enzo has lost his permanent grin and flirty eyes.

I'm totally fucked.

I can feel it in my gut, my stomach twisting in knots as the SUV pulls up outside a restaurant I'm not familiar with.

Vito opens the door before the driver can even get out of his seat, Enzo shuffling after him to wait just outside, offering his hand to me. I take it without pause, letting him lead me out into the street. The weather, thankfully, is dry for the first time in days but dark clouds loom above us. Matteo follows me out of the vehicle, his hand brushing the base of my spine as he moves around me, making my body tingle with the slightest of touches.

"Stay by our side, *Stellina*. I will keep you safe," he murmurs against my ear before stepping to the front of the group. Vito is hot on his tail, while Enzo offers me his elbow to link arms with him as we make our way into the restaurant.

It's dark and quiet as we enter, like the place isn't open, and my assessment is confirmed as we step further inside. There's just one table set up in the middle of the room, the rest of the chairs are tidied away on top of the other tables, confirming no one else will be joining us.

But the matter causing me the most trouble is the reason Luna told me to abort. The meeting the De Luca brothers have brought me to is bigger than they realize. The entire reason I'm here *with* them is because of the person already sitting between four men at the table.

Luna.

My heart threatens to pound out of my chest as I keep my face neutral, my pulse ringing in my ears uncontrollably.

Roman, Parker, Luna, Kai, Oscar.

The five of them are sitting around the circular table, and four seats remain free. Matteo takes the one across from Luna, Vito to his left, while Enzo offers me the chair beside Matteo, leaving him to sit next to Oscar.

Fuck. Fuck. Fuck. Fuck. Fuck.

"I'm unsure why you feel this meeting is necessary, Miss Steele," Matteo starts with a bored tone. "I'm aware you'll do anything to interfere, but there's nothing you can say or do that will make me listen. You're wasting our time and yours."

I look at Enzo, not wanting to seem like this is completely normal for me, and to my surprise, he places his hand on my thigh and offers me a reassuring squeeze in comfort.

If only he knew.

"It's *Mrs*. Steele," Oscar grunts, slumping back in his

seat, his body language matching Matteo's tone as Luna places her elbows on the table.

"We're trying to keep the peace, Mr. De Luca, and whether you believe it or not, we're trying to keep everyone safe," she explains, her green eyes widening with the truth as Roman scoffs.

"Well, everyone but the Russians. They've already gone too far," Roman spits, his lips twisting in distaste. It's weird seeing him now, sitting across from me like he's done so many times. Only this time, I don't have my mother forcing me to push myself on him.

It's a relief, a weight lifting from my chest that I never knew was there. I expect these people to hate me forever, and that's something I can live with.

"We can work together. Then we can discuss whatever it is Totem promised you," Luna offers, her voice remaining calm as she looks at each of the brothers, completely overlooking me as she waits for a response.

"None of this would be an issue if you hadn't killed him. The day I learned of his death, I vowed to avenge him," Vito spits, and my blood runs cold. My eyes squeeze shut before I can stop them, but Enzo's hand tightens, like he assumes I'm scared by Vito's words.

This is a mess.

A huge fucking mess that I should never have agreed to.

I'm tangled in lies, a web of my own making because I suddenly felt something for the first time in my life.

Sitting at this table now, I know I have a decision to make.

Loyalty.

But to whom?

Lust or redemption?

It's one or the other, no in-between.

"Let's not waste time on such bullshit. In fact, maybe I should be done with you now?" Matteo grunts, pulling a gun from his pocket and training it on Luna. Each of her men are about to move, but she raises her hand, halting them in place against their will. "An eye for an eye, Mrs. Steele. The consequences for *killing* Totem."

Luna's eyes land on mine for the first time since I walked through the door, and I immediately know what she's saying.

Show me I wasn't wrong for trusting you.

Lust or redemption?

Redemption or lust?

Releasing a breath, I let my body take over, rising to my feet in one swift move with my hand wrapped securely around the grip of my gun. With precision, I press the end against Matteo's temple, pain ricocheting through my chest at what I'm doing, praying this doesn't go any further.

"What the fuck?" Enzo mumbles behind me, his hand retreating from my leg as my eyes settle on Vito. The shock is unmistakable on his face as he stares back at me.

"What if your vengeance starts with me? What if my name isn't Ava but Wren? *Wren Dietrichson*. And what if it was me who killed him? Killed Totem? Killed my father?"

My chest heaves with every word falling from my mouth, the sound of my own voice not registering in my ears over the sound of my thundering pulse.

Matteo turns to face me, the end of my gun aimed right between his brown eyes as he peers up at me in disgust.

"Then you have until the count of five to run before I put your own bullet through your skull."

EIGHT

Matteo

The tension was already high before we stepped in here, that hasn't changed, nor has the fury in Vito's gaze and the tightness of Enzo's jaw. One thing that has drastically changed is the protective stance I felt toward the woman who is now holding a loaded XD that is pressed to my forehead.

I knew something was shifting the second Mrs. Steele turned her gaze to Ava's for the briefest of moments, a knowing glint in her eyes. It took all of two seconds for everything to unravel before me, but it's not the barrel against my skin that pisses me off. No. It's the fact that I didn't react quick enough, caught completely off-guard by the platinum-blonde vixen staring at me with vacant eyes.

The words that swept from her mouth so casually floor me, but I refuse to let it show as I lay down my demand. "Then you have until the count of five to run before I put your own bullet through your skull."

I mean every word. I won't be derailed by a willing body that writhed between the three of us. Never have, never will.

She's not Ava, the hot-as-sin woman who fell apart between us last night. She's Wren Dietrichson, the bitch who killed Totem and ruined all our plans in the process.

Slowly blinking, I make sure her gaze is set on mine as I purse my lips. "Five," I begin, feeling the tension around the table heighten, but it doesn't go unnoticed that the five people sitting across the table don't immediately jump to her defense.

I hold that thought, focusing on the actual task at hand.

Her pulse is throbbing in her neck, her chest heaving with every breath she takes, like she knows very well it could be her last, and it makes my cock stir in my pants.

"Four." The word comes out clipped as I internally berate myself for still having a reaction to this woman who has caused so much trouble for us. My nostrils flare ever so slightly, and I know she spots it the second a glimmer of hope flashes in her eyes. How does this crazy-ass woman get hope from my anger? It doesn't make any sense. "Three." This time, the number falls from my lips far less aggressively as I rein myself in.

The hope that was there seconds ago diminishes as she frowns at me. I can sense the itch in her to look at Enzo or Vito, but she knows the second she takes her eyes off me, I'll put an end to all of this.

That thought stirs my gut in a way I've never felt before, like my instincts are wavering on the next course of action, and that only adds to the building fury inside of me.

The next number is on the tip of my tongue when she finally speaks. "I don't want to run." Her words are raspy and raw, her eyes wide with shock, like she's surprised even herself with the truth that tumbles from her mouth.

"What?"

The question comes in unison from both Vito and Enzo, threatening to tear my gaze from the killer standing over me, but I manage to keep everything focused on her. She doesn't lower the weapon or take her eyes off me as she responds to their outburst.

"I said, I don't want to run." This time, she's firmer, more sure of her words, but a hint of vulnerability is there too. She has an ability to catch me off-guard entirely. It's almost refreshing, but the circumstances haven't changed.

"*Stellina,*" I murmur, clenching my hands on the arms of the chair as I remain seated. "You're not going to want to stay if what you're saying is true."

Anger courses through my veins even hotter as I sense the hope inside of me that this is all a lie, a ridiculous joke that has gotten out of hand. Why don't I want her to be the villain in my story? Why do I want to keep her at my side? Even if it's only for the next two days.

My plans are blown, my hopes of restraining and exploring her completely dwindling.

But I have to remember the most important fact. She's Totem's daughter.

Fucking daughter.

Why would his own blood kill him? That is the highest of all sins within the De Luca code.

Blood is blood. No matter what.

Pursing my lips, I wait for her to respond, but instead her mouth falls open and closes a couple of times, yet nothing comes out.

I can feel Vito's eyes glaring into the side of my head from his spot to my left, and I sense his desire to communicate with me. I have no idea what it is, or if I'm even right, but I offer the smallest of nods, trusting in his judgment no matter what as I continue to stare at Wren.

Fuck, that name suits her so much more than Ava.

"If you're not going to run, Av—Wren, then your only other choice is to come with us." My heart stills at Vito's words. He's taken this in an entirely different direction than I was expecting, and I most definitely regret giving him the signal to say something.

"No, she isn't," Luna blurts, interjecting in the mess tempting to swallow us whole.

The chair scrapes as she rises to her feet, and I can't stop myself from glancing in her direction out of the corner of my eye as Roman holds her back.

Never one to be left out, Enzo's chair scrapes across the floor just as quickly as the pounding of his fists on the table vibrates around the room. "It's her, or a bullet through your brains. We said, an eye for an eye, which would you prefer?"

Wren's eyebrows pinch together as I meet her gaze, at the exact same time Vito knocks the safety off his gun.

Finally. One of them wants to pull a weapon to help a brother out.

Fuckers.

But I know in my gut that it's not aimed at the one putting me in danger right now; it's aimed across the table instead.

"I'd like to see you even try to put a fucking bullet anywhere near her." That statement comes from a growly Oscar, and when I glance at him, I spy the dagger he's twirling on the table top.

Releasing a heavy sigh, I try to remain calm amid the clusterfuck that's unraveling before us. None of this was supposed to be happening. We're completely off track and I need a moment to fucking think.

I'm ready to move, counter attack, or god knows what to get this over with, but before I can settle on my next step, I'm caught off-guard once more by Wren as she pulls the gun from my skull and drops it back into the oversized pocket on her blazer.

Surprised by the vulnerability in her move, my eyebrows rise to my hairline as she takes a step back. I assess her every move as she cracks her neck from side to side before squaring her shoulders.

"Let's go."

It's my turn for my brows to knit together as I twist my neck to follow her walking away from the group. Is she talking to us?

It's almost fucking cute that she thinks she can give out orders, and the way no one fucking stops her only confirms that she's used to being in charge. I almost scoff at the actual fact that she's stepping away and I'm not raising my own gun at her.

Something is stopping me, but I don't understand what.

The Featherstone men flick their gazes between us and Wren, while Luna stares at her with a hint of concern in her eyes as her hands clench on the table.

The muscles in my neck bunch as I follow her line of sight to find Wren standing by the door. Her stance is too fucking casual, too fucking intriguing, yet too fucking willing.

This doesn't make sense. As if reading my thoughts, Wren shrugs her shoulders as she nods at the Featherstone members sitting across the table. "I promised redemption. This is it."

Like that makes any sense to me or either of my brothers. "Didn't you hear me? If you were the one to put the bullet in Totem, you're not going to want to go anywhere with us." My tone is almost bewildered as I stare her down, but her demeanor doesn't change at all. Not even a twitch of her eye.

"I was dead under his rule and order. I've been sitting for the past six months, waiting for Luna to put the final nail in my coffin, but she didn't. If you're going to kill me, then do it. I'm already gone."

My heart ricochets in my chest despite my better judgment. Her words give me more questions than answers, but none of that matters as Enzo strides toward her.

Vito follows suit, which leaves me no choice but to get in line. We operate as one. Always. Even if we don't like it. I'll have a lot to say later when it's just the three of us.

"What's happening?" Luna asks as I adjust the lapels of my blazer and head for the door. She just wants to hear it from our lips.

"Wren." Her name is hot on my lips as she whips her head in my direction. "Tell Luna what's happening. Where are we going?" How I'm able to keep my voice so calm is surprising, even to me, which is likely why my brothers are remaining quieter than I am, because they'll reveal their hand quicker than I would.

Without missing a beat, Wren glances at the table, to whom in particular, I don't know, since I don't look away from her. Her gaze turns back to me before she speaks.

"Wherever you're fucking taking me."

NINE

Wren

I stare blankly at the palms of my hands, repeating the past twenty-four hours over and over again in my mind as the De Luca brothers murmur among themselves like I'm not here.

It suits me fine. I need a minute, an hour, fuck, a whole week, to process this shit, but more than anything, I could really do with a shower so I can properly delve into my thoughts.

What kind of a woman agrees to leave with three brothers that run a fucking mafia? Not a sane one. But I've never claimed to be one. Not with my past. I wasn't born for a calm and easy life, and I don't think I would survive one even if I tried it.

It's been a little over nine hours since I walked out of the nightclub with the De Luca brothers, leaving Luna and Featherstone behind. As much as I'm questioning whether I made the right decision, the reality is that there wasn't an alternative.

My thighs ache from my time with Vito earlier, my heart pounds with a mixture of fear and excitement, and my head aches from the very quick shift in dynamic between the four of us.

Lifting my head, I look out of the window as the engine continues to rumble. Land has come into view again after a long time looking at the ocean below, but seeing the building tops doesn't offer me any reassurance.

No.

Because I didn't expect to be boarding a private jet immediately after leaving the restaurant. I sat silently as I watched Matteo make one single call, bark a handful of words in Italian, and put everything into motion.

I thought we would go back to their hotel or a property they own nearby in New York. I never imagined we would be flying halfway around the world to their home.

Italy.

The wonder in that one word ripples through my veins. The heritage of the country has always intrigued me and has forever been on my bucket list. I just didn't imagine going under these circumstances.

At least I'm not dead. Yet.

There's time, I'm sure, and placing me on their home soil will likely make it a lot easier than dealing with Featherstone and the US legalities instead. The fuckers haven't even bothered to take my loaded gun from me. My phone remains in my other pocket too.

It's clear they know I'm not going anywhere, especially after hearing the truths I spilled earlier. I hate that I left myself so vulnerable, but it's true. There's nothing for me to fight for. The only thing keeping me alive was my redemption. Have I obtained it? Not likely, but did I start making progress? Sure.

I pulled a gun on a man who only brought me to the meeting so he could protect me.

Protect. Me.

Those two words have never been used in the same sentence as me. Ever. And when it finally did happen, I had to ruin it all by following my gut and proving to Luna that

I'm not the worst bitch in existence.

A heavy sigh falls from my lips as I pinch the bridge of my nose. My thoughts are going around and around in circles and it's driving me insane. I need to get off this damn plane and breathe in some fresh air.

Vito grunts from across the small cabin, drawing my attention to the three of them as they sit on the plush white leather seats. There are four chairs facing each other with a large table between them. Matteo and Enzo sit in my line of sight while Vito sits across from them with his back to me. Enzo has undone the top button of his shirt, Vito has lost his jacket altogether, and Matteo... looks as put together as he did when I had the barrel of my XD pressed against his head.

They haven't uttered a single word to me since we stepped out onto the street in New York, which likely isn't helping the insanity swarming in my mind. But if they were to speak, I'm not sure I'd appreciate what they'd have to say anyway.

I don't want to see the disappointment on their faces, the surprise in their eyes, or the anger in their demeanor. As much as I may deserve it, I just can't face it.

Which is frustrating as hell because I've known them

for less than twenty-four hours. In that short span of time, I've climaxed between the three of them, slipped a tracker into their possession, and agreed to continue the rest of my stay with them while keeping my location a secret. Only to have Vito show up unannounced, nearly blowing my cover before fucking me into oblivion, followed by Matteo and Enzo's arrival and the rest... is a total disaster.

"Do we need to cuff her?" The question comes from Enzo, a hint of teasing in his tone as my eyes lock with his. As much as there's a lightness to his tone, the glare in his brown eyes is unmistakable.

I feel another two sets of eyes glance my way, and despite my better judgment, I look to both Matteo and Vito, who are glaring in my direction.

"Cuff her? She's harmless and completely at our mercy. I don't think that will be necessary," Vito bites out, and his hands clench on the table before him as he shakes his head at me dismissively, which only makes me smirk in response.

It's a natural response when someone underestimates me. As much as I enjoy this new, fresh feeling of being the underdog—something I never felt with the power moves my mother always played—I still manage to smother the smugness from my face.

I'm a bitch. A heartless, damaged, twisted bitch, and that's never going to change.

"It's cute that you think you're strong enough to take us on," Matteo states, drawing my attention toward him as he laces his fingers together on the table in front of him. I drag my eyes over every inch of him before I reply.

"It's cute that you think I'm not." I lean back in my own white leather seat, quirking a brow at him as Enzo chuckles in response.

"Yeah, she's definitely begging for death." I don't know how he manages to say that with a hint of humor, but he does. Despite the light-heartedness in his tone, my breath lodges in my throat.

I'm out of my depth here, there's no doubting that, but I will never sink without at least attempting to swim with all of my might first.

Show no fear.

Show no pain.

Show no mercy.

Show no weakness.

Show no vulnerability.

If it wasn't my mother muttering one of those statements

to me on repeat, it was my father whenever he made an appearance. But despite my hatred for both of them, I can't seem to shake those five mantras they instilled in me.

"I've begged for death before, but it never came." The words fall from my lips like stone as I meet every one of their gazes, but they give nothing away. "I told you already. If you're going to kill me, then get on with it. I don't fear death. I don't fear the darkness, and I don't fear the afterlife in Hell I'm destined for."

Matteo purses his lips as Enzo tucks a loose strand of hair behind his ear, while Vito huffs, leaning back in his seat so I can no longer see his expressionless eyes.

When it's clear none of them are going to pull the trigger or offer me any kind of response, I turn my attention back out the window. We're getting closer to landing, the flight attendant doing a quick sweep through the cabin as she murmurs about our seatbelts, but I ignore her as the world gets closer and closer.

I don't know what my future holds in this foreign land, but it can't be worse than the hell on earth created for me back home. My parents' decisions will haunt me forever, and if anything, this is a luggage-free vacation away from it all.

As the wheels touch the ground, my chest relaxes slightly with each breath. I've taken far more on today than I expected, but I'll hopefully stop thinking about that on loop in my head once I get in the goddamn shower.

It's not until the door opens and the steps are dropped that the De Luca brothers rise from their seats. I hold my position, remaining comfortable as I wait for their next order. Better to give them the illusion that I'll follow them blindly, rather than wait by the plane for further instruction.

This is their game now, and I'm simply a willing participant.

Vito walks by first, ignoring my existence, which hurts far more than I care to admit. Especially after this morning, but I get the feeling that is all long forgotten now. Enzo follows, his usual smirk fixed in place, but he doesn't turn it in my direction either. Instead, he pauses beside the stewardess at the door. The green-eyed monster gets the better of me as he kisses her cheek before murmuring something in her ear, making her giggle in delight.

My hands clench together in annoyance, but I keep my lips tightly shut, refusing to give them any kind of response.

It's Matteo who comes to a stop beside my seat, hands

tucked into his pants pockets so I can't see if they're clenched or not. I stare at his perfectly polished black shoes, traveling up the length of his legs, before casting over his blazer and settling on his face.

Once again, I'm drawn to the scar that runs down the right side of his mouth, my tongue eager to run over the mottled skin to feel the texture against my touch. I did say I was a crazy bitch who was obsessed with just as crazy men who make all the decisions. And that's exactly what this is. Except my life is on the line and the foreplay is not leading toward sex.

"Move."

That one word has me sighing as I rise to my feet. Fucker had to go and spoil my little daydream. Now I want to bite the scar with an extra pinch of pain to make him pay for it, but I obviously don't as he stomps to the exit and marches down the stairs, not waiting for me.

Running my fingers down my blazer, I take a deep breath as I feel a pair of eyes on me. Lifting my gaze, I find the stewardess squinting at me in a mixture of jealousy and disgust.

Bullshit from the De Lucas, I can take, but from this bitch, definitely not.

I move toward the door, looking at her from the corner of my eye, and when a sneer touches her lips I spin on the spot, gripping her throat in my hand before I slam her back against the cabin wall behind her.

A gasp falls from her lips, a beautiful sound in my fucked up head as I add a little more pressure to my grip. "You don't fucking know me, and you certainly don't know what I'm capable of. So if you ever see me again, you keep your eyes down and mouth shut. Do you understand?" Venom drips through my words as fire burns in my veins, the ability to unleash some of my pent-up anger feeling like heaven as it tingles down my spine. When she doesn't answer, her eyes bulging a little as her face turns red, I pull her toward me a little before slamming her head straight back into the wall once more. "Do. You. Understand? Or do I need to make an example out of you?"

She instantly nods the best she can, a small sob breaking past her lips as a tear trickles down her cheek, and I grin, pleased with myself.

"That's enough, *Wren*." At the sound of Vito's voice, I slowly release my hold on the stewardess, offering her a sickly sweet smile before I turn for the steps. I refuse to bring my gaze to his as I brush past him, heading down the steps to the waiting SUV.

The heat that clings in the air catches me by surprise, but I still manage to tilt my head back and bask in the feeling on my face before I slip into the vehicle. The satisfaction I felt moments ago continues to flood my veins as I find Matteo looking down at his phone and Enzo smirking at me slightly before Vito joins us. With the layout allowing the four of us to face one another, I feel a hint of uncertainty, but it dwindles moments later when the SUV starts to move and the three of them continue to ignore me.

Perfect.

I'm only as lonely as I was in Philadelphia. At least there's some eye candy and a bright sun gleaming down on me here.

One minute draws into the next as we travel through cities, small towns, and stunning countryside. It's a little over an hour later that the vehicle slows to a stop at an opening among rows and rows of trees.

I lift out of my seat a little to see that the forest-like setting is framed by a stone wall with black iron, adding height to the whole thing. Shifting my gaze, I look through the front window to see a large double gate made from the same iron on the walls, and with a tap from the driver, it opens moments later.

None of the brothers utter a word at my nosiness, not even when I watch as we drive down a stone lane through more trees and a house slowly comes into view.

House is too small of a word, it's a freaking mansion for sure. I've stayed in enough of them to know what one looks like, but this is way more rustic and Mediterranean in comparison, and I'm in complete awe.

The forest seems to circle the entire property, while acres and acres of open space sits before us. As the SUV rolls to a stop in front of the mansion, my eyes light up at the sheer size of the place.

The sound of the door opening to my left pulls my gaze, and Vito climbs out first. Neither Matteo or Enzo move, making the silent order heard loud and clear that I follow after him.

The entire place looks stunning in the setting sun, a sense of calmness casting over us as I follow after Vito. Someone appears to open the front door of the house for Vito, who steps through without a word, and I can't help but run my hand over the stone wall as I step through too, murmuring my thanks as I go.

"Oh, you're home. I wasn't expecting you for a few

more days, but I can whip something up for dinner right away." The sound of the woman's voice makes me pause as I stand in the open doorway. A small woman with graying brown hair wraps her arms around Vito tightly as he lowers himself to embrace her in response.

I almost feel intrusive on their moment and consider turning and heading back outside, but her brown eyes find mine before I can even take a step.

"And who might this lovely *Bella* be?" she asks with a smile, making my eyes widen as she approaches me with her arms open as they were for Vito.

I glance over her shoulder at Vito who is staring at the two of us in confusion, but he must take pleasure in the discomfort clearly flashing on my face as she hugs me, because he doesn't urge her away from me or make her stop. It's like he's enjoying my pain, and the slight tilt to the corner of his mouth tells me I'm right.

Fucker.

"Don't hug her, Nonna. She pointed a gun at Matteo's head this morning," Enzo states from behind me, making my body stiffen even more, but to my surprise, the woman clinging to me throws her head back with a laugh as she rubs my arms.

"It's about time someone put him in his place. What I would have done to see that." She continues to giggle as she takes a step back, swiping her hands at her face as someone grunts from behind me. *Matteo.*

"I can show you again if you like," I blurt with a wide smile and a waggle of my eyebrows, which makes her laugh even more.

Unfortunately, Enzo wraps his arm around my shoulder tightly, pinning me to his side in a silent order to keep my gun where it is. "I'm sorry, Nonna. She can't, not today," he starts, taking large strides to guide me from the room. "Until we decide what to do with her, she's on room arrest."

My brows pinch as I look up at him, managing to keep my pace up with his. "Room arrest?" I repeat, the confusion clear in my tone as he offers me a dark smirk in response.

"It's exactly what it sounds like, *Bella*. A lot has happened today, and until we decide what to actually do with you, you're going to remain in here." As he stops speaking, his feet also halt before he swings open the door to his right.

I can't get a single word out before he shoves me into the room and slams the door shut behind me, the sound of a key turning in a lock following moments later as I gape at the panel of wood in surprise.

I shouldn't be shocked. They're mafia, for fuck's sake.

I'm just not used to being the one ordered around instead of giving the orders. But I'm alive and breathing, and as I tilt my head to the left, I see an open door leading into an ensuite, and I smile wide despite the circumstances.

Shower.

Think.

Plan.

Survive.

TEN

Wren

After my shower in the lush ensuite, I feel lighter. As if a huge weight has been lifted off my shoulders now that I've had time to properly process the day's events. I'm never going to know whether I made the right decision in that restaurant, which means I will stand by the actions I took.

It's dark outside now, the time difference making it later than it was back home so I'm still wide awake, and from the occasional noise I hear from the other side of the door, I know I'm not the only one.

Crossing my legs as I sit at the end of the bed, I take in

my surroundings. A pale, dusty pink paint covers the wall, cream curtains hang around the window, and hardwood flooring shines on the ground. All the furnishings in here are made from solid oak, from the closet and drawers, the bedside tables, to the desk in the corner of the room and the bedframe beneath me. The cream colored satin sheets crinkle underneath my body. The softness is a dream against my skin as I pull apart my gun again, inspecting it.

It's cute as hell in here, nothing like the bland holding cell I was expecting. Shit, I've had worse bedrooms in general. As a child, nothing was ever mine or just for me. It was always pieced together by my mother, with occasional input from my father whenever he made an appearance.

Shaking my head, I focus on the task at hand. Once I'm satisfied, I tuck the weapon back into the pocket of my oversized blazer. After my shower, my only option was to step back into the clothes I've been wearing all day. Maybe in the morning, when I reconfirm my lifespan with the De Lucas, I could discuss the alternatives.

My cell vibrates in my other pocket again. It's been going off more than usual, and after the first glance when I saw a message from Luna, I didn't bother looking again. I don't need her pity or worry about my safety. I signed up for this, we all did, and we know exactly how this goes.

Maybe when I don't feel guilt from her concern, I will look at them, but right now, I just can't face it. Who knew a simple emotion could cripple me so much?

"I don't care what you say. The light is on. I can see it under the door." There's no mistaking Nonna's voice. She sounds as if she's standing toe-to-toe with the door.

"Not my problem." That sounds like Matteo, but he's not as close to the door as she is.

As much as I've heard them in passing, this is the first time I've felt anyone this close, and within the next second, the lock is turning and Nonna is standing in the open space.

A wide smile spreads across her face as she keeps one hand on the door handle and the other balls into a fist and rests on her hips. "Come, eat." Two words. An order, not a request, even with it spoken so kindly and softly, yet I still falter, hesitating in my spot as I look up at her. When I seem to take a moment too long, she quirks her brow at me. "Please, you'll regret hesitating when you get a taste of my famous cannelloni." Her Italian accent thickens as she says cannelloni.

Her sass is amusing and I can't deny that I love it.

With a roll of my eyes, I rise to my feet, moving toward her with my gun and phone secured in my pocket, and as soon as I get within an arm's reach, she's linking her arm through mine and dragging me down the hall. The kitchen comes into view to the right as Nonna hums happily beside me.

The guys are sitting at the dining table at the far end of the room beside the patio doors leading out into the garden, but I ignore them and take in the kitchen first.

It's rustic, with cream cabinets and an olive green paint on the walls, which matches the wooden worktops perfectly. The terracotta tiles on the floor completes the vibe as a chandelier hangs above the dining table. Countertops frame the room with an island set in the center, and with the amount of pots and pans scattered around, it seems Nonna likes to use every inch of space available to her.

My gaze finally returns to the three brothers glaring at me from across the room as Nonna shuffles us toward them. I have to clamp my lips shut when I realize not one of them is wearing a suit, not even Matteo.

Vito is wearing a fitted black t-shirt with a pair of matching shorts. Sweat beads at his temple, and his veins protrude on his arms, hinting that he's been working out since I last saw him. But what holds my attention the most are the scars that are scattered all up his wrists to his elbow, each one as deep as the next, resembling those that also frame his neck.

Enzo looks hot as ever with gray sweatpants and a matching tee. His mousy-blond hair is curled behind his ear as usual, but the mischief that usually shines in his eyes isn't there.

Matteo is the one who catches me off-guard. I've seen the other two undo something when wearing a suit, hinting that it's not their favorite choice of clothing, but he's usually the one who remains poised and held together. Not now, though. In a black polo top and a pair of jeans, he almost looks like a different man altogether.

If they sense me taking them in from head to toe, not one of them utters a word as I sit across from Enzo, where Nonna places me before she takes the seat to my left, facing Matteo.

I run my tongue over my bottom lip as I look up through my lashes at Enzo, watching as annoyance hoods over his gaze. The smell of hot food makes my stomach rumble, reminding me I haven't eaten anything since last night.

When I reach for my cutlery, no one says a word

until my hands are poised, ready to bring a forkful of the cannelloni to my mouth.

"Hostages shouldn't be sitting with us at the table while we eat, Nonna." The disdain on Matteo's tongue is undeniable, and Nonna scoffs at him in response.

"We don't hold hostages around here, Matteo. They're either dead or they're not, and as far as I can see, her heart is still working." She clicks her tongue, like that's the end to that, and it's my turn to scoff as I shake my head at her.

"My heart has never worked, but I'm still breathing," I correct, before taking my first bite of her cannelloni. I groan with satisfaction at the deliciousness in my mouth, making Nonna smile from ear to ear as she waves her fork at me. *I told you so* flashes in her eyes, but she keeps it off her lips, and I appreciate it as I dig into my food.

Surprisingly, no one comments, and we continue to eat in silence. Every nerve in my body is vibrating with awareness, my past making it impossible to relax when I know my life still hangs in the balance. My right hand keeps drifting to my pocket, feeling the weight of my gun like a safety net, until I clear my plate.

I murmur my thanks to Nonna before turning my full attention to the De Luca brothers across from me. Now that there's food in my system, I'm more than ready to leave the table again, but there's one thing on my mind first.

"So, I'm wondering what the likelihood of me dying in the next twenty-four hours is? Because if the odds are low, I would appreciate an alternative set of clothes." I quirk my eyebrow as I look at Enzo first, before trailing my gaze over to Matteo, then Vito.

"Maybe I would prefer you in none," Enzo blurts with a smirk before clearing his throat and adjusting himself in his seat. I have to bite back a smile as Nonna chuckles beside me.

"We did. Things changed. Remember?" Matteo's terse tone makes my body tense, but I keep it hidden, not wanting them to see my reaction.

"I don't recall at all since I wasn't there," Nonna interjects before twisting in her seat to face me. "So, I will most definitely help you with some clothes tomorrow." Her warm smile relaxes my shoulders, making me smile at her in response.

"Thank you," I breathe, an understanding flashing between us, which is crazy since this is the most fucked-up shit I've been involved in for a while.

Matteo clears his throat as he leans forward, nudging his empty plate out of the way as he crosses his arms on the table top. "I didn't say whether you were dying or not."

Nonna rolls her eyes, making me desperate to do the same, but I manage to refrain. My gaze travels to Vito instead. He hasn't said a word since I walked in. This morning is a far too distant memory amidst everything else now, and I have a feeling I've hurt him the most. Or I would have if they actually had any feelings and emotions to begin with.

"How about we have a go at a quick draw, see who pulls their weapon first and get this bullshit over with?" The words slip from my mouth, my father's voice echoing in my mind in memory of the number of times he said those exact words to me.

Matteo shakes his head, his version of an eye roll, as he turns his gaze away from me once again.

Tension sits tight in my spine, the offer still on the table. I refuse to be caught off-guard if one of them opts to pull a weapon without notice.

Pursing my lips, I place my palms on the table, ready to stand, when the shrill sound of a phone rings through the house, making Nonna groan in agitation. "I'll help you with the clothes, *Bella*, if you respond to Mrs. Steele because she hasn't stopped calling since you arrived, and the ringing is starting to get on my last nerve." Her smile is tight, the irritation clear in her features as I nod, wincing with a hint of guilt.

I take that as my cue to leave, slipping my hand into my pocket, wrapped around the gun as I give the De Luca brothers my back.

I'm surprised no one follows me to the bedroom to ensure the door is locked behind me, but relief courses through me as I close it shut and drop down onto the bed. I pull my gun from my pocket first, laying it on the sheets beside me before I dip into my other pocket to retrieve my phone.

Twelve unread messages.
Thirty missed calls.

I roll my eyes at the ridiculousness that is Featherstone, or Luna, more specifically. I thought we were on the same page that I was a bitch and everything was even now, but apparently not. With a heavy sigh, I shuffle back on the bed, leaning against the headboard as I open the messages.

Luna: Where are you? Are you okay?

Luna: Wren, where are you?

Luna: Let's not do this silent shit, it doesn't suit you.

Luna: Have you taken her phone? You fuckers better get her on the line. Now.

Luna: Can you at least confirm that you're not dead?

Luna: Where. Are. You?

Luna: I can't come and find you if you don't help me out!

Luna: This wasn't the plan, Wren. What on earth is going on?

Luna: Goddammit, Wren.

Luna: Maybe I should just leave you to rot like you did to me after you jumped me in Ace Block if this is how you're going to be.

Luna: Fuck, Wren. Answer me. That's a fucking order.

Fuck.

I'm used to being on the harsher end of Luna's wrath, but not where she's fucking worried for my safety. What the hell is that about?

A yawn teases at my lips as I tap out my response.

Wren: Unfortunately for you, I'm still breathing. It's like a vacay; accommodations are good and the food is fabulous. Stop worrying and focus on the Russians.

I hit send, but another thought buzzes at the tips of my fingers, and before I can think better of it, I add another message.

Wren: Jumping you was a simple decision.

Attack you or feel the wrath of my father. I made the decision we would all make in that situation. It isn't worth shit, but I'm sorry that happened, and in the grand scheme of things, I think we went through far worse in the months that followed. We each had our roles to play whether we liked it or not. But now we're even. Don't worry about me, and I won't have to worry about you.

REDEMPTION

ELEVEN

Enzo

I wipe my hand over the steam covering the glass mirror as my reflection comes into view. My tired eyes are evident, and the deep frown on my forehead is still there. It hasn't moved since Wren stood up from the table last night and sauntered out of the kitchen so seamlessly, I had to remember whether this was my home or hers.

Readjusting the navy towel at my waist, I take a deep breath, attempting to relax my muscles before I push my damp hair back off my face. I was hoping a quick shower before our meeting this morning would freshen me up, but it seems I need a little more reviving than I thought.

I don't know what the hell happened to us on American soil, but it messed us up something crazy. We've made that trip hundreds of times, and I didn't expect this one to be any different, but fuck was I wrong.

Never would we have allowed anyone to live after drawing a gun or any other kind of weapon on us, but here we are, with the accused in our goddamn home.

My hands clutch the edge of the marble vanity unit, my knuckles whitening with the strength behind my grip as I shake my head in annoyance.

American soil made us soft as fuck. Weak beyond words for a piece of pussy.

Pursing my lips, I push off the vanity, dragging my hand down my face at the same time a knock sounds from the door to my right. I gaze in that direction, even though I know it's locked and no one in their right mind would try to come in here right now, and a moment later, Vito's voice echoes.

"Hurry up, *Stronzo.*"

There's no need to respond when I can already hear his footsteps retreating down the hallway. Instead I do exactly as he says, despite my preference to be the biggest pain in the ass they've ever seen. It's no secret my brothers tend to have a stick firmly lodged up their ass ninety-nine percent of the time, and now is no exception.

But Matteo called a slightly earlier meeting time for the three of us so we can address the elephant in the room before our men arrive and we discuss the pressing matters affecting the De Luca family. So I know now isn't the time to rile them up, even if it is my favorite pastime.

Especially when we all opted to hold off the conversation until this morning so we might attack it with fresher eyes and less jet lag, but I didn't sleep very much. My thoughts were replaying everything that happened since the moment the Russians stood us up, but the part I kept coming back to, time and time again, was the taste of Wren's sweetness on my tongue.

Fuck.

Unwrapping my towel, I dry myself off. Reaching for my suit hanging on the back of the door, I add one garment at a time until I'm looking at my reflection in the mirror again.

In my midnight-blue Brioni suit, a crisp white shirt underneath, and a dark blue tie, I look every inch the man I'm supposed to be. Who I was born to be.

Enzo De Luca.

Youngest brother and least likely to ever take the reins, just the way I like it. Although Matteo will always want both Vito's and my input on all things, I love the fact that the responsibility doesn't fall entirely on my shoulders, as it does his.

Happy with myself, I grab my wallet, phone, and sunglasses off the vanity and tuck them into my pockets, except the latter, keeping them in my hand, knowing the mid-morning sun is going to burn my eyes the second I step outside.

Making my way downstairs, I slow my pace as I pass the room I know Wren is in, but I somehow manage to fight the urge to peek inside and leave through the front door. I don't take two steps before I put my sunglasses on, wincing at the glare of the burning orange ball in the sky as I make my way down the stone path to the separate building beside our home.

We never wanted to conduct business in our home, but having another property off-site seemed to be causing issues with threats and vulnerabilities when in transit. So, we opted to construct another building on our grounds and conduct business from there.

It's a single story, stone structure, with no windows

and only two doors. As I step inside, I breathe a sigh of relief from the Mediterranean sun as the air-conditioning kicks in and the lighting dims.

All that stands in the room is a large conference table in the middle of the space, surrounded by multiple seats, while the far wall to the left houses screen after screen of surveillance cameras.

Nothing more, nothing less.

Anything that needs housing is handled at the warehouse on the outskirts of town. We might want to keep our business close, but we're not so crazy that we would put anything incriminating right on our doorstep.

"What took you so long?" Matteo's voice draws my attention to him and Vito already sitting at the table, waiting impatiently for me.

I pause on the spot, lips stretched into a grin, striking a pose as I playfully flick the ends of my hair that have crept free from behind my ear. "Sorry, boys, I was a little busy curling my hair."

Matteo only glares harder as Vito tuts at me with a slight shake to his head, but I see the glimmer of humor flash in his eyes, and I take that as a mission accomplished.

"Sit the fuck down. The others will be here in less than

ten minutes for us to discuss general upkeep and the shit that went down in New York, so there isn't long for us to get on the same page about the *other* issue at hand," Matteo grunts, reaching for the fresh mug of coffee in front of him as he sighs.

I fight back the eye roll that's so desperate to come out as I take my seat at the table. Matteo sits at the head like always, Vito to his left and me to his right. There's coffee in front of me too, but I don't reach for it straight away, too eager to see what their initial thoughts regarding Wren are going to be.

Unfortunately, neither Vito nor Matteo seem to get the memo because neither of them utters a word as they choose to sip at their coffees instead.

"For someone so eager to talk and rush me over here, I really expected the conversation to flow a little smoother than this. It's not like either of you to be so speechless." I raise a brow at them, noting the tightness to Matteo's jaw and the crinkling of Vito's brows.

It's Vito who relents first, sighing heavily as he sinks back in his seat. "That's because I don't know what to even fucking say." He rubs at the back of his neck in annoyance.

"I don't think any of us do."

Matteo nods slightly in response as silence takes over us once more, but I manage to push through it and get straight to the point. "The reality of the situation is we were played. Big time. By the Russians when it comes to whatever game they have up their sleeve, but most importantly, by Featherstone." My fingers run back and forth slowly over my chin as I relay my thoughts. "Which seems to include Wren. But bigger than that, the person we vowed revenge on, for the death of Totem, is the exact same person we took to the damn meeting because our instincts told us to protect her."

Understanding shines in their eyes. The truth. The fact that we all felt something strong enough for this woman to want to protect her, when it was us that needed protecting from her all along.

It feels like an eternity before someone else speaks, and this time, it's Matteo as he leans forward, bracing his elbows on the table. "A promise is a promise."

I nod, knowing the words he's going to speak next, but it's Vito who beats him to it. "Blood is blood."

"Death is never the end," I say, completing the statements my father used to tell us when he was still alive and breathing.

Tapping my fingers on the table, I can't help but wonder why those words feel so flat when it comes to this topic? We've applied them to every aspect of our lives, but this... this feels different somehow.

"Is a promise really a promise to a dead man that never kept his end of the fucking deal anyway?" I turn my gaze to Vito, his question lingering in the air as I mull the words over in my head.

I hum in response, at a loss for words as Matteo clears his throat. "Wren Dietrichson is the daughter of Totem, as well as his killer. Something about that doesn't sit right with me. The darkness that flashed in her eyes, followed by the swift plunge into nothingness, caught me completely off-guard."

My brows rise in surprise, not expecting him to take notice of anything like that from her, but I guess being on the gunpoint, these things are taken into account.

"I also don't know what she meant when she spoke of redemption to Luna. I feel like there's a lot we don't know about her and Totem when it comes to their dynamic," I state, watching as my brothers nod in agreement. "But more than that, there's a lot of information that I'm sure *she* knows and we don't. We could use that to our advantage."

Matteo and Vito look between each other for a second before glancing back at me. I can't tell if it's surprise in their eyes that I have an idea like that or something else, but either way, I sit patiently and wait for one of them to answer me.

"Agreed," Matteo finally says with a sigh, downing the rest of his coffee before continuing, "Maybe we can pause everything until we can see what information we may be able to gain from her. *Then* we can revisit the decision on her life."

His last statement makes my gut clench and my chest tighten, but despite the emotions swirling inside of me, I nod, willing to pause the conversation for now as I turn my attention to Vito to see what he thinks.

When he doesn't respond, Matteo calls out his name, but just as he opens his mouth to add his opinion on the matter, the door I stepped through moments earlier swings open and ten of our men saunter inside. They're laughing and joking among themselves, completely unaware that they just interrupted something important, but the three of us shake it off, rising to our feet as they close the door behind them.

The second our feet are firmly planted on the ground,

we're in full work mode.

Jaws tense.

Eyes sharp.

Shoulders rolled back.

Feet shoulder-width apart.

If the way this man stood could kill, there would be a trail of dead bodies in his wake.

"Torres, how are current operations running?" Matteo asks, looking to the highest ranked member. The rest of the men find a seat at the table as the room quietens.

Torres is our most trusted lieutenant, that's why he came to New York with us, and the same reason he has the role of overseeing the smaller operations here in Italy. While we retreated when we returned home, taking a much-needed break, he was tasked with touching base with every member of our *famiglia* instead.

"Everything is looking good, Boss. The warehouse has a steady flow of stock coming in and out, the new Beretta 92's are looking good and pleasing the clients," he informs, referencing our gun business as he comes to a stop at the empty chair beside me. "There seems to have been a slight issue with the drugs coming out of Naples, but we rectified that before we came over here, and there is a new man overseeing the quality checks now." No further words are required; if he says he's handled a situation, then he's handled a situation. "And the distillery just confirmed first profits for the year," he adds with a smile on his face, and my own lips turn up with the news as I reach my hand out to shake his.

He takes it instantly, before doing the same with my brothers. Knowing the distillery is running at a profit is excellent news. It's the one thing my father always refused to do—a legitimate business—but the three of us knew it was necessary when he passed, leaving the business in our hands.

I don't think the De Luca family will ever go fully legit in our lifetime, a thought that has crossed my mind a time or two, and I'm fine with that. We were made for this life. Real life is far too mundane in comparison to the adrenaline we get from this.

"That's good news, Torres. Good news," Matteo murmurs, releasing his hand as he takes his seat at the head of the table again, and I follow suit, reclaiming my spot as I finally have a gulp of my coffee.

Fuck, that's good.

American coffee and Italian coffee are definitely not

the same thing. This tastes delicious. Like home.

"Now, with that taken care of, we need to discuss the shit that went down in New York, which has meant we're home a few days earlier than planned." A heavy quietness falls over the room as each man looks at Vito for him to continue. Even Torres has his brows quirked because he has no clue either. We got the fuck out of there as soon as possible while he was still in a meeting with our men who are permanently situated there, so he had to grab another flight home.

"With the Russians?" The man sitting beside Vito is the one to speak. I'm not too familiar with what he does. He's one of Torres' newer recruits called Antonio and he's an absolute beast with his fists.

"Yes, but also with Featherstone."

The gasps and grunts are audible around the table. We all know exactly how we felt when we learned of Totem's passing, and how it felt to lose everything he promised us before he even harnessed it himself.

Torres knocks his fist on the table, leaning back in his seat with wide eyes as he looks from me to Vito, before settling on Matteo.

"Did you find the person responsible for Totem's

death?" His question guts me, the air stolen from my lungs as I blink at him.

We don't keep our men in the loop on everything that happens within the business, but we kind of have a silent rule that when asked, we don't lie.

But as that thought runs through my mind, I shake my head at the exact same time I give my answer in complete sync with my brothers.

"No."

TWELVE

Wren

A heavy sigh falls from my lips as I look up at the ceiling in a daze. In the same clothes as yesterday, with my hair pulled back into a slick ponytail at my neck, I'm freshly showered and bored.

My cellphone is on the nightstand, drained of battery and no longer useful, while my gun is two inches away from my hand in my blazer pocket. I have no idea what time it is, but the sun is shining outside and I'm refreshed from sleep. I'm not foolish, I'm very aware that everything isn't perfectly okay and I am in danger here, but subconsciously, I think everything is fine because I slept hard.

The click of the lock from the bedroom door pulls me from my thoughts as I turn to see Nonna fill the space. I'm not sure when they actually locked it, but somebody did. I checked as soon as I woke up this morning, hoping I might have free rein of the house at least, but alas, I wasn't that lucky.

Nonna's smile spreads from ear to ear as she looks at me. She looks cute in a long-sleeved floral summer dress that falls all the way to her ankles, with sunglasses perched on top of her head.

"Come, I've got us some *saccottinos* to eat on the way." I blink at her in awe for a second, loving the way her voice switches between languages so effortlessly as she waits patiently for me to respond.

Slowly rising to my feet, I remain at the bottom of the bed as I cock my head to the side and meet her gaze. "On the way to where?"

Without missing a beat, she rolls her eyes at me dramatically, stepping out into the hallway as she waves her hand at me to follow. "Clothes shopping, obviously."

I rush to catch up, falling into step beside her. "It's not obvious at all. I'm here because they said so. Technically as a prisoner. My life is hanging in the balance and my survival instincts are heightened. So, when you're nice to me, I'm left wondering if it's because you really are that nice or whether the De Luca brothers have roped you into the darkside and are setting me up for something."

She pauses mid-step, right by the front door with her hand resting on the handle as she meets my gaze. A chuckle falls from her lips as she shakes her head slightly at me. "I definitely like you."

Without another word, she swings the door open and heads outside, leaving me to follow, again in a complete state of shock. She climbs into the waiting SUV, not checking if I'm still there, and I silently make my way around to the other side of the vehicle to join her.

A man dressed from head to toe in a black suit with a matching shirt and tie waits to close it behind me. I recognize him. I saw him in New York for the briefest of moments, but he's never uttered a word to me. He still doesn't when I climb in and he closes the door securely behind me before taking the driver's seat.

Nonna is buckled in already. Once I am buckled in, I turn to her, only to find her already looking at me. "Oddly enough, I seem to like you too," I blurt, making her grin as she offers me a small platter of pastries to choose from.

Saccottinos.

I murmur my thanks as I take one, opting to nibble on it while I watch out of the window, the vehicle pulling away from the house as Nonna hums her response.

The SUV is quiet as we drive through the winding roads leading to the nearby town she plans on taking us to. Eventually, the greenery turns into small buildings before we arrive at a busy area and the SUV pulls over to the side of the road. Shop after shop lines the street to our right, big glass displays advertising what lies inside.

"Are you ready?" Nonna asks, a quirk to her brow. She climbs out as I nod.

Reaching for my own handle, I barely open it an inch before the driver is at the door doing it for me. It doesn't feel like a polite gesture though. With the way he glares at me, his body tense as he points to follow after Nonna, it seems as if he's just making sure I don't run. There's an underlying vibe from him that tells me he would love for me to do just that so he can put me in my place.

I keep my eyes fixed on his as I climb out, making sure to let him know that I'm not scared of him. I don't look away until I have to round the back of the SUV, and my attention is then quickly grabbed by Nonna who is waiting on the pavement to link her arm through mine and drag me to the store directly in front of us.

It's a high-end store, because the outfits in the window are somewhat familiar. I'm not out of my comfort zone in a place like this, not at all, but as we step inside and the luxurious scent fills my nostrils and the perfect lighting hits us from above, I wonder why she would bring a so-called captive here?

Nonna must see the skepticism on my face as I glance around at the separate areas laid out for each designer. "This is my favorite pastime, so we're going to have some fun. Don't worry about a thing," she states, and I smile.

If I'm going to die, at least I'll be wearing something cute.

"I can afford to pay for this, you know," I grumble, giving Nonna a pointed glare as she wags her finger at me in front of the cashier.

We've been in here for hours, and although she may have picked out a few items for herself, the majority of the items in the bags are for me. It's laughable, the amount that's there, it looks like I don't plan on dying at all, but I just couldn't help myself. While staying in Philadelphia, I kept my head down and never entertained the idea of going shopping, so I've definitely made up for it.

"You shouldn't *have* to pay for it, Wren, that's my point. Like you said, it's not your fault you're in this situation to begin with." She winks at me before mumbling to the cashier something about the purchases being settled on the De Luca account.

I can't argue with a statement like that, especially when I know it's not her paying but them. It makes a small smile tease the corner of my mouth as I turn to face the door, watching as the driver/bodyguard, who hasn't left our side the entire time, takes the last of the bags out to the vehicle.

Nonna links her arm through mine once more before dragging me to the SUV. Climbing in, I sink back in my seat, exhausted from trying so many clothes on as she turns to face me.

"Shall we have lunch?" Her voice is eager, and it makes me feel like there isn't usually a female presence around for this kind of thing.

It's on the tip of my tongue to agree with her, when the driver takes his seat up front, slamming the door shut behind him as he shakes his head. "No can do, Ms. De

Luca, I have a call for you."

Her lips pinch in irritation as she takes the cellphone from his hand, pressing it to her ear with a huff.

"What?... No, we're busy actually... doing none of your business..." Her eyebrows knit as she sighs. "Fine, but you owe me." She ends the call without another word before tossing it into the empty front seat as the driver joins the traffic. "It seems we'll have lunch at home, but not to worry, I have the perfect idea for us." She smiles wide, like her plans haven't just been changed, and I nod, still slightly caught up on the fact the driver called her *Ms. De Luca.*

How have I not yet considered who she is? With a name like Nonna, you would assume she's their grandmother, but she really doesn't look old enough for that.

Could she be their mother?

Something tells me it's not quite that.

"Tell me what's on your mind, dear. You're pinching your brows so tight we may have to do emergency botox to relax the damn muscles." There's a shimmer of humor in her eyes as I shake my head at her dramatics with a glint of a smile touching my lips.

"Who are you to them?"

Understanding washes over her face as she nods lightly in response before speaking. "They bestowed me with the name Ms. De Luca six years ago when their father died. It was the first order of business they put through when Matteo became the head of the family." She glances off almost wistfully, her eyes tracking the world as it flies by us before she turns to look at me again. "I was their nanny until Enzo was fourteen, then I was no longer needed. But those boys… they never knew their mother, not even Matteo seems to have a memory of her, and their father… Well, he was a different kind of mafia man altogether." Her eyes then draw to the driver, like she's aware he's listening and she doesn't want to give too much. "They came to me years later, pleading for me to come home, and honestly, I had no true life of my own without them. I had spent so much of my time dedicated to those boys that I didn't have a family of my own. So, as they get lost in the world of violence, blood, and gore, I provide stability, safety, and a home."

Her words melt my frozen fucking heart.

How are they so lucky to have her in their life? For her to seemingly drop whatever it is she was doing when they reappeared in her life. The love they must feel between them... God, I can only imagine what it would feel like.

I press my lips together, not wanting to show any hint of vulnerability or weakness in my response, so I choose to offer none at all as I turn my attention out the window.

I've technically been held hostage for over twenty-four hours now, and I feel less trapped than I did as a child. Being in the care of my parents didn't offer me any kind of stability or safety, never knowing what a true home feels like. Under the rule of my mother and the almighty asshole, Totem, I spent every waking day imprisoned under their thumb. A version of a daughter they wanted to mold perfectly in their image as opposed to being who I wanted to be.

My bloodline, my heritage, that placed me in Featherstone Academy, was highly regarded because of my mother's family, but they were just as treacherous as my father's. No morals, no values. Just greed, death, and destruction.

Who knew there was another way?

Soon, the SUV pauses at the iron gates and we make our way up the dirt path, coming to a stop outside the beautiful home.

I make sure to climb out and shut my door before the

driver even gets a chance to place a foot on the ground, and I round the back of the SUV in time to head inside with Nonna. "We'll get the bags in a little while, let's eat first," she declares. My stomach grumbles in response too, giving her my answer as we head inside, straight for the kitchen.

I'm frozen in place as we enter the open space that seems like the heart of the entire house. A gathering space, a family hotspot, a room that has an atmosphere that continues to catch me off guard, but worse this time, as I spot two out of the three De Luca brothers sitting at the dining table.

Vito and Enzo.

I wonder where Matteo may be, but that's squashed as I note the tense facial features of both men.

Vito's blazer is thrown over the back of his seat, his shirt sleeves rolled to his elbows as his fingers are laced on the table. His jaw is tense and the lines around his eyes almost seem like he's trying *not* to glare at me. Confusing.

Enzo, on the other hand, has his black blazer still on, although the top button of his shirt is undone and his tie is long forgotten. And even though his lips are parted, making it seem like he's relaxed, his brows are knitted harshly.

I run my tongue over my lips as I gulp, but it's Nonna who breaks the silence first. "Boys, nice to see you. I told you on the phone we're about to have lunch. Do you want something too?" She turns her back to them, moving around the kitchen effortlessly as she fastens an apron in place before searching for the ingredients she needs.

"That can wait, Nonna. We have some important questions for Miss Dietrichson," Enzo answers, his eyes remaining on the back of Nonna's head instead of flicking to me.

That must be a purposeful move, just like the fact that I'm suddenly not Wren, or Ava, or *Bella,* and just *Miss Dietrichson.* Clearly, something has changed since yesterday evening, and it leaves me a little uncertain. There's something in the air, I can sense it.

"Well, you can wait until I've fed her. We've barely eaten at all today and it won't take much time." Nonna's reply is much more tense as she turns to face them, spatula in hand as she raises her eyebrows.

"She can wait," Vito grunts, leaning back in his seat as his hands remain on the table.

"No. She. Can't." My eyes widen as I glance at Nonna. Vito and Enzo are talking about me like I'm not even here, while Nonna is defending me in the same manner. What the actual fuck is going on?

"I'm not above starving her." Vito's shoulders bunch as he adjusts in his seat, and I don't miss the way Enzo glances at his brother out of the corner of his eye with a hint of concern teasing the edge.

That's my cue to interject before Nonna blows a blood vessel. She's practically boiling, vibrating with anger as I step toward her. I place my hand on her shoulder for the briefest of moments, a silent thank you mixed with a hint of assurance, before I move toward the table where the brothers wait.

It's not until I'm right near the chair facing Vito that I scoff, shaking my head dismissively as I pull it out to take a seat. "You think I haven't been starved before?" My head tilts to the side, a mocking smile gracing my lips as I drop down onto the chair.

As I flick my gaze between the two of them, I notice Enzo likes to talk with his eyes because once again, I can see his emotions and the surprise flashing in his brown orbs at the statement I just made.

It takes a beat before Vito manages to muster up a response, but getting a read on him is far more difficult.

"That probably happened because of your lack of loyalty."

Fuck. You.

My hands clench in my lap as my nostrils flare, the strength and willpower to not blurt those words out at him taking control. As much as I want to fire them at him, I don't want him to know he's getting under my skin like that.

Shaking my head dismissively, I keep a smile on my face as I stare directly into his eyes. "I did show loyalty, just not to you. It's a decision I could regret down the line, but I made the right call for everyone involved."

Vito purses his lips as Enzo leans forward in his seat, assessing me until I look in his direction. "What does that mean?"

"It means absolutely nothing to you."

Enzo leans back in his seat, running his tongue over his teeth as he openly glares at me. He clearly doesn't like my response, but I can sense it triggered a thought to run through his mind as he continues to eye me. "When we left the restaurant yesterday, you said something about redemption. Does that have something to do with it?"

His observation catches me off guard, but I keep my

emotions in check. "My life as Wren Dietrichson didn't begin yesterday when I revealed who I was. I hadn't been playing the role of Ava my whole life, Enzo." I scoff, shaking my head at him. "Have you ever lived under the rule of someone you didn't have the same moral code as? Have you ever been forced to take actions that will forever haunt you?" I raise my eyebrows in question, looking between the two of them as neither attempt to answer. "My loyalty wasn't connected to my redemption, my loyalty was connected to the fact that I gave my word. I have never, and will never, offer my word without meaning it. Redemption be damned."

My chest is heaving with every breath, my emotions rattling in my veins as I clench my hands in my lap, wishing like hell that there was a glass of something strong in my palm instead.

"I think you're forgetting that it's us that should be asking the questions right now, Wren. Not you." Matteo's voice comes from behind me, but I don't turn to look at him, especially not when I hear Nonna gasp.

Don't let them see your emotions, Wren. Don't let them see.

I repeat the words in my mind, even as Vito adds to

his brother's statement. "You're our captive, Wren. Ours to decide what to do with, and your answers may determine the overall outcome of your life. You should be mindful of that."

A bark of laughter bites my tongue as I shake my head at him again. This motherfucker. "I think you're forgetting who my father was. I've *felt* the repercussions of far worse threats in my life. It takes a little more than that to scare me."

THIRTEEN

Vito

I don't know what the fuck is going on with me. My mind and body are at war with every word that tumbles out from her sweet, delectable mouth.

Every. Single. One.

I've never been so conflicted in my entire life. I was completely wrapped up in this woman, leaving meetings to protect her because I couldn't stop the urge from overwhelming me, taking her to another meeting so she wouldn't be out of my sight, and yet… here we are.

I want to hate her, with every fiber of my being, that is how we were raised, and the fact that she's still breathing right now is a miracle in itself. Anyone else and they would never have left that restaurant alive.

My fingers twitch in my lap as I continue to stare at her, the overwhelming need to wipe my hand down my face almost unbearable, but I refuse to let her get a glimpse of what she's doing to me.

I'm still struggling to look at her and not just see the beautiful Ava that we initially met. She doesn't exist, not really, but I'll never hate that version of her. In that moment, even if it was beyond brief, we'll always have the memories.

The pain I see swirling around in her eyes tells me there's more to her past than we know. The way she spills little truths about her past, her words about her fear of her father outweighing anything and anyone else confirms she's not lying.

As I glance at her now, sitting perfectly still in her seat with her hands resting in her lap, she appears calm and unrattled. What I wouldn't give to see what is going through her mind right now. She's a master at hiding her emotions, and it's driving me insane.

How much fear must she have felt to kill her own father?

Our dear old papa wasn't the best, not at all. He was a bad example most of the time, putting us in shitty situations, but I sense her pain runs much deeper than that.

It doesn't mean anything though. It shouldn't. Yet here I am, with an overwhelming need to reach across the table, pull her sweet ass into my lap and cradle her in my arms. Instead, I focus on the matter at hand, and that's delving into the questions we have for her now that the revelations of yesterday have dwindled down a little.

I don't think I'll ever truly get over the surprise of her being Totem's daughter, but I can at least think past it now.

My hands clench in my lap again, the need to do something, *anything*, right now taking over, so I shake my head, sitting taller in my seat as Matteo finally joins us at the table. With the three of us focusing on her, you would expect Wren to falter, but she doesn't miss a beat.

I can feel Nonna glaring at us from where she still stands by the oven, but for now, she's keeping her distance. Although I get the sense she'll jump in if necessary, just not likely to our defense. Especially since she has taken a liking to our new guest.

Enzo adjusts himself in his seat beside me, undoing the next button on his shirt before wiping his fingers across his chin like he does when he's deep in thought. But it's Matteo who continues to guide the situation.

"Now, we're going to ask you some questions about Totem, and you're going to answer them." I almost roll my eyes at the tone he uses, like she's a fool who needs time to process what he's saying, when all she's actually shown us is that she's resilient, smart, and somewhat calculated.

Wren doesn't respond, doesn't move an inch, except for flicking her gaze over the three of us once more. If anyone were to walk in now and see the situation from the outside looking in, they would likely assume that Wren is actually the one conducting the conversation. There's power in her posture, fueled by the pain that ripples through her veins, and I get a sense of pride from that for some reason.

Matteo taps his fingers on the table as he thinks for a moment, before diving straight in. "What control did Totem gain over Featherstone before you killed him?"

A scoff slips from her lips as she shakes her head at my brother, the corners of her lips tilting up in a mocking smirk. "None."

My jaw clenches at the short and blunt answer she offers, while Enzo works to cover his mouth to hide the grin that is likely taking over his face. Matteo remains stoic, just like Wren, the two of them perfectly mastering their poker faces.

"We know he gained control of the games."

I recall that fact, the news circulating like wildfire around us. Apparently, part of being a bloodline within Featherstone meant taking part in trials and tests that, if won, can make you a member of the Ring, aka the leaders of Featherstone.

We never truly got the hows and the whys of it all, his death coming soon after, but among those he had made promises to, it was a win everyone was cheering about.

"He didn't gain control of shit," Wren says with a burst of laughter, her head falling back as she moves her hands over her hair. "He literally gate-crashed one of the trials, shot someone in the shoulder and fled like the weak man he was." Her words quickly turn to acid on her tongue as she lifts her head to look at us once more.

I try to process her words and the fact that's not what I was expecting to hear, and Enzo must agree because he chimes in too.

"You're lying."

Wren whips her gaze to his, staring straight into his eyes without missing a beat. "What do I have to gain from lying?

The man is dead, and I'm not about rewriting someone's history." She lifts her hands from her lap, placing them on the table in front of her as she casts her gaze over each of us. "If you're at war, in a trial, or under attack, and one of your brothers goes down, what do you do?"

My head tilts to the side slightly as I observe her. "What do you mean?" The question falls from my lips before I can stop it, but when neither of my brothers interjects, I know they're just as confused as I am.

"I mean, you're in a blood bath, your brother is bleeding out on the floor surrounded by gunfire, men are continuing to drop around you, yet you're luckily unscathed. What do you do?"

"Get my brother out of there." The answer tumbles from my lips, my filter not working as I blurt the truth. Her lips form a thin line as she nods slightly, bringing her hands to her lap again.

"I was part of the trial that my father interrupted. Smeared in blood and surrounded by people he forced me to make my enemies. Yet when it got too much and he ran, do you think he made sure to take me with him?" Her tone is answer enough. That would be a firm no, and it makes my heart ache for her.

Nobody asks to be brought into this crazy world we call life, but to not even have your family there to support and protect you? Shit, I can't even begin to imagine how that must feel, which only serves to piss me off even more because I'm not supposed to feel compassion for her. Not at all.

Matteo clears his throat as he adjusts his tie, trying to hide the fact that he's affected by her words, just like I am, and by the way Enzo shifts in his seat too, I would say he's feeling the same.

"None of that is relevant now," Matteo grumbles as I hear Nonna scoff from where she's standing with her arms folded over her chest, watching us intently.

"You guys were the ones to bring up the games. I just wanted to give a reality check." Wren's fake smile widens as she stares Matteo down.

God, I hate how fucking fantastic she is with her sass and attitude, and the way she carries herself tells me she's not all mouth either. We have to remember she was trained at Featherstone Academy, and the way Totem spoke of it, it's something to definitely watch for.

"Totem promised us—"

"For fuck's sake. I don't care what my father promised

you. You were fools for thinking he would follow through on whatever bullshit you agreed on, and you're even more foolish for thinking you are still going to get it." Wren's jaw tenses as she stands, her chair scraping across the floor behind her as she plants her palms flat on the table.

I can't decide if she's mad or frustrated, but either way, the red tinge to her cheeks is undeniable. I'm sure anyone else in front of her, hearing her tone and venom coating every word, would sink on the spot, but not Matteo. He's just as sadistic as she is when it comes to this fucking power play.

Slowly, Matteo rises from his seat too, matching her stance right down to placing his hands on the table the exact same width apart.

"He promised me an heir from his daughter," he spits, his voice low and murderous as he tries to keep his anger at bay. "He was quite a fan of selling women, including you it seems."

His words are a lie. A push at her. We would never do anything in exchange for a woman. Ever. Human trafficking is where we draw the line. We're not angels. Fuck, we know which afterlife we're heading to, but we'll go knowing very well that we stayed true to that rule.

I expect Wren to gape in horror, bark back in anger, or maybe even sob like a heartbroken girl, but she does none of that. Instead, she does what she keeps doing. Catching me off guard.

A scoff falls from her lips, followed by another and another as she pushes up off the table, shaking her head in disbelief at Matteo's words, before it suddenly morphs into a burst of laughter. It's my turn to stare at her as she laughs, all the way from her gut, swiping her hands over her cheeks to discard the tears that have escaped, before she looks Matteo dead in the eye. All her humor is gone, and in its place, stands a stone-cold woman.

"Then he played you, Matteo. Well, he played you or you're downright lying to me because my motherfucker of a father didn't want me to be distracted. Not in any way, shape, or form, and that involved him having my tubes tied when I was fifteen years old." Her words hit me square in the face as I see the truth shining in her eyes and my jaw falls slack.

Silence blankets us. But even if Wren is pleased with the fact that she's rendered us speechless, it doesn't show in the fake smile plastered on her face. No. It's as fake as her name being Ava.

She clenches and unclenches her hands at her sides a few times, before she rolls her shoulders back and turns away from us. "Sorry, Nonna, I'll take a pass on the food right now," she states before turning for the door, not waiting for a response from the woman nodding with a scowl firmly set on her face.

She's not mad at Wren, I can sense it. She's mad at the words that just spilled from her mouth.

It's only when Wren gets to the doorway that Matteo hollers after her, but we all know it's too little, too late. "We're not done here."

But it's not Wren who spins around and puts him in his place, it's Nonna.

"You're more than done here, and I don't want to hear another word about it."

REDEMPTION

FOURTEEN

Wren

My body aches from the tension that hasn't stopped vibrating through me since I stormed out of the kitchen. If my childhood taught me anything, it's that the only person that is going to protect me, is me. I don't have to lie or exaggerate, my life really was that shitty, which then made me even shittier. Although it did give me truthful horrors that stop people in their tracks.

I needed to get out of that room, away from the three of them and the hint of pity that flashed in each of their gazes as they stared at me in shock.

Looking out of the window as the evening sun sets,

I run the towel over my damp hair, my body missing the pounding of the water even though I've hopped in three times already. Those fuckers had me turning into a damn prune. I can't stop stepping under the spray as I think, think, and think again about everything happening around me.

Once I'm satisfied with my hair not dripping down my spine on my new clothes, I move over to the mirror. I found a hairdryer in the closet earlier when I started unpacking all of the shopping bags. It feels ridiculous that I removed every item from the bags and found it a home.

It's like I'm deluding myself and assume I'm going to survive long enough for their chosen places to matter, but it was the only thing I could occupy myself with so I didn't step into the shower again. Besides, I've learned to control what I can, and this is something I have the power over. Small or not.

The reality of the situation is I'm getting antsy. I don't do well doing nothing, getting the opportunity to get lost in my mind, tear it all apart, only to fail miserably at piecing it all back together again.

Not that any of that matters to the De Luca brothers. No. They are dead set on trying to extract pointless information from me. Information I likely don't have or know, not that I'm going to tell them that, not when it may be the only thing keeping me alive.

Shaking my head, I focus on the new clothes I'm wearing, attempting to pull myself from my thoughts as I run my hands over the cute *Mom* jeans I picked out today. They're frayed slightly at the hem, a distressed color adding to the effect, and I love them. With a fitted white tank top tucked into the waistline and an oversized sweatshirt, I feel comfy and relaxed for the first time since I got here. Despite all of the bullshit I'm sinking in.

There's makeup sitting on the desktop now since Nonna insisted we organize it while we were at the store, but I'm in no mood to mess around with it. Knowing my mood, I'll be jumping back into the shower in no time.

That thought plays in my mind as I glance at the hairdryer again, trying to decide if it's actually worth doing, but despite my uncertainty, I reach for it. If anything, it will keep me busy for a little while at least.

Plugging the gadget in, I reach for the hairbrush and drag it through my ends, thankful that my center part is starting to form more naturally now since I've been training it into this style for what feels like an eternity.

As I reach for the hairdryer once more, I startle when the bedroom door swings open and Nonna stands in the open space. She's still wearing her pretty summer dress from earlier. I have no idea what she's looking for, and I don't bother to ask, but whatever it is, she seemingly nods to herself before moving toward me.

She stops on the other side of the double bed, twirling something in her hands as she rolls her shoulders back and smiles gently. "I can sense you don't want to talk right now, Dear, and that's okay. I'm never going to push you to talk about anything or do anything that makes you uncomfortable," she states, making me confused as hell as I remain rooted to the spot. "But, this is a twenty-minute warning that food is going to be done, and you bet your cute butt you're coming out there to eat with me. Understand?"

This woman is somehow becoming my kryptonite because I find myself wanting to obey her, but I also remember who else lives here, who this home belongs to, and I wave my hand dismissively. "Thanks, Nonna, but—"

"No buts. They're gone. It'll just be the two of us. Those assholes can sort themselves out, they're not my problem tonight." The truth is thick on her tongue and it makes me grin despite my uncertainty, and before I even realize it, I'm agreeing.

"Okay. Twenty minutes is enough time for me to sort my hair out."

Her smile spreads wide as she throws the thing in her hand on the bed, before turning and heading for the door. I frown at whatever it is she just left, but it only takes me a split second to realize it's a cellphone charger.

When I glance back up to thank her, she's already gone, so I reach for the charger. The second it's in my hands, I cringe a little. I don't have anyone to call or text, to reach out to or ask for help. No one. And over the past six months since I left Featherstone, I've loved it. No constant presence from my parents monitoring and controlling my every move. No fake friends feeding me gossip I don't care for, and no stresses from the academy life either.

The one thing I do want to charge my cell phone for is my latest obsession. Playing fucking Sudoku. I have the app hidden in my health and fitness folder so no one can see my guilty pleasure, but it keeps me going more than I care to admit.

Plugging in the cord beside the hairdryer, I quickly insert it into my phone and place it on the nightstand so it can charge, before focusing back on my hair again.

I feel calmer and more relaxed now that Nonna has stuck her head in to see me. I don't know how she does it. I used to take my privacy very seriously and would have gone crazy if someone waltzed in like that, but not only did she just appear, her presence soothed me, too.

It's insane.

Slightly bewildered by the whirlwind that is Nonna, I grab the handle of the hairdryer at the exact same time my cell phone screen lights up, showing notifications with Luna's name written all over them.

This is another thing bothering me, and I don't know how to handle it. I told her to leave it in the dust, yet here she is... continuing to push me despite everything I've done since we first met.

Now isn't the time for me to go through those messages, otherwise I'll be back in the shower and I'll exceed the twenty minutes Nonna gave me. She might be here on the dot if I don't make an appearance.

As if sensing my thoughts, the screen lights up again, but this time it's an incoming call. I consider pretending I don't see it, but Luna would keep hounding me if I don't pick up.

Taking a deep breath, I reach for my cell, answering

the call as I bring it to my ear. I don't utter a word, but there's no need because Luna calls out my name.

"Wren, are you there?"

"I'm here." Her sigh of relief is apparent, and it only adds to my confusion. I don't know how to handle someone reaching out to be... nice? Caring? Forgiving?

Shit, I don't know what it is, but I don't deserve any of it.

"Why has your cellphone been turned off?" I raise my eyebrows at her like she can see me but keep my silence. When she realizes I'm not going to indulge her, she sighs as I settle back on the bed with my back against the headboard.

"What were you calling for, Luna?" I ask, my tone bleak as I wait for her to reply.

"I wanted to make sure you were okay," she says, like it's really that simple, and it makes me shake my head in disbelief.

"I'm fine."

My short and blunt response does little to dampen her mood. "Are they treating you well?"

After a quick survey of my surroundings and mental comparison of the things I've experienced prior to this,

I realize I'm being treated far better than I deserve after the shit I pulled with the De Lucas. I don't tell her any of that though, that would be showing vulnerability and weakness. "Does it matter?"

"She cares about your safety, Wren."

Jessica Watson. I would know that voice anywhere.

Luna's best friend, the redheaded sunshine from Featherstone Academy that somehow manages to see lightness in everything and everyone. Except me, of course, it's only Luna that continues to push at me like that.

Hearing Jess's voice does little to settle me though, making me feel like I'm under a microscope with the two of them, and I can't bear it. "I really wouldn't care about my safety or anything else, Luna. It's not fucking worth it. I did my job like you asked and protected you when needed. I'm done now. That was the agreement."

My words are tight, my jaw clenched and my eyes slammed shut as I try to regulate my breathing. Admitting what my father did to me earlier to the De Luca brothers has my emotions twisted up in knots and I feel like I'm a live wire ready to blow a fuse.

"You're right. You did what was agreed, but you also did more. You didn't have to raise a gun to protect me, but you did and that means something to me," Luna explains almost soothingly down the line.

"Well, it shouldn't," I blurt, feeling more and more sensitive with every passing second I stay on the call.

"We're going to help you, Wren. I'm dealing with the mess Totem left behind with the Russians as well as the De Lucas, but the Russians are getting completely out of hand at the minute. Once I have them under control, or at this stage, dead, then I can focus on what seems to be a problem with the Italians. But above all that, I want you back in one piece." There's a bite to her tone that I'm familiar with. Her determination and willpower is like nothing I've ever seen before, not even from my own father.

"Don't waste your resources, Luna." My words sound bored, desperate to protect the emotions swirling inside of me, as Jess scoffs on the other end of the line.

"Remind me why we're helping her?" she mumbles, the question exactly what is floating through my mind, but thankfully, to my relief, Luna doesn't answer her.

"Sit tight, Wren. I'm figuring this out," Luna advises instead, likely waiting to answer her friend when she's off the call.

"Don't rush," I mumble, which is met with a pause

from their side for a moment before Jess speaks.

"Why?"

That one word holds so much weight that I almost choke on the answer as it stumbles past my lips.

"There's literally nowhere else for me to go."

With that, I end the call, not wanting to feel another hint of pity from anyone.

I've lived through worse.

I've survived harsher circumstances.

Who knows, maybe surviving this is my ultimate challenge because being around the De Luca brothers, when all I feel is their hatred aimed at me after feeling their soft and delicate caresses, may just be the death of me.

REDEMPTION

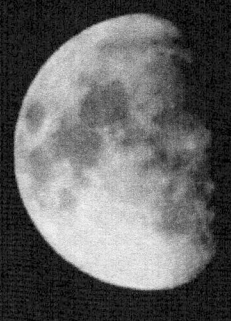

FIFTEEN

Wren

I feel dazed as I'm ripped from the depths of sleep, encouraging me to squeeze my eyes shut tighter for a second before attempting to blink them open. When I feel blinded by the light in the room, I realize my error. I didn't close the curtains last night, and now the mid-morning sun is crisp and clear but trying to burn my retinas.

With a huff, I roll over, turning away from the glaring light in an attempt to fall back asleep, but after a few minutes, I know it's useless. I'm awake now, whether I like it or not, but I'm definitely blaming Nonna for this interruption. It was her amazing food that put me in the most perfect food coma last night when the two of us sat at the table and ate until I couldn't fit another single bite in my mouth.

I had stumbled back to my room like a drunk woman, and only just managed to slip into a pair of pajamas before I collapsed on the bed. Sleep beckoned me from my food coma, leaving me to fall victim to the effects of the blistering morning sun through the uncovered windows.

Unable to remain in my cocoon of blankets with my thoughts being the only thing to keep me company, I lift the sheets and swing my legs over the side of the bed. I yawn, stretching my hands above my head as I arch my back.

The second I stop, my thoughts drift to jumping in the shower, but I decide against it as I can see that the bedroom door to my room is slightly ajar, which means I can leave and roam around for a while.

Rising from the bed, I waste no time reaching for some yoga pants and a tank top in the closet that we bought yesterday for me to do some exercise in. Hope blooms in my stomach at the desire of being able to get some fresh air and feel the wind on my face. Running wasn't a pastime of mine before I was cooped up in Philadelphia, but I fell in love with it out there. Even though it may have only been a week since I was there, it feels like an eternity.

I slip my socks and sneakers on next, before reaching for a light jacket in case it's not as warm as it looks outside. The reality of the weather in Italy is lost on me, but back home, things weren't always cooler than they originally looked.

Glancing at my cell phone, I consider taking it with me, but there's no point when I don't have my earphones. So I leave it on the charger and head for the door, slipping out and shutting it closed quietly behind me as I practically tiptoe toward the kitchen.

My muscles tense with every step I take, worried that one of the De Luca brothers will be around, and I immediately regret not grabbing my gun.

Fuck.

I'm at the open doorway to the kitchen now so turning back is pointless, but with one deep breath, I step into the room, only to find it empty. Not even Nonna is here, but I do notice a small note propped up on the table with my name written in bold black pen.

Wren, I had some errands to run and I didn't want

to wake you before I left.
I won't be gone too long, but I did make some fresh sfogliatelle for you to try.
Here is my number if you need me.
Nonna.

I run my fingers over the number that she jotted down, before glancing at the covered plate behind the note where the *sfogliatelle* is. I grab one of the sweet flaky breakfast buns, taking a big bite, before I head for the door. I'm ready to get my legs moving, and this will fuel me enough to keep me going.

I've eaten the entire thing before I even make it to the front door, and I make a mental note to eat the other two still on the plate when I get back because they're too delicious to waste.

Swinging the front door open, I cringe as soon as my eyes lock on the man pacing back and forth in front of a SUV. It's the driver from yesterday, and the second he looks up, I know he's going to be an asshole.

Instead of the suit he wore yesterday, he's wearing a pair of black combat pants, a fitted black tee, and combat boots. He looks like someone in the military; likely has the training of someone of that caliber too. If he wasn't sneering at me, he would almost be handsome with his slicked back black hair and olive skin.

Men always ruin themselves with the aura they give off.

Well, that's not technically true since the aura I got from Vito, Matteo, and Enzo when I first met them was enticing and exciting. It was when the truth about me came out and they opened their damned mouths that it all went to shit.

"Back inside. Now." His bark is sharper than I initially expected, but it doesn't mean I'm going to follow his order.

"I'm good, but thanks." I plaster a fake smile across my face as I shut the door behind me, and he really must have thought I was going to do as he said because he gapes at me in surprise for a second.

When he finally musters a response, I've already taken two steps to the right in the opposite direction of his parked SUV.

"I said, back inside. Now." He folds his arms over his chest like he means business, clearly hoping I'll be shaking in my boots at his mere presence, but instead, I roll my eyes, exasperated with him.

"I heard you, and politely declined. I'm not trying to escape if that makes you feel any better." I'm itching to start running, the added chase from this fucker would be exhilarating, but at the same time, I don't want to put my back to him and leave myself at a disadvantage.

"Listen, bitch—" he starts, but I turn to face him head-on, lifting my hand to halt him, and like a good little puppy, it works.

"I dare you to call me that again and see how far it gets you." I don't want to say who I am in case that hasn't been revealed to the members of the De Luca family, but if this guy puts another foot out of place, I'll show him what I'm capable of. He must be able to sense it in my tone, his throat bobbing, but the anger in his eyes is venomous at the same time. "I'm going for a run around the property."

There. That's nice enough of me. I didn't have to share my plans, but I did in an attempt to compromise, but the way he starts shaking his head pisses me off.

"You can't do that."

Nope. I refuse to be told what to do by someone whose name I don't even know. Not after everything I've been through. He's not my captor and I'm not his to control.

With my mind made up, I drop my hand, offering him

another fake smile, before I turn on my heels and run. I don't stop to look at him as I hear him call out to me. Instead, I focus on putting one foot in front of the other as fast as I can.

The stones beneath my feet quickly turn into perfectly mowed grass as I get to the edge of the house and the rear of the property comes into view. A large open field is framed by the dense trees that shelter the entire land, and I use them as a guide as I continue at the same pace, smiling from ear to ear. After a few minutes, I glance back over my shoulder to find no one following me, and my smile only spreads wider as I drop my stride a little now that I know I'm not being chased.

I wouldn't be surprised if the distance around the perimeter is about a mile. It's nowhere near what I was hoping to cover, but it'll do for today. With that in mind, I drop my pace to a jog, wanting to savor every ounce of the freedom I feel as the wind brushes against my face and the sun beats down on my skin.

Although I may be alone, there is one sinking feeling that stays with me no matter how many steps I take. The feeling of someone watching me. I can't see anyone, and I'm on high alert, focused on my surroundings. My ears are perked, ready to catch the sound of anyone over the pounding of my heart in my chest, but I get nothing. Not even a glance of someone in the distance, but my gut tells me someone is there.

Keeping my pace as I move around the back of the house, I almost come full circle when I find a dozen men gathered at the front of the property. There are three more SUVs now, and every single guy is dressed exactly the same as the driver, so I instantly know they're members of the family.

As I approach them, the asshole who lives to piss me off steps forward, others following his lead as he looks smugly at me. "Here she is. The 'runaway.' Let Matteo know we found her and are keeping her locked in the outer building until they can come and beat some sense into her."

My eyebrows knit in confusion at the fact that this motherfucker is talking utter bullshit, but before I can call him out on anything, another guy steps forward, smirking at me. "Maybe he wouldn't mind if we had a go at beating some sense into her first." He runs his tongue over his bottom lip, and my jaw instantly tightens.

"You could try," I state, raising my eyebrows at them as they all snicker in response.

That's all the confirmation I needed. These fuckers definitely don't know who I am or why I'm really here, but if they continue to push, I'm more than happy to show them. The tinge of a threat in the air has my shoulders dropping back, my stomach clenching, and my feet inching to shoulder-width apart.

If they notice the shift in me, they don't say anything about it. Their vibe screams they believe they're bigger, better, and more powerful than they actually are. *Push me, I dare you, and let me put you back in your place.*

The driver steps forward another inch, wagging his finger at me as he gets ready to give me a piece of his mind, but he's interrupted by the sound of a vehicle making its way up the driveway. With the blacked out windows, no one can tell who is in the SUV until it rolls to a stop beside me.

If this is one of the De Lucas, then I know I'm fucked. Even if this asshole is lying, they're not going to believe a word that comes out of my mouth over their men.

To my relief, as the door opens, a pair of small legs stick out, revealing white cropped pants and a red flowy blouse as Nonna comes into view.

"What's going on here?" Her tone is sharp, her chin

slightly tilted up as she looks down her nose at the men before us.

"Ms. De Luca, we were just handling the woman as advised. We're going to take her to the outbuilding until Matteo arrives," the driver explains, waving his arms around as he talks to her, but she shakes her head at him.

"I don't think so. I'm here now and Vito is aware our guest has been on a leisurely run on the property and doesn't require any further action." My eyebrows shoot up to my hairline at her words.

How the fuck does he know that? The eyes I felt. Were they him? A camera? I have no clue, and it doesn't really matter if it gets me out of this bullshit. Without waiting for a response, Nonna turns her attention to me with a tight smile on her face. "Go and wash your hands, Dear, then you can come and help me in the kitchen."

She saunters off and every single man watches her move. They start mumbling among themselves, and then disperse. Everyone but the driver, that is. He stands in place, glaring at me like I spat in his mother's face or something.

"What's your name?" I ask, needing a name for the fucker that is purposely causing issues for me.

"Teto," he states as he tilts his head to the side, his jaw so tight and tense he could cut through glass. Taking a step toward him, I make sure to keep my body language neutral, unfazed, and guarded until I come to a stop before him so we're almost toe to toe.

Keeping my voice low, I smirk. "Excellent, I know what to put on your gravestone when I bury you if you continue to fucking push me."

SIXTEEN

Wren

I place my hands under the faucet, letting the soap suds run off my hands, before toweling them off and reaching for a hair tie. Scooping the top half of my hair off my face, I secure it in place and glance at my reflection in the mirror above the vanity. Half up, half down will do. I have a feeling Nonna is going to kick me into gear when I get into the kitchen, and I'm ready for the distraction.

Leaving my bathroom, I close my bedroom door behind me before cutting across to the kitchen, where Nonna is already standing by the counter with a selection of ingredients laid out. When she hears my footsteps, she lifts her head to glance in my direction, a smile spreading across her face immediately, and my shoulders slump at once.

I don't know how she does that, and sometimes, it leaves me a little worried that she has the ability to leave me exposed like this. For now though, I'm willing to accept it.

"How is it I leave for two hours, *Bella*, and you have the ability to cause such a ruckus?" Her grin stretches even more as she offers me a playful wink.

Coming to a stop beside her, I take the apron from her outstretched hand and tie it around my waist as I respond, "I went for a jog on the property. I didn't realize I'd cause such a stir."

"Oh, Teto likes to think he's more important than he actually is. You just gave him the perfect opportunity to flex his weak muscles and get in the brothers' good books. Although, that doesn't seem to have worked out too well in his favor."

I hum in understanding as she organizes the peppers, onions, zucchinis, and carrots in front of me. She nods at a knife beside them, hinting for me to take it and begin chopping the vegetables, and I do so without a word.

I take the zucchini first, slicing it lengthways before quickly dicing it with precision that can only be obtained with a perfectly sharpened blade. Nice. I might keep it. Twisting the tip of the blade on the chopping board, I reach for the next one, before glancing at Nonna out of the corner of my eye.

"Was it true what you said before? That Vito knew where I was and what I was doing?"

She doesn't look up from the garlic she's slicing, but gives me a short, "Uh-huh."

Nothing more, nothing less, no sense of an explanation, and I push her for more. "How?"

This time, she pauses what she's doing to tilt her head, looking at me with a pointed stare. That's all the answer I'm going to get, I know it. She continues to stare me down until I give in, sighing as I shake my head and focus back on the task at hand.

I move from the zucchinis to the carrots before I delve into the peppers and onions. It's only when I'm dicing the onion up finely that Nonna clears her throat.

"You're good with a knife," she states, making me scoff slightly in response.

"I was trained to be." Silence settles over us, not

uncomfortable though. There's no point hiding who I am and I'm only stating the truth; I'm good with a knife because I was trained to be. Just like I was with every other weapon you can think of.

My family's vault, back at Saints Academy, is filled with weapons upon weapons of every variety. Handguns, nunchucks, shit, I'm quite sure there's a rocket launcher on the wall rack too.

"What was that like?" Nonna's question catches me off guard for a second as she pulls me from my thoughts. I glance at her out of the corner of my eye, but she's focused on the meat she is cutting into the cubes.

"What was *what* like?"

I don't miss the way she rolls her eyes at me, shaking her head with a hint of a grin on her lips. "You're a handful."

A smile touches the corner of my mouth as I lift my free hand to my chest with a gasp. "Me? Never." Nonna chuckles as I clear my throat, dropping my hand back to the onion. "I know I am, but I also don't know how much you're aware of, so this conversation is going to have to be led by you."

Nonna turns to look at me head-on, and I'm not sure if it's a dose of pride that flashes in her gaze, but she quickly blinks and it's gone. "Okay then, what was it like going to an actual academy for criminals? I've seen mafia training, but you actually went to an academy and trained for that?"

A sense of relief washes through me as I release a small breath. I was worried we might start on topics a little more difficult, but this... this I can handle.

Keeping my focus on my knife work, I feel a tight smile touch my lips before I answer. "Nonna, I was training well before the academy. Shit, it was a more informative and controlled environment if anything," I admit with a shrug. "I went to Featherstone High as well, but that was almost a safe haven amidst the crazy I was surrounded by. My father had plans for me before I was born. I had a role to play, so I played it."

I feel Nonna's eyes assessing me, but I don't turn to look at her. I don't know what I may see in her eyes and I'm not ready to find out. After a beat, Nonna clears her throat, and I catch a glimpse of her bracing her hands on the countertop out of the corner of my eye.

"It's so crazy to me. The boys... they were trained from a young age too. Immediately knowing the ins and outs of how the De Luca family worked, but their sister... she was kept as far away from it all as possible. All the women were." My eyebrows cock in surprise at the mention of a sister.

"They have a sister?"

I turn my attention to Nonna properly in time to see her shake her head at me again. "Of course that's what you take away from that."

I twirl the handle of the knife in my hand. "What do you expect? I've grown up learning how to kill, survive, and to reign supreme over everyone around me. It's not a natural progression. We don't all take our first breath in life and know how to do these things. They're taught to us. I just happened to grow up in a world where the women were pushed just as hard. Something as mundane as having a sister I didn't know about is far more informative than the trials and situations the De Luca brothers had to go through. They wouldn't be the men they are so highly regarded to be if they didn't come with a tough background. It's all par for the course."

Nonna's eyebrows pinch ever so slightly, and I feel the initial bite of pity swirl between us, but the moment is broken by the sound of a deep raspy voice.

"What would you know about the course?"

My heart rate spikes at the interruption, and I act before

I can think better of it. My hips shift to the left, gaining me a better stance as my hand tightens around the handle of the knife for a split second, before I throw it through the air. It's only when the tip of the blade thrusts into the wall beside the open doorway that I finally cast my eyes over the cause for my surprise.

Vito.

His hands are tucked into his pockets, one eyebrow raised at me as he slowly looks to the handle of the knife sticking out of the wall. "You missed."

I wipe my hands down the front of my apron as I shake my head. "I hit exactly where I was aiming. A threat isn't a threat if I actually do it."

"What's there a threat for?" The next voice belongs to Enzo as he comes to a stop beside his brother, but it only takes him a few seconds to realize what has Vito's attention.

Without missing a beat, Enzo grabs the knife and pulls the blade from the wall. He takes purposefully slow and calculated steps toward me, before offering me the handle of the knife. I take it, placing the everyday kitchen utensil down on the countertop before I answer him.

"The threat could be for many things. Creeping up on

us while we were talking, tracking me while I was running. I'm sure I could think of some other things if you like?" I tilt my head to the side as I wait for either of them to respond, and it's Enzo who makes the first noise.

With a small burst of a chuckle, he wags his finger at me as he steps backward toward the dining table. "I don't recall hearing your warning because you're being held here against your will as a prisoner. Care to add that?"

Vito moves to follow his brother too, and once they're both seated, I scrunch up my face as I shake my head. "No, I'm good. While I'm still breathing, it's not all that bad."

Back in New York, I told them I didn't want to run and I meant it. I felt something before that meeting, and I'm drawn to them now. That's not going to change on my end, no matter how much they may feel betrayed.

Before either Enzo or Vito respond, Nonna claps her hands beside me with a laugh. "I love this girl. Imagine her and Valentina together?"

Enzo's eyes widen with mock-horror for a moment before he shakes his head. "Do not put that fear in me." His response only seems to make her laugh more while Vito stares straight at me.

Nonna must sense I have no idea who she's talking

about because she steps closer, hip-checking me as she grins. "Valentina is their sister."

The reaction from Enzo has me ridiculously intrigued. "Now I *have* to meet her," I state, just as the third and final grizzly De Luca brother steps into the room.

His frown is locked in place as he glares at me, continuing toward Vito and Enzo. "You won't be meeting anyone," he tosses over his shoulder, before taking a seat and directing all of his attention at his brothers like I'm not here. "We have issues with the Russians."

"When don't we?" Vito grunts, folding his arms over his chest as he tears his gaze from me and turns to his brother.

"No, not like this." Matteo's tone says something isn't right. While Nonna takes the ingredients from the chopping board and starts adding them to a pan, distracting herself, I assess the three of them.

"Can we at least eat first? Whatever's cooking over there smells good already," Enzo pleads, the smell of garlic filling my nostrils as Matteo shakes his head, but before he can utter a word to his brother, Nonna interjects.

"I won't take no for an answer, Matteo. You need to fuel your bodies if you plan on exerting energy," she states, a sharp tone to her clipped voice that leaves the three of them staring in her direction for a second, before Matteo's gaze finds mine.

"We can discuss it while we're eating if necessary, but I don't trust the ears around us." It's clear I'm the target of his words, but I maintain my silence, continuing to stare at him as I raise my brow in question.

"Who do you think she's going to tell, Matteo? She chose to be here, remember? That's more the reality than us actually taking her as a captive," Enzo grumbles, wiping his fingers over his chin as he takes me in, and I simply plaster a smile on my face in response. I'm not confirming or denying anything right now.

With a heavy sigh, Matteo loosens his tie at his collar as he speaks to his brother. "They have taken us leaving New York without a follow-up meeting as a sign of war against them. In retaliation, they have hit two of our cargo ships that arrived in port last night, taking all the goods and killing every single one of our men."

"How do you know it was them?" The question comes from Vito as I eagerly wait for Matteo's response.

"No matter how each of our men were killed, a V was carved into their chests afterward."

Yep, that's definitely the Russians, all right. But I'm also intrigued by the fact that the Russians feel betrayed.

"Fuck," Enzo bites, hands clenching on the table. "We can't allow moves like this in our territory to go unanswered." Tension radiates off him, the cool, fun, and collected side of him concealed behind his dark eyes.

"Agreed," Vito adds, his jaw so tight it could cut steel as his nostrils flare with each breath.

"I think we need to put everything into place so we can head back to New York as soon as possible and confront them." The palms of Matteo's hands hit the table with force, making my heart race slightly. Not from his show of anger and frustration, but from the way I can see the picture more clearly than them.

"You need to see the bigger picture," I interrupt, watching as Matteo, Vito, and Enzo each turn their gaze to mine.

"This has nothing to do with you." Matteo's voice is tight, but he doesn't turn away, which tells me he's going to listen if I speak.

"I know it doesn't, but that doesn't mean *I* don't know things. *Important* things that could be of use to you." My blood pumps through my veins like it's on fire, the feel of a battle or war between men spiking my very soul for the first time since I put a bullet in my father.

When none of them respond, each one looking me over with a wary, yet inquisitive look, I take a step toward them. "The Russians are calculated, right down to the very last detail. They won't make a move like hitting your cargo without predicting your response and preparing their next move. More so, one thing the Russians hate more than anything, apart from bad vodka, is the feeling of betrayal. If that's the reason behind the plays they're making, then they will have observed how you have handled this kind of situation before, so they can keep the upper hand." I stop at the chair next to Matteo, settling my gaze on him as I lower my voice, trying to keep myself calm and relaxed even though this entire thing is far more thrilling than I care to admit. "If going to your enemy for a confrontation is what you would usually do in this situation, then you'll need to prepare for the fact that they know this and are already anticipating you."

Matteo purses his lips, flexing his fingers on the table as he looks at me. "You're wrong."

My body tenses at his words, frustration threatening to get the better of me as I scoff. "If you say so, but what I think you're forgetting is the fact that my father knew what *everyone* was doing at all times. Without fail. How do you think that worked? He couldn't be the one with his eyes on every single group he was handling now, could he?" I grip the back of the chair in front of me, my knuckles wrapping around the wood as I lift my brow in question.

A couple of beats pass, and it's Vito who speaks this time. "You were watching them."

"I was." The truth slips from my mouth without pause. With all my training in other matters, I also have the skills to embezzle, negotiate, and all that bullshit, yet here I am, giving it away for free. What a fool.

"What is our next move, then?" Enzo asks, leaning back in his seat as he undoes the top button of his shirt.

Pushing up off the chair, I fold my arms over my chest as I think for a moment. "I'm not standing here making moves for the De Luca mafia, Enzo," I say with an eye roll, but I'm serious. The last thing I want is for them to think I'm making their plays or trying to infiltrate them or whatever other bullshit might run through their minds. "What I do know is that betrayal outranked anything else with the Russians. They would hit you in one way, only to draw you out of hiding to put the real stinger on you,"

I state, remembering the deaths I witnessed at their hands. "Their secret move is always the double hit. Hit you once, make you mad, let you play out your usual response, only to be one step ahead and ready to bring you to the depths of hell at their hands. So, from my experience, you need to come at them hard and fast before they even realize it, but you can't play the same hand you always do because that's what they're expecting."

All three of them look away from me, silently speaking to each other with only their eyes, but the moment is interrupted as the rapping of knuckles sounds on the kitchen door.

"Boss, we have an issue." I don't need to turn around to know it's Teto interrupting us, and I don't give him the satisfaction of my gaze, not when I can see the smallest hint of anger and frustration flitting across Enzo's face.

"Fuck."

REDEMPTION

SEVENTEEN

Enzo

"Let's roll out," Matteo orders as he rises from his seat. Whatever the situation is, it doesn't look great by the look on Teto's face. If Torres, our second-in-command, has sent him in here, things can't be good.

My stomach grumbles, hating that we are being interrupted before I can eat a single forkful of what Nonna is putting together. But despite my disappointment, I follow Matteo's lead, as does Vito, while Wren waves her hand to stop us.

"I'll come with you." Her words make my eyebrows lift in surprise, but any response I may have is cut off by

Matteo as he breezes past her and heads for the door.

"Like fuck you will!" he grunts, but that doesn't seem to dissuade her.

"But—"

"No." This time, the refusal comes from Vito as he saunters past her and she flops her arms at her side like a petulant child. Fuck, she's too much fun, and far more adorable than she even realizes. Behind all of her walls and anger that she projects to prevent anyone from getting close, there's a lost soul underneath, trapped by whatever haunts her.

I have an inkling it links to her father, but that's not for me to say. I simply watch and explore, and I can't deny the fact that I'm learning much more about her from the small interactions we continue to have than I thought we would.

In my gut, I know she's right, we're not doing too well at keeping her as a prisoner, a captive, but that's a little hard when she chose to come with us.

As I near her, I flash her a wink, making her glare at me as I slide up beside Nonna to place a kiss on her forehead, before hightailing it out of there.

I'm only a few steps behind the others as Torres explains the situation. "The men operating the nightclub called in an emergency because there's been a break-in, and the only other word I got out of the message was that it was the Russians."

Fuck.

They are not happy with us, which pisses me off more because these fuckers think the world revolves around them. We didn't leave because of them, we left because of *her*, but they'll never believe us unless we tell them who she is. The mere thought of that alone twists my stomach, and I know that's not the answer to the situation.

Despite that, they've hit our cargo now, taking action before asking questions, and there's no coming back from that.

"Do you want me to come in the *dark*?" I ask, moving in to step with Vito as we walk through the front door, my gaze fixed on Matteo as he nods. There are three SUVs parked outside ready to roll, and without another word, Matteo, Vito, Torres, and the men waiting outside begin to pile in. I, however, move around to the left of the house where our garage is.

The door is already open from the SUVs being rolled out, and a grin takes over my face when I spy my matte-black Ducati parked in the far corner. With its two hundred and thirty-seven horsepower, paired with its one hundred and eleven newton-meters of torque, it's my new favorite toy. Any excuse to climb on board and I'm there for it.

Grabbing my helmet from the hook beside it, I waste no time throwing my leg over the seat and climbing on. I can't imagine what I look like in my full suit on the back of a sports bike, but I couldn't give a shit. Revving the engine as I kick up the stand, I can feel myself vibrating with excitement despite the issues we're going to face.

I roll the bike out of the garage to find the SUVs waiting, but once they see me approaching, they start to move and I take off down the stone path behind them. The second we get to the front gates to the property, they take a left turn and I go right.

With nothing but a clear open road before me, I floor it. Set up in the hills like this means the winding roads are surrounded by trees and nature, and it only increases the care-free vibe that washes over me as the wind hits my body.

My mind wanders back to Wren. The damn woman has fucked with my brain. I want her. I've wanted her since the very first night we saw her in the sex club and believed her name was Ava, and even with the revelations that have followed, I am still drawn to her.

I'm like a moth to the flame, and I'm not afraid of getting burned.

But what does that say about me? A De Luca doesn't allow anyone to pull the rug from under their feet. We make examples of them. So what does that make me when she's still breathing, sleeping in my home, and eating food at my fucking table?

So. Fucked.

Shaking my head, I focus on the task at hand and whatever the Russians think they're going to accomplish at our downtown nightclub. Luca's has been the base of our business for as long as I can remember. My father's favorite spot was always called his headquarters because he liked to entertain those he was in business with there in the VIP area.

As the country lanes turn into busy roads, I tamp down any thoughts but those that matter to the business. Despite being on the bike and feeling the euphoria I get from riding it, I push it all down, becoming a shell of the man I am as my mind only envisions the enemy.

Taking a right turn, I see the nightclub up ahead. I believe it was once a warehouse, standing on its own, which is likely why my father was so drawn to it. No one to hear gunshots, no one to complain about noise, yet a hotspot that everyone wants to gain an access to.

My knuckles tighten around the handlebars as my spine stiffens. The three SUVs pull up at the front of the building, while I slow myself down and circle around to the back.

Whoever has stepped foot on our property and caused a commotion is going to fucking regret it. Because we're poised, well collected, and dressed in suits. More so than not, others may see us as easy targets, but that only makes destroying them all the more fun.

Underneath our designer suits and polished shoes are bones of steel, hardened hearts, and soulless men. It's a pity they only get a glimpse of that for a small moment before we end their life.

Around the back of the building, a metal fencing acts as an added layer of security, locked with a high-tech system, which I open with a fob on my keys as I roll toward the gate. The second I'm inside and pushing down the kickstand on my bike, the gate closes again.

Hanging my helmet off the handle bar, I straighten my blazer and run my fingers through my hair before checking my weapons. There's always a gun at my hip and a blade at my ankle, and the feel of both of them helps me relax a little as my shoulders roll back.

I glance around me, making sure my Ducati is perfectly placed in front of the security cameras we have set up, before heading for the metal emergency exit door. Slipping the key out of my pocket, I twist the lock and pry it open slightly, listening for any noise on the other side. When I don't hear anything, I open it further to slip inside before shutting it quietly behind me. I make a conscious effort to let as little light in as possible, my palm resting against my gun as I scan the dark hallway.

Pleased I'm alone, I move straight ahead toward the door I know leads out into the main area of the nightclub. There's a small panel of glass in the door, offering me a glimpse of the room, but I don't see anybody from this angle.

I peer through the window to make sure there's no one down here, and although I can't see anyone, I hear voices. Confident they're not located near me, I twist the door handle and silently slip through the small opening I created for myself before plastering my back to the wall at my right.

It's strange as hell to see the nightclub in the daytime without it jam-packed with people moving and grinding together. There is usually no space to move for people enjoying the buzz of alcohol thrumming through their veins, but thankfully, no one is here right now, which means if there are going to be casualties, it's not going to be someone completely innocent. It also helps that the resident DJ isn't here blasting music too, so I can understand what's going on.

The stairs leading up to the VIP section twist around to my right, and I can tell that's where the hushed conversation is coming from. I strain my ears, focusing all my attention on them in hopes of hearing what it is they're actually saying, but I come up short.

Fuck.

Inching along the edge of the wall, I stop when I reach under the staircase where another door leads back into the shadows of the building, and I waste no time slipping through it. Confident no one is in here, I race to the end of the hall before finding the private metal steps that also lead up to the VIP area, but from behind the bar instead.

I know exactly where to step on the stairs to keep the noise I make to a minimum, and as I reach the top, I stop altogether when I hear the sound of my brother's voice echoing from the other side of the door that stands before me.

"Uri, explain what you're doing on our property." His voice is void of any emotion, but the dark tone is enough to make a grown man shiver. He's not in the mood to be fucked with, none of us are, but an explanation for his arrival would be greatly appreciated. I'd like to know why this motherfucker is even in our country, let alone here specifically, but Matteo will always get straight to the point.

The window on this door is a small square, angled perfectly for me to have a clear view of what is going on in there.

Uri, and what looks like four men, are standing with their backs to the bar where I am, while my brothers, Torres, and a few of our men are facing them head-on. With the empty bottles of liquor and smashed glasses dotted around the bar, it looks like Uri and his men may have had a good time before we arrived.

Excellent.

Uri must be close to seven feet tall. His wide frame and bald head make him look bulkier. I'm sure he's feared among others, but we fear no one.

No. One.

"Ahh, how nice of you to join us, Mr. De Luca. We were entertaining ourselves while we awaited your arrival." He waves his arms around him, noting the mess before shrugging. "Maybe next time, don't keep your guests waiting so long, huh?" His accent is thick but understandable, the mocking tone highly noticeable as he shrugs his shoulders once more.

Asshole.

Matteo takes a step toward him, straightening the collar of his shirt as he looks at the intruder. "Had I known we were having guests, I would have been here to greet you, but I don't believe this is a friendly visit."

Uri chuckles, head falling back as his shoulders bounce with the movement, his men joining him. Vito sneers at them. He's not the most smiley man to begin with, but it pisses him off when he sees grown men take their cues like that from their leader. Don't laugh because your boss is, don't crack your neck because they do. You're supposed to still have individual thoughts even when you're part of a team. Idiots. They need better training, that's for sure, and a lesson or two in class, but that's not likely to happen.

That's your biggest sign that your men are fuckers and aren't being true to themselves and the business, the family, they are choosing to be a part of.

"Whatever gave you that idea, Matteo?" I catch a glimmer of a smile on Uri's mouth as he turns to one of his men, giving me his side profile, and I want to slice his face up with the anger and frustration rushing through my body.

Fucker.

"What happened to our two shipments at the port, Uri?" A smirk teases my lips at Vito's question. Never the one to fuck around.

"I don't know what you're talking about," Uri replies with *another* shrug, irritating the hell out of me, but not as much as it agitates Vito because in the next breath, he pulls his gun from his hip and points it at the Russian. "Now, now, Vito, don't go waving weapons around if you're too afraid to use them."

I scoff at his words and the fucking audacity he has to say that about Vito of all people, but I realize too little too late that his words were a distraction as he reaches for his own gun. In the blink of an eye, it's aimed at Torres who stands beside Vito, and as the next second follows, a bullet hits Torres right between the eyes.

My jaw goes slack at the fast move, before chaos breaks out on the other side of the door. That's my fucking cue to join the action and catch them off guard. As I swing the door open, I hear the sound of another gunshot, but I can't be certain who it was from or where it was aimed, so I keep my focus on the closest one of Uri's men to me. He's standing at the entry point to get behind the bar, so there's nothing between us.

With my hand gripping the gun at my waist, I take quiet, calculated steps toward him, but as I get within an inch of him, he spins on the spot with his gun poised in his hands, but the barrel is aiming down.

I take my opportunity to elbow him in the throat, the sound of him sputtering and choking meeting my ears as the grip on his gun loosens. Kicking my foot out, I collide with the back of his legs, and he topples forward, gun slipping from his hands and gliding across the floor as he hisses in pain on his hands and knees.

Since we're blocked from everyone else in the bar, I drop to my knees, not wanting to use my gun just yet if I'm still unnoticed because the noise will give me away. Before this fucker can attempt to attack me, I wrap my arms around his neck and my legs around his waist as I roll us to the side.

He grunts in my hold, fingers digging into my arms as he attempts to loosen my hold, but this isn't the first time I've strangled someone, and it's not the first time I've done it in this position either. Come to think of it, I've probably strangled someone to death behind this bar before, too.

The guy tries to kick his leg over his head at me, and I smirk, adjusting my legs, so they're between his, holding them apart and pinning them in place. With him firmly locked in my grip, I tighten my arms at his neck, feeling his fight against me draining until there's nothing but a lifeless body in my hands.

As I let him go, tossing him to the side, the noise of the room quickly comes back into focus as I hear shouts and grunts coming from the other side of the bar. Before I even attempt to get mixed in with them, I reach for his gun and tuck it into my blazer pocket, appreciating the extra round of bullets if necessary.

Pushing my hair back out of my eyes, I take a deep breath as I move to the opening at the side of the bar, crouching. Another one of our men lies out cold on the floor a few feet away from me, while Matteo and Vito have flipped a table and are shooting from behind it.

I'm not sure if they see me or not, but that's not my priority just yet. I need to know what's going on with the rest of these Russian bastards. However, the angling of my brothers hints that the Russians are firing from the other end of the room.

Shuffling back behind the bar, gun poised ready to take aim, I move as quickly and quietly as I can to the opening on the left. When I reach the other side, there's only one man remaining.

Uri.

His attention is diverted. No. He has another table turned, his gun in hand as he peers to the right to attempt another shot at my brothers.

Rising to my feet, I press the barrel of my gun against the back of his skull, and he freezes at the contact from the cool metal.

In a split second, my gaze flicks from Vito's, to Matteo's, over to Torres's dead body lying amid the blood and carnage, before I settle on the bald man before me. Without wasting another moment, I pull the trigger, watching as the giant crumbles to the floor in a heap.

My chest heaves with the adrenaline coursing through my veins as silence finally settles over the room.

"You good?" Matteo asks, rushing from behind the table, blood smeared over his crisp white shirt as his angry eyes take in the mess around us.

I shake my arms out, trying to release the tension that's wound up tight within me, but it's a little harder than I expect. Without answering my brother, I step over the lifeless bodies as I make my way to Torres, crouching at his side when I reach him.

The bullet hole in his skull will forever be seared into my head. None of this was necessary. No one needed to die today, and especially not Torres, but here we are, sitting in the middle of a blood bath once again. Only this time, we've lost one of our most loyal and trusted men.

I sense someone moving toward me, but I don't look up. Vito pats on my shoulder. "Torres will be taken care of with pride and honor, brother. Someone, get word to his family, a display of respect is necessary. Whatever financial support he provides to his family will be met by us."

"Yes, sir." With that, someone races down the stairs.

These deaths... they never get easier. We can honor and respect the dead man before me, but it still won't bring him back to life. Some may say these are the consequences of the life we've chosen, but I would call that bullshit.

With a sigh, I rise to my feet, moving back to the bar on autopilot as I reach for a random bottle of liquor that hasn't been destroyed, unscrewing the lid and bringing it to my lips.

"What are you doing?" Matteo asks as the liquor burns down my throat, and I scoff.

"Drowning my fucking sorrows, brother. Drowning it all."

REDEMPTION

EIGHTEEN

Wren

I stand locked in place, glaring at the back of the De Lucas' heads as they all storm from the room. Fuck. I never wanted anything to do with the bullshit my mother and father were involved in, but being away from everything for the past six months has left me itching to sink my nails back into the gritty lifestyle.

I was a fool for thinking I could have a low-key life, not needing the blood or outlet to project my rage. I can't stay cooped up in the house forever. I won't survive it.

Nonna clears her throat from beside me, pulling me from my thoughts. "You look like your eyeballs are about to fall out of your head." She quirks a brow at me as I exhale harshly.

"They just might," I grumble, placing my hands on my hips as I lower my chin to my chest, attempting and failing at taking a deep breath as she moves closer to me.

"You need to burn off some steam, *Bella*." That's an understatement.

Tilting my head to the side, I offer a tight smile. "I need to burn something, that's for sure. Maybe Matteo's bedsheets? That might make me feel better," I offer with a shrug, and she chuckles at me in response before heading for the door and waving for me to follow her.

"Come on."

I don't miss a beat, upping my pace to catch up with her before I fall into step beside her. I'm slightly hopeful she's going to show me to Matteo's room so I can get my hands on those bedsheets, but as she steps past the door to my room, she comes to a stop at the one just past it.

There is no way that man has been sleeping this close to me, I know it. My gut would know.

My assumptions are right when she twists the handle and opens the door to reveal a gym. I can't decide if this is better or not, but the way my shoulders relax and my heart rate slows, I know this is by far the winner.

Directly facing us at the door is a full-length window overlooking the side of the garden, while three treadmills line the wall to the left, followed by three bikes, and three rowing machines. To the right of us are a wide variety of weights and equipment to help build muscle that I'm familiar with from the gym back in Philadelphia.

I've seen a few of them at Featherstone Academy too, but that was a lot more about being physical like sparring on the mats or in the ring. It didn't matter, just getting blood was the end game.

"This might work for you. At least this way you can burn off whatever is going through your head without stepping outside and causing mayhem with the men permanently on guard," Nonna says with a soft smile, and I offer her one of my own.

"I like you more and more every day, Nonna." I reach out before I can think better of it, squeezing her shoulder in appreciation. What catches me off guard even more is the way she places her hand on top of mine for a moment, rooting me to the spot as I blink at her.

"Same." That one word from her lips breaks the tension rising within me as she takes a backward step. "I'll finish food while you... do whatever it is people do in here," she states, waving her arm around the room with a twist to her lips.

"You don't like working out?" It's clear from her stance already that she couldn't think of anything worse, but her pinched eyebrows and scrunched up nose confirm it.

"I would rather stick pins in my eyes, Wren. Pins. In. My. Eyes," she repeats, making sure I get the message.

Without another word, she shuts the door behind her as she leaves, and I turn on the spot, my gaze immediately landing on the Bluetooth speaker in the corner.

If I can't go with the De Luca brothers and cause mayhem and Nonna won't let me burn Matteo's sheets in defiance, then I guess this will have to do.

I lose myself in the motion of each workout, before Nonna calls me to eat. We sit side by side, our conversation leaning more on the lighter side in comparison to earlier, and I appreciate it. But the second we're done, I make my excuses and head back to the gym.

Hours pass me by in a blur as sweat beads at my temples and my heart pounds in my chest, but I love it.

Even when the sun goes down outside, I continue to push myself a little more before I finally call it quits for the day.

My legs feel like jelly as I head back to my room. The house is silent and I can't hear Nonna anywhere, which only makes me even more concerned that there's been no news from the guys. Not that they owe me any, but my concern has me intrigued.

Closing my door, I sag back against it for a moment before using the remainder of my strength to make it to the bathroom. I switch the shower on and undress on autopilot, a soft groan slipping past my lips as I step under the spray and let the water engulf me.

The second it touches my skin, my brain kicks into overdrive. While the shower is the perfect place for me to think, the gym is where I do the opposite. It clears my brain down to nothing, my focus solely on the moves I'm making until there's no room for anything else.

I can't believe they didn't let me go with them. They know who I am, where I was raised, and what I have learned. Surely, that could be of use to them?

Fuck.

I'm not supposed to want to be of use to them, not in any way shape or form. I'm supposed to just want to take care of me, *just* me, no one else. Just like it's always been. My resources were wrung dry by my parents, my skills and abilities pushed to their limits, and when I sent them to hell where they belong, I vowed to not play that role again. Yet this feels so different.

Running my fingers over my wet hair, I pull the hair tie from the ends before reaching for the shampoo. Thoughts of the De Luca brothers continue to drown me as I go through the motions of washing my hair before using the coconut and shea butter body wash all over my skin. There's no avoiding it, and the madder I get at myself for being mad at them, the worse it gets.

Goddammit.

Frustrated, I shut off the shower and reach for the fresh navy towel in the cabinet before stepping out onto the plush bath mat. I wiggle my toes in the fluffy material for a second as I wrap the towel around my body, then head for the door.

Maybe I can find something fun and distracting to watch on television. Just anything to occupy my mind.

Steam seeps out of the bathroom with me as I move to the edge of the bed, when the door handle for my bedroom door begins to twist, shooting adrenaline through my body as I instinctively reach for my handgun on my nightstand.

What the fuck?

My body is on high alert, my arms clamped at my side to keep the towel in place as I aim the barrel toward whoever the fucking intruder is. As the door swings open, I frown in confusion when Enzo stumbles into the room.

His blazer is unbuttoned and falling loosely at his sides, his shirt is half untucked from his pants, and his tie is nowhere to be seen as he looks at me. "Why the fuck are you pointing that at me?"

I assess him, my eyebrows rising in confusion right along with him. "Why the fuck are you coming in here without knocking?" My response doesn't really seem to register with him as he steps further into my room, shutting the door behind him.

"This is my house."

I scoff, like hell is that reason enough to barge in here. Hell. No.

"Your house or not, I'm not entertaining visitors," I bite back, my gun still aimed at his chest, even as he folds his arms in front of him.

Without a word, he takes another step closer, followed by another, until we're standing almost toe to toe. The only thing between us being the barrel of my gun that presses into his chest. His hand reaches out, his fingers wrapping around the barrel of my XD as he murmurs softly.

"Drop the gun, Wren."

My heart lurches, my eyes widening ever so slightly at the sound of my name on his tongue, and I gulp.

Fuck.

I shouldn't allow him to have this power over me.

With that thought in my mind, my eyes roam over him from head to toe, searching for something, anything, to push back at him with.

He's been drinking.

I don't know how much. He's not completely inebriated, but his pupils are dilated and his balance seems a little unsure. It would also explain the state of his clothing compared to usual, along with the way his hair is sticking up in some spots too.

My body gives in and I lower the gun to my waist, pointing the end at the ground instead of at him. Relieved, both of our shoulders sag.

"What happened, Enzo? Are you okay? What about Vito and Matteo?" I keep my voice low as I look at him, his eyes downcast.

"Hmm, fine. They're fine. I'm fine. Bloody... but that comes with killing people, doesn't it?" The word has my gaze drawing to the dark spots on his blazer, the dried red marks on his hands and the slight splattering over his shirt. How had I not noticed them a moment ago?

"It does," I breathe in response, slowly lowering my gun to the bed beside me. My fingers twitch with need, wanting to reach out to him, but I refrain as he takes a seat at the foot of the bed.

I continue to stand, holding my towel in place the best I can as I look down at him.

"Do you want to talk about it?" The words slip from my mouth before I can think better of it, and he shrugs in response.

"What's the point?"

Shit. Something must have happened, but what?

Clearing my throat, I shuffle from foot to foot. "I don't know, but someone told me once that talking about it can make a difference."

It's Enzo's turn to scoff this time as he looks up from his hands in his lap to meet my gaze. "What difference is that going to make? Dead is still dead whether I talk about it or not. I couldn't give a shit about the Russians we brought down today, or the backlash that may cause, but..." He trails off as he wipes a hand down his face, and my chest tightens.

Pushing my gun further up the bed, I take a seat beside him, releasing a heavy breath as I consider my next words.

"How many men did you lose today?"

"Three."

His response is instant, and the tightness to his tone and the way his body stiffens tells me that's where the pain lies for him right now.

"That must be hard," I murmur, glancing away from him as these foreign words fall from my mouth. I don't know how to do this... whatever this is... compassion? Fuck, I don't know.

"The hardest part of it all is that one of the men we lost today was my closest friend outside of my brothers, and our most trusted guy."

"Fuck, that's not good." I cringe at myself internally over my choice of words, but I've never had to handle the death of someone I've cared about. Which is probably because I've never actually cared about anyone.

"Yeah, fuck is right." Enzo's response drops the tension from my body, the surprising worry running through me that I had just pissed him off with my poor choice of words, but it goes unnoticed.

"I'm sorry that happened to him." I rub my lips together, hoping I'm saying the right thing, and as much as he doesn't seem mad, the pain in his eyes is unwavering.

"Me too. But we'll take care of his family. We always do, and that's what matters."

My brows knit as I turn to look at him. "That doesn't bring him back though."

He looks down at his hands again, a slump to his shoulders as he replies, "I know. That's why I decided to spend some time with my other friend instead." Other friend? His eyes lift to mine, and he must see the question dancing across my face because he continues, "Tequila."

Ahh. Quirking an eyebrow at him, I smirk. "It looks like you didn't really have the best of times," I admit, indicating the state of him.

"I'm past the stage of knowing."

Silence descends over us for a moment, a heaviness surrounding the man that is usually so happy-go-lucky and vibrant.

Clearing my throat, I tuck my wet hair behind my ear as I nudge my shoulder against his. "I'm not very good at this whole consoling or being sympathetic thing," I start, waving a finger between us. "But if you need anything from me, just say the word. I can shoot a motherfucker up close or with a sniper rifle, however you prefer," I start, listing them off on my fingers. "I can beat someone to death and make it look purposeful or by accident, again, whatever your preference. Shit, I can go after them where it really hurts too—their money."

A smirk tips the corner of his mouth up. "That is hot as fuck."

I shake my head in disbelief at him as his hand moves to my shoulder. "Only a crazy mafia man would think so."

No sooner do the words leave my mouth does he inch closer and closer. I'm frozen in place, unable to stop what follows, but when it comes down to it, I don't want to anyway.

I've been dying for it since the night I met him, even more so now with the raw and vulnerable version of him sitting in front of me. It's like I've slowly been suffocating, one breath at a time, before his lips touch mine in a punishing crush.

REDEMPTION

NINETEEN

Enzo

She smells so fucking sweet, looks like an angel fallen from heaven, but with the skills to bring the world to its knees.

How can someone be so damn tempting and addicting without even trying?

I felt this pull toward her the first night I saw her moving across the room to take a seat at the bar. There's no way she could have known we had eyes on her yet, not with the way her head was focused on her destination. She couldn't have known where we were, even if she was sent there for us, but with each sway of her hips, she reeled us in.

I don't even realize I'm leaning toward her until my lips crush into hers, magnetized together, and she doesn't hesitate against me.

Fuck.

Her mouth molds to mine, her fight for control instantly noticeable, even when I lift my hand to grip her throat and hold her in place. I recall her telling me she wants a man who can make decisions and take control, and I'm more than willing to deliver right now. It's all I've been able to think about, which is exactly how I wound up in her room instead of my own when I returned home.

When she hums in approval at my touch, I groan. I'm playing with fire, but fuck the consequences.

Our kiss deepens as we battle for control, until I take the leap needed and sink my teeth into her bottom lip. She gasps before it melts into a deep moan, which hits me straight in the dick. Pulsing inside of my pants, I almost cry out with her, need vibrating through my veins.

Fuck.

I need more.

Of this.

Of her.

Without further thought, I drop my hand from her throat,

gripping her hips, before I toss her up the bed, making her let out a small yelp. She bounces on the sheets as she looks up at me, her eyes swirling with heat and desire, just like I imagine mine are reflecting back at her.

Her palms are flat against the sheets, her fingers digging into the material as her towel falls open a little, revealing the peak of her taut left nipple. My mouth waters as my heart thunders in my chest.

I need to calm myself down before I get too ahead of myself.

"What sin did I commit to deserve you?" The question falls from my mouth as I kick off my shoes and climb onto the bed, slowly crawling up the length of her until my face is in line with her exposed tit.

"All of them," she breathes back, running her tongue over her bottom lip as my cock presses into the waistband of my pants in response.

"Ii vali tutti." She doesn't ask what it means. *You are worth all of them.*

Reaching forward, my fingers glide over the soft skin at her chest, slowly swooping down to the swell of her breasts before I lean in and take her pretty pink peak into my mouth. The second my lips lock around the sensitive skin, Wren's back arches up off the bed as a moan falls from her mouth, which only makes me tighten my hold before I sink my teeth into her flesh.

"Fuck," she whimpers as I ease my pressure and lap my tongue at the spot I just feasted on.

She's so fucking responsive, I love it, *crave* it.

With my cock eager to be released from my pants, I distract myself by trailing kisses up her chest until I'm sucking at the skin at her neck. Pleased with the mark I leave in my wake, I move my head so I'm hovering directly above her, looking down at her dilated pupils. She pants with every breath she takes and it only makes me want to devour her more.

"I just need to confirm something with you," she mumbles, her words barely audible over the need pounding in my ears, but I nod for her to continue. "How much fun did you actually have with your good friend Tequila?" My brows knit, but before I can say a word, she presses her fingers against my lips. "I just don't want to be blamed for taking advantage of you in the morning. You may regret this."

Her chest continues to heave with every breath as she stares straight into my eyes. It startles me that she's not overly concerned about me regretting it in the morning; it's almost like she expects that of me, but her priority is wanting to make sure I'm not completely under the influence.

Did I need the strength of the liquor to help with Torres? Yes.

Did I need the courage of the liquor to come in here? Yes.

But am I only here because of it? Hell. No.

"I know exactly what I'm doing, Wren." I place one hand right beside her head to keep my balance as I drag my other hand down her side. She shivers against my touch, goosebumps rising in my wake.

"And what is that exactly?"

Her question makes me grin, the temptation in her tone making my dick scream for attention in my pants as I lean forward to whisper in her ear. "I'm taking exactly what I want."

Without another word, I find her core with my exploring hand, and I almost bounce on the bed with raw excitement when her thighs spread for me.

Holy. Fuck.

She's slick against my touch, her sensitive folds wet

from her need as I find her clit with my thumb. Pressing against the magic button, I drag small circles over the eager nub as her hands lift to my arms, her fingers biting into my skin as she groans. I recall the feel of her when she was positioned between my brothers and I, yet she somehow feels even sweeter now.

I continue to tease her folds as she struggles to keep her eyes open. I want to see all of her, and I need it more than my next breath.

Sitting back on my knees, I continue to glide my fingers over her pussy as I use my other hand to remove the remainder of the towel that was hiding her from me. Her neck and chest are flushed, and she has a death grip on the sheets instead of my arms.

Slowly, I circle her entrance, teasing her, once, twice, before thrusting deep into her with two fingers, and she makes the most perfect 'O' with her mouth that I almost come on the spot.

"You're so fucking beautiful, *Bella*," I murmur, my voice huskier.

"Those are some sweet words, Enzo, but it's your dick I need to feel euphoria," she retorts, making a grin spread across my face.

Without a word, I slip my fingers from her and stand at the bottom of the bed. I don't miss the way she moans and pouts at the loss of contact, but that only spurs me on.

Shaking my blazer off, I toss it blindly over my shoulder before undoing the remaining buttons on my shirt. Wren tracks my every move, watching as inch after inch of my muscled chest is revealed to her. As I drop the material to the floor, I can sense her gaze lingering on the scars at my abdomen, but that's not a conversation for now, or ever to be exact, so I continue to distract her by unbuttoning my pants.

As I lower the zipper, I peer up through my lashes at her, only to find the vixen playing with her core as she watches me.

Fuck.

I should demand she stop, claim her pussy as mine, and only allow her pleasure at my touch. But she's just too fucking delectable as she is. With her pupils blown, her damp hair fanned out around her on the pillow, and her skin heating from our activities, I've never been more intrigued to watch a woman pleasure herself than I am right now.

Kicking my pants off, I take my socks with them, but

when I rise to my full height once more, slipping my hands under the waistband of my black designer boxers, Wren shuffles toward me and stops me.

"Let me." Her words freeze me in place as she drags the material down my thighs, her gaze locked on my rock-hard cock as she licks her bottom lip.

She doesn't move when my boxers gather at my feet, hypnotized by the slow pull I give my dick again and again. She inches closer, her breath running over the tip of my cock, and I have to squeeze myself tighter to stop the tingles racing up my spine.

Just as she begins to open her mouth, I bring my free hand to her chin, stopping her in place as I shake my head. "I want to lose all of my problems in you, Wren, and that's not going to happen if your mouth touches me right now," I admit, watching as her teeth sink into her bottom lip.

She doesn't utter a single word as she leans back, dropping down onto the bed as she spreads her legs wide, perched on her elbows, and looks up at me. "Then do it."

I climb onto the bed with her, and the moment I'm close enough, she wraps her thighs around my waist as I hover over her. She takes her sweet-ass time to lie back on the bed, my lips a breath away from hers as she continues to intoxicate me with her delectable scent.

Seconds merge into one another as she tilts her head and pinches her lips. "Don't make me say it again, Enzo."

Fuck.

I have no more restraint, not an ounce, and in the next moment, my cock is plunging deep into her core. My head hangs forward, my cock pulsing inside of her as I feel the telltale signs of her fingernails biting into my skin again as her moans of pleasure ring in my ears.

My body feels like it's on fire from head to toe, ecstasy vibrating through me as Wren gasps, only this time, it makes me pause and look up at her.

Her eyes are wide and mouth agape with pleasure as realization washes over me. "Oh my god, there's no condom. There's no condom." My brain spaces out as I process what the fuck is happening right now, but it's far harder than I care to admit when I'm absorbed in her entirely.

No condom?

It takes an extra fucking second for me to even remember what a damn condom is as Wren nods up at me.

"Fuck, no wonder it felt so good." I shake my head even though I remain deep inside her.

She doesn't respond right away, staring up at me with as much confusion as I'm feeling at the moment. Instead, our chests heave with every breath we take.

My cock flexes involuntarily inside her, and we gasp as my fists clench the sheets. "Shit. I've never…" My words trail off, but the understanding must be there because Wren nods.

"I have… with Vito."

"Shit," I mumble, my head falling until my chin lands on my chest and that slight movement causes my cock to move inside her again, making us both groan.

"Yeah." Wren sounds out of breath, her pussy clenched around me, but the rest of her body doesn't seem as tense.

I slowly lift my head to stare into her eyes better, each of us waiting for the other to make the next move. It should be me. I'm hovering above her, I should pull out. I should… Instead, my hips flex, my cock dipping deeper inside of her as ecstasy continues to cling to every inch of my body.

"Fuck. Please thrust into me hard and fast like the first time. Just once more before you pull out," Wren pleads, her words like a prayer in my mind.

Slowly, I pull out all of the way, the head of my cock

resting at her entrance as I look up at her, waiting for her confirmation. The second she nods, I move, thrusting deep into her core once more, only harder and faster than last time.

Her pussy clenches around my cock, milking me for everything I am, and I can't stop the next thrust or the one after from taking over. My hands move, one to her waist and the other to her breasts as I grip onto her, shuddering, as her hands clutch my arms. *Finally.*

"Fuck, yes, Enzo. Yes." Her cries of pleasure are like a symphony in my ears, encouraging me to go harder, faster, deeper. Gone is the worry of the condom, and in its place, remains the raw need between us.

My body heats from my toes, the pleasure coursing over my skin is undeniable as my movements become more stuttered. Wren feels so tight around me, her cries turning into screams as she climaxes around my cock, taking me over the edge with her.

Wave after wave of euphoria crashes into me as she chants my name, adding to the ecstasy flooding my veins. If I die right now, it'll all be worth it.

Panting for breath, we cling to each other as our sweat mingles. My head is nestled in the crook of her neck when

I pull out of her warm core.

Sleep clings to me like a second skin, begging me to fall into slumber, but I fight through it as I look up at the platinum blonde goddess in the sheets with me. I don't want to screw it all up with my next words, so I try to come across as calm as possible.

Lifting up onto my elbow, I use my free hand to stroke a finger down her face, gaining her attention as she peers up at me. "Please tell me you have some kind of protection so you don't end up—"

A dark chuckle falls from her lips as she places her hand over mine at her chin, halting my movement. "I was sterilized at my father's orders as a teenager, remember?"

The memory of the story she told us yesterday sours the mood as I glare down at her, the alcohol in my veins momentarily wiping that piece of information from my mind. There's something in my gut right now that hates the idea that nothing can be created from this moment, but that leaves me confused at my own thoughts, and I force it to the back of my mind.

Sleep clings to me harder now, pleading with me, but before I fall into the void that is my dreams, I can't help but state a single truth that has been in my thoughts since yesterday.

"If he wasn't already a dead man, I would kill him for that violation alone."

I think I hear her gulp or gasp, I'm not sure, but I feel her fingers squeeze around mine before I slump on the bed beside her and drift to sleep.

TWENTY

Wren

I stretch my limbs out, the feel of the sheets covering me smooth over my skin as I groan. Everywhere aches but in the best way possible. Once each of my muscles relaxes, I roll over in bed to find the spot beside me empty. I'm not surprised, not even a little bit, but for some reason, it causes a twisting pain in my chest.

Fuck, last night was… intense, yet reckless, while also feeling like I was exactly where I was meant to be.

The De Luca brothers have a way of exposing me in ways I've never experienced before, but somehow, that doesn't scare me away like I would usually expect. Instead it draws me closer, intoxicating me with every breath I take.

"If he wasn't already a dead man, I would kill him for that violation alone."

I'm not sure Enzo was even aware he spoke those words to me, but they haven't left my mind since. Repeating in my dreams just as much as they did in my head when I stared at his sleeping form beside me.

He said it with such sincerity that there was no room for doubt. But he was talking about the man who promised them the world, the man they vowed vengeance for.

Did that change anything for us? For me? I don't know, but I can't lie here and assume I'm safe now because Enzo fucked me. That's not how the world works, especially not ours. If anything, he may have fucked me out of his system and I'm no longer of use.

Frustrated with myself and the train of my thoughts, I shake my head before propping myself up on my elbows, my fingers clenching the sheets against me as I sigh. Last night was a whirlwind. After his speech, Enzo passed out, leaving me to slip from the bed and clean myself up, something I've only had to do once before… with Vito.

Shit.

Without a condom. I don't know what we were thinking. Too drunk on each other to consider any consequences, and even though a child may not be one of them, there are plenty of other things that you can get from unprotected sex. First Vito, and now Enzo. I might make a joke about not being able to reproduce, but I've never been careless like this before.

Until them.

Releasing a heavy sigh, I force myself to relax. It was clear he had never done it before either, so I have to take that as my assurance that everything is okay.

When I re-entered the bedroom last night, I was half expecting to find him gone, but there he was, passed out under my sheets. It left me nervous as I tiptoed closer and delved beneath the material, opting to turn away from him and lie on my side, but in a split second, the heat of his chest was pressed against my back.

Despite my usual stiffness around others, I melted into his hold and fell asleep. I felt guarded, protected, and fucking important, which is crazy as shit because he's supposed to be one of my captors. That title doesn't really sit well though, not when I want to be here. I think that's the fact that's keeping me alive at this stage. My deliriousness.

My stomach grumbles, and I sit up and swing my legs over the side of the bed. I have no idea what the atmosphere will be like when I step out there, but I'm starving. All of that late night activity on top of the exercise I put myself through yesterday has drained my energy, and I need refueling.

Standing, I glance at the bathroom door, then to the closet. I probably should shower, but if I step in there, my brain will start overthinking and I'm really not ready to assess everything in great detail just yet.

So I move toward the closet, grabbing a pair of loose black shorts and a gray tank top. I boycott underwear and get dressed. Pulling my hair back off my face, I reach for a clip and secure it to keep my face free of any loose tendrils, before I turn to the door.

The second I reach for the handle, uncertainty kicks in. Hopefully, Enzo won't be there. Hopefully, none of them will be there and I won't have to deal with any of their bullshit.

With my fingers crossed, I open the door and step out into the hallway, my eyes and ears alert as I listen and search for them, only to come across nothing. My shoulders sag in relief as I head for the kitchen, but my hopes are shattered the second I walk into the room to find the three De Luca brothers huddled around the dining table. To top it all off, Nonna is nowhere to be found.

Fuck. Me.

I track my gaze over each of them, frozen in place as I scramble for my body to freaking move. They're all in their usual suits, with their ties perfectly in place and not a speck of lint to be seen. Vito observes me, like he's trying to pick me apart, scrutinizing every detail. The question hovers over whether he would piece me back together or not.

Matteo is glaring at me as per usual, his brows furrowing in the middle, with his jaw so tight he could cut through ice. While Enzo… fuck, he's grinning at me like the cat who got the cream. *My* cream.

My fight or flight is being triggered, but the need for coffee outweighs everything, and before I can think better of it, my feet are moving toward the coffee machine. The hairs on the back of my neck stand on end with the attention as I open the top cupboard to pull down a mug.

The second my hand latches onto the handle, Enzo speaks. "I made you a coffee, *Bella*. I was on my way to bring it to you before Matteo insisted on a brotherly meeting."

He's far too cheery. Far too pleased with himself. And making far too much of a show.

I can feel it.

Clearing my throat, I turn to face him, and my assessment wasn't wrong. His smile is more prominent on the left side of his face, his eyes sparkling with mischief like I remember from the first night I met the three of them. The way he leans back in his chair, with his arm draped over Vito's chair beside him, makes him look like a motherfucking king beckoning me closer.

I'm clearly a glutton for punishment because I'm moving toward the table for the caffeinated goodness without another word. Vito glances back and forth between Enzo and me, obviously sensing a shift, but I keep my eyes trained at the mug Enzo is pointing at.

As I near them, I notice there is a selection of pastries, cookies, and cakes scattered on the table, and at the sight of them, my stomach grumbles. Matteo is at the head of the table to my left, with Vito taking the seat beside him and Enzo facing me head-on. I stop behind the chair I usually take, not willing to walk around the table to get the mug, and Enzo thankfully slides it across the wood to me.

I lift it off the table and take a step back, ready to hightail it the fuck out of here when Vito clears his throat, drawing my attention toward him.

"Nonna said we had to make sure you eat." His gaze drops to the treats scattered on the table, and I gulp past the lump in my throat. I had always heard Italians started the day with sweet foods instead of savory.

Nodding, I lean forward to grab a cookie with my free hand when Matteo grunts.

"Sit."

It's not a request, and despite the uncertainty around Enzo and I right now, I'd rather face the wrath of Matteo's annoyance than discuss what I was up to last night.

I take my seat and a large gulp of my coffee before snatching a cookie or two. None of them utter a word as I eat, giving me a moment to relax, but I don't lower my defenses, not with these men.

The silence is surprisingly not as awkward as I would expect and if I wasn't so hungry, I might be worried about them watching me eat, but any concerns about that have gone straight out the window. When I'm satisfied, I sip the remainder of my coffee and offer a tight smile.

"Thanks. I'll take myself to—"

"You look truly fucked, Wren." Enzo's words shouldn't catch me off guard like they do, but they take me by surprise whether I like it or not, and I find myself choking and spluttering on thin air.

Motherfucker.

Plastering a wide smile on my face, I lean back in my seat, lacing my fingers on top of the table. "*Truly* seems like too strong of a word."

I expect my reply to make him falter, but his grin only spreads wider.

He inches forward, elbows braced on the table as he looks deep into my eyes with a raised brow. "You're telling me that you're not sore this morning? Because I can definitely rectify that."

Holy. Fucking. Shit.

This is actually happening.

I fuck and run. Fuck. And. Run. Until them. Until Vito. Until now.

And the way Enzo tilts his head slightly to the side tells me he's enjoying watching me squirm far too much. This situation is unlike any I've faced before.

"Wait," Matteo interrupts, waving his hand between Enzo and me. "Did you two—"

"Truly fuck? Yes. Yes we did." My sass shines through with every word, and it gives me the confidence to embrace it and push back, refusing to give Enzo the response he was enjoying so much moments earlier.

Matteo's hands clench on the table, knuckles white as his nostrils flare. Rolling my eyes at him, I look at Vito, but he's assessing me just as intently as he did when I first stepped into the room.

"She's the fucking enemy, Enzo," Matteo bites, fists slamming down on the table and making the plates clatter from the force.

"She's not *my* enemy." Enzo shrugs as he says the words so casually yet so confidently, and my heart skips a goddamn beat.

What is he doing to me?

Between them, they evoke feelings in my chest that I can't decipher or make sense of and it's far more unsettling than having a gun aimed at my head.

Despite enjoying seeing Matteo so wound up, I know getting between the three of them is not going to help me out in this situation, so I clear my throat and look intently at the eldest brother of the De Luca family.

"It's not like we were declaring marriage to one

another, Matteo, we were fucking. Get over yourself." I roll my eyes dramatically at him, not wanting to lose the harsh and confident front that I always feel so comfortable behind, even when I'm doing something to help them.

Enzo's eyes are burning into the side of my head, and I turn and face him. The second my eyes latch on to his, the crazy idiot climbs up onto the table.

"What—"

My attempt to understand what the fuck he's doing is cut short when he jumps down beside me, before sweeping me up off my seat and taking it for himself with me firmly in his lap.

Gaping at him like a fool, I can't deny that my heart is galloping like crazy in my chest because of him.

"It definitely could be marriage, especially if you two are over it," Enzo states, looking over my shoulder at his brothers as my eyes bug out of my head.

This man can't be for real. Can he?

Before I can even understand what he truly means, Vito responds without missing a beat, "I'm not over it."

I look over my shoulder at the man in question, my eyebrows pinching in confusion as his gaze remains fixed on me.

"You both need to stop saying shit like that," I grumble, weakly attempting to move out of Enzo's lap, but when he pulls me into his chest, I'm a goner.

"You know you like it, *Bella*," he breathes against my ear, lips dancing over my skin as I shiver. I can't find a response when his hand creeps up my thigh, goosebumps lying in its wake as he inches higher and higher. The entire time, I can sense both Matteo and Vito watching us, and I'm desperate to know what their faces look like, but I can't bring myself to turn around and face them.

"Maybe jetting off to America is a good idea. It will help cool you off, Enzo." Those words come from Matteo, forcing me to lean back and glance into Enzo's deep eyes as he scoffs at his brother.

"You're going to the US?" Enzo nods, his hand frozen at the hem of my shorts as he looks at me inquisitively. "I think you're making a mistake with that." The truth falls from my lips whether I like it or not, and his nose crinkles in a mixture of confusion and hesitation.

"Then it's a good thing *your* opinion doesn't matter," Matteo replies, his tone firm, leaving no room for argument, so I don't bother. Until Enzo grabs me by the waist and places my ass on the table, moving effortlessly between my thighs as he cups my chin and tilts my head back.

"Why?"

His eyes are laser-focused, waiting for an answer as he works his jaw. Wetting my lips, I take a split second to consider my choice of words. Fuck it, if he wants the *why*, he's going to get it.

"The Russians are making all these moves while continuing to ruffle the feathers of the Ring at Featherstone. They're playing bigger games here, games you need to understand before you can respond properly. They literally swept into Italy and killed some of your men, on *your* property yesterday. I think going to the States is too dangerous because all it does is expose you."

My chest rises and falls with every breath I take. I can sense Enzo is about to speak when a knock sounds from behind him. "Boss, you're all set."

Teto.

I know that sleazy motherfucker's voice without needing to see his face now. Asshole.

The sound of chairs dragging over the floor draws my attention to the right as Enzo's grip on my chin slacks. Both Matteo and Vito are standing, eyeing each other, speaking without using words as Matteo shakes off his blazer.

"Thank you, Teto. We'll be out in a minute." Matteo doesn't even bother to turn and look at him, but that doesn't stop Teto from pushing for more.

"Sir, if you don't mind me confirming, I just wanted to be sure that you didn't want me to join you. Especially with Torres being—"

"Fuck off, Teto." The words are spat from Enzo's mouth, his teeth grinding together as the muscles in his neck bunch.

"We're sure," Matteo adds in a calmer voice when Teto clearly doesn't seem to get the message, and I shake my head in disbelief at his audacity. If anyone faltered at my father's word like that, they wouldn't have made it to the door. He's lucky this family business is run better than his was.

Tension radiates off Enzo, and I have a feeling it links back to the mention of Torres. Before I can decide against it, I lift my hands, cupping Enzo's cheeks. It's only when his eyes are set on mine that I speak.

"Think about what I said."

He blinks down at me for a moment, before offering a subtle nod and leaning down to press the softest of kisses to the corner of my lips.

Without a word in response, he turns on his heel and heads for the door, hands clenched at his sides as he storms from the room. Matteo glares at me, while Vito looks just as confused by me as ever, but neither of them speak. Instead, they follow their brother, leaving me alone in a kitchen that isn't mine, with worries and fears for men that aren't mine either.

If I knew offering Luna redemption would get me so tangled up in them, I would've taken a pass. They're playing with my emotions, emotions I didn't know I had, and I'm far too scared to be left so vulnerable by them.

Vulnerable *for* them.

REDEMPTION

TWENTY ONE

Wren

Motherfucking men and their motherfucking need to take charge of shit.

I thought the De Luca brothers were different, but they're not. I understand I'm not here because of my abilities and skills. However, my fuck up doesn't change the fact that they're setting themselves up for failure by charging into New York right now. I know it, but apparently, that doesn't matter.

What matters is *they* are the De Lucas, and this is their family business that they're running, so whatever they say, goes.

Fuck.

My breath comes in short, sharp bursts as my feet pound on the treadmill. Sweat has my tank top clinging to me like a second skin, but it doesn't stop me from continuing to push.

My muscles scream from the strain, but the longer I'm in here sweating my ass off, the more time I'm actually avoiding rinsing it all away in the shower and letting my thoughts consume me.

I started the morning worried about what would happen when I ran into Enzo. For the first time in my life, I didn't want to be discarded or feel rejected by him. Instead, I got the complete opposite and that has left my head spinning even more.

Sweeping a loose tendril of hair back off my face, I grunt, forcing myself to focus on my actions. It doesn't help that Nonna still hasn't come home, or if she has, she hasn't made her presence known. Which sounds like the least Nonna thing to do in existence.

Is it weird that I miss her even though I haven't really been here that long? It's crazy to me the connection I feel with her and the impact her smile has on my life.

If the De Luca brothers don't fuck me over emotionally,

then it will be Nonna instead.

Fuck, I need to do something else. With a sigh, I slow my pace, the beeping of the buttons on the machine echoing in the otherwise silent room as I glance around at the other equipment available to me.

The hair on the back of my neck stands on end. I glance from the door to the window and back again. It feels like someone's watching me. My spine stiffens as I strain my ears, but there's nothing.

Shaking it off, I bring the machine to a stop and step down, reaching for my water bottle as I guzzle half of it in one go. My gaze settles on the rowing machine over by the floor-length window and I stretch my neck from side to side as I make my way over to it.

I drop down into the seat with a mixture of a groan and a sigh, my body begging me to stop despite my efforts to continue. Linking up my chosen weight, I grab the handles and take a deep breath before pulling back with all of my strength.

Fuck, that feels good.

I repeat the motion in a perfect rhythm as I control my breathing. Seconds spin into minutes, my limbs ready to crumble into a heap. Then I hear the sound of the door clicking open behind me.

Nonna?

Glancing back over my shoulder, I pause my stroke to see if it's her, but to my dismay, it's Teto I find in the open doorway.

Fucker.

I really don't have the time or energy for this asshole today. By the glare on his face, he looks like he wants to end me rather than deal with me.

When his gaze doesn't falter as he stands with his arms folded over his chest, I release my hold on the bar and turn in my seat to face him better. His black cargo pants and fitted black tee make him look every inch of the henchman or *henchboy* he thinks he is.

I can't say *man;* it doesn't feel like he's earned his stripes for that.

Rolling my eyes, I brace my hands on my knees as I watch his every move. "I wasn't aware there was an issue with me being in here, and to be honest, if there is, I'll hear it from one of the brothers, not you. So, unless you're here about something else, you can fuck off." The saccharine smile on my face is fake as hell, and it does nothing to stop the sneer spreading across his face.

"You talk a big game for a little girl." What is it with assholes thinking they can call me a bitch or a little girl when it's them getting their panties in a twist? I'm not offended by the names they throw in my direction, I've dodged far worse.

Raising my eyebrow at him, I take my time dragging my gaze from the tips of his black boots all the way to his slicked back hair, before settling on his eyes.

"I'm sure I do talk a big game, Teto, but why don't you come closer and see if my bite is as good as my bark?" I snap my teeth at him, watching as his sneer turns into a grin while he shakes his head at me dismissively.

He takes two steps toward me, unfolding his arms and tucking his hands into his pockets. A clear sign to show me he isn't worried about having to defend himself against me.

"Big words for a little bitch. All this mayhem going on around us leads back to you somehow. It only seems to have intensified since you arrived. Am I wrong?"

I flutter my eyes innocently, remaining bolted to my seat even though every fiber of my being wants to stand so he can't have the advantage of looking down at me. But this will only make catching him off guard all the better.

"What mayhem?"

He scoffs at my response, shaking his head again as he takes another step toward me. "Torres."

My gut twists from the pain I remember seeing in Enzo's eyes last night, but I tamp it down, refusing to let this fucker see any kind of emotion from me. "Nope," I reply, popping the 'p' like a child as I shrug. "That one had nothing to do with me, and believe me when I say, I don't lie about this shit. If I take a life, I make sure to take all the credit."

His sneer reappears on his face as he grunts, cutting another two steps toward me as my hands start to clench in my lap. "You have no idea what you're getting involved in, bitch."

I chuckle despite myself, cocking my brow at him as I point my finger in his direction. "Are you sure? Because you just said I'm the problem behind the mayhem. I can't be the problem *and* have no idea what I'm getting involved in. That fails to make sense."

Fucking idiot.

Without any warning, he lunges for me, and I'm far too eager to see what it is he's going to do. So when his hand grabs the neckline of my tank, I don't stop him, letting him haul me to my feet.

"Don't play games with me, little girl. I'm the big bad wolf and you don't want to get on my bad side. I don't mind cutting out your fucking heart whether the De Luca brothers allow it or not," he grunts, our noses nearly touching as he glares at me.

Adrenaline pumps through my veins, my body igniting to fuck him up, so it takes everything within me to remain calm and still.

"I've killed people for far less than this, Teto," I breathe, my voice void of any emotion or bite as I keep my eyes fixed on his. "So, I'm only going to ask you this one time. Let go before you regret it."

He barks out a laugh as he shakes his head at me. "I'll put you down when and where *I* please." His grip tightens on the material of my top as he yanks me closer, eliminating the final bit of space between us. "If that's on the tip of my blade, then so be it. If it happens to be on my dick first, then so be that too."

It's my turn to chuckle this time, my head falling back for a moment before I return my gaze to his. "I'm sorry, I shouldn't laugh, but it's hard not to when your threats are so shitty." I run my tongue over my teeth, and his jaw tightens with annoyance. "But to clarify—are you threatening to cause me pain at the touch of your small, moldy green dick as well as insinuating that you're going to stab me, like, to what? Death?"

My words don't seem to spark any amusement in his eyes, instead, they only seem to make him angrier. In the next moment, he rattles me, shaking me back and forth on the spot as he spits out his words. "I'm saying that I'm the fucking boss right now, and you'll do well to follow my orders."

I want to ask him what fucking orders he's talking about because he hasn't actually given a single one, but I'm not down with him and his bullshit. He waltzed in here, pushed all of my buttons, and I wasn't finished with my workout.

"I'm sorry, but it's a no from me." My hands clench at my sides as he shakes his head.

"You don't get a fucking choice."

I know my eyes are likely giving away my anger now as my tone darkens. "You see, that's the thing. We always have a choice, you're just not appreciating the fact that mine doesn't align with yours."

Teto yanks my top again, the material tearing a little

under his harshness as he leans in closer. "You don't know my fucking choice."

Just because he has a hold of my top doesn't mean he has all of the control, and I make that point clear when I rise up onto my tiptoes. "I know that you walked in here with intention. I know that I asked you to remove your fucking hands from me and you haven't. And I know that you threatened me against what *must* be your better judgment." Anger burns in every word, my body ready to attack as I hold myself back from the edge by a sliver of a thread.

He smirks, tilting his head to the side. "Like I said, I'm the fucking boss."

That's it. That's the final drop of acid from his tongue that I needed to dissolve the tether holding me back.

"Not mine. Not today. Not ever."

The words have barely left my lips before I smash my skull into his face. His nose crunches beneath my pounding head as he grunts, stumbling back a step and releasing his hold on me to cover his face.

I blink past the pain ricocheting through my head, but my body immediately moves into position to bring this fucker down.

"You fucking bitch."

I roll my eyes at his attempt to throw harmless words in my direction, and a dark smile taints my lips. "Yes, I am. I thought we covered this. No wonder the De Lucas don't give you any responsibility. You're nothing more than an errand boy."

"Fuck you," he bites, charging toward me in the next breath. His arms band around my waist, knocking me to the floor with him following along as my back smacks harshly into the ground, taking the wind from my lungs as I gasp for breath.

Despite my pain, I fight blindly against him, refusing to let him get his legs and arms over mine so I'm restrained. Thrusting my knees up, I hit him in the back twice before the motherfucker manages to grab both of my wrists in one of his hands, while bringing the other down to my breast.

His fingers grip the flesh through my sports bra, and I wince, the instant feel of bruises forming under his hold only fueling my anger. It feels like my rage was only simmering beneath the surface, contained at my command, and he's just flicked the fucking switch to unleash it.

I knee him in the side, at the same time, I use all of my strength to pull one of my wrists free of his hold. I groan in relief when my right hand slips free, but he tightens his hold on my left. It's a struggle to block the pain out as I rear my free hand back and punch the motherfucker in the face.

"Fuck," he spits, blood dripping down on me from his nose as I hit the wounded spot twice more. When it doesn't allow me to gain an advantage over him, I change tactics, kneeing him in the side again, pushing him forward as I plunge my thumb into his eye.

I know the perfect pressure point; it was one of the first things my father taught me. As he cries out in pain, I yank my captured arm down toward my face, bringing his arm along with it, before sinking my teeth into his tattooed flesh.

There's always a barrier in our actions when we sink our teeth into that of another human, a moment where you hesitate whether you should push further, and in this instance, I blast right through it.

I taste the coppery essence on my tongue as I continue to sink my teeth into him, his cries turning into wails as I feel his body slack a little above me, and I use the opportunity to buck my legs and twist my hip at the same time. Rolling the pair of us, I release my teeth from his flesh as I come to settle on top of him.

"What the fuck?!" His voice is hoarse as he struggles to defend himself. Blood pools in his eye which tells me I hit him exactly where I wanted to. His nose is a mess, and his arm is draped in blood too. The same blood that dribbles down my chin.

I can't imagine what I look like, but I couldn't give a fuck. This asshole deserves it all. I might have been trained to assassinate the enemy and make it look effortless, but I'm also well-versed in fighting as dirty as I need to.

The taste of copper is still heavy in my mouth, and despite my usual thoughts on spitting, I quickly aim it in his direction. The splatter makes me cringe despite him fucking deserving it, before I spot him moving for the blade holstered at his hip.

How had I not seen that there before?

Without wasting a single moment, I grab the handle before he does, pulling it from its sleeve before quickly thrusting it into his thigh.

"Ahhh! Fuck!" His cries of pain are like a symphony to my ears, his grunts making my mouth tick up at the corner. "You're going to fucking pay for that, bitch."

The smile teasing my lips drops instantly, a familiar

sense of numbness washing over me as I become consumed with bringing this fucker to his knees.

"No, you are."

When I rip the blade from his thigh, he cries out once more, and I stab the bloodied blade into his stomach, twisting for good measure as he whimpers and gargles beneath me.

His hands lift to my hair, pulling at my ends as he tilts my head back, and I blindly ball my hands into fists and aim for his face. My knuckles meet his flesh three times at full force, blood smearing across my skin as his hold relents.

My body already aches from the exercise I put myself through earlier, and now with this on top of it, I'm completely drained. I've had enough, but this doesn't end until he's dead.

With a groan of my own, I grab the handle of the blade again, tearing it from his body, before slamming the sharp edge into his throat, not stopping until the tip hits the floor through him.

The gargled sound of blood in his throat is all I can hear as he struggles to breathe, the sound vibrating off the walls around me until the noise comes to a complete stop.

His body wilts beneath me and I know he's visiting his maker in hell.

I fall from my position above him with little to no grace, using my hands and knees to keep me up off the pool of blood surrounding him. A small sob of anger and relief bursts past my lips as I gasp for breath.

I frown as the sound of approaching footsteps filter through, kicking my heart rate into overdrive as I force myself to stand.

Looking down at Teto beside me, my body vibrates with uncertainty. How the fuck do I explain this? My mind is in survival mode, but I know no matter how I attempt to get out of here, it's going to involve a fight with whoever is approaching first.

I flex my hands at my sides as I try to inhale through my nose and exhale through my mouth, but any attempt to regulate my breathing and remain calm is short-lived as Matteo appears in the open doorway.

His gaze flicks from me to Teto and back again a few times over, before it settles on me. There's no tell on his face, no hint of an expression to guide me to whatever is going through his mind.

My chest heaves with every breath I take, until he takes

one step into the room, hands clenching at his sides before he turns a glare toward the dead man beside me.

"What did he do?"

What did he do? What did he do? I repeat his words in my mind over and over again, trying to comprehend what the fuck he's saying. It almost sounds like… he knows this wasn't my fault. I think? But this is Matteo, and that's not usually the case. Also, why the fuck aren't they halfway to New York by now?

When he doesn't storm toward me, waiting patiently for me to respond, I relax. His eyebrows lift, encouraging a response when he can sense my body is no longer on alert.

With a shrug, I take in the blood dancing along the edge of my sneakers and sigh. "It doesn't matter, Matteo. What matters is this carpet because if we don't get some cleaning supplies right now, this fucker's going to stain."

TWENTY TWO

Matteo

"**W**hat matters is this carpet because if we don't get some cleaning supplies right now, this fucker's going to stain."

Did she actually just say what I think she said? I can't be right, she really can't be *that* crazy. Can she?

Anger vibrates through every inch of my body, seeing the blood smeared all over her skin and the battle she must have fought. I want to put a bullet through his fucking brain for good measure.

Observing Wren, it catches me off guard how still she's standing. There's no shake to her bones, no anxiousness making her bob on her feet. Nothing. She stands cold and calculated just like Totem would. If this was the first time meeting her, I would instantly know she was his daughter. That stance is undeniable and completely untrainable.

How many times has she done this? How many times did Totem use her as a weapon or force her to take someone out whether she liked it or not? My father did it too many times to count, and he was a far better man than Totem.

Shaking my head ever so slightly, I continue to gaze at her. If there was any confirmation needed to clarify that staying in Italy was the right decision, this is it. We listened and didn't make the trip to New York, and seeing her before me, I'm flooded with relief, but it doesn't last all that long when I think about how none of this would have happened if I hadn't left the house.

This is not something anyone ever wants to return home to.

Clearing my throat, I ask her again, "What did he do, Wren?"

Her gaze drops to Teto's lifeless form beside her, before her empty eyes meet mine again. "He pushed."

It's as simple as that. Her response is monotone, her pain squashed, and her rage depleted.

"Pushed what?" I take a step toward her slowly, wondering if she'll become skittish, but to my surprise, she remains as she is.

"Me."

It's clear I'm going to have to be more specific if I actually want any information from her because she's happy enough to give me the bare minimum, and I can't stand it.

Taking another step, I keep my arms relaxed at my side in case her demeanor does change. "Is this what happens when people push you?"

A lifeless huff falls from her lips as she shakes her head. "When someone repeatedly threatens me and hints that they're going to touch me with their mangy dick against my will, then yeah, this is what happens." Her gaze lowers to him once more, no remorse flashing in her eyes or even a hint of sadness. Just like if it was me looking down at someone I killed, she has the same stance.

Before I can ask anything else, Enzo calls my name from somewhere in the house. "I'm in the gym," I holler without hesitation as Wren lifts her gaze to mine. It's like she's trying to see into my soul, see if she can guess my next move, and I know that's my fault more than hers. It's been me pushing at her too, just not quite like Teto did.

Fuck.

Following the sound of my voice, Enzo and Vito appear in the doorway behind me a few moments later, a curse falling from Vito's lips as they notice the scene before us.

"What the fuck happened in here?" The question comes from Enzo as they stand beside me. Vito to my left, Enzo to my right.

Wren shrugs, like it's not her place to answer, and I immediately take the weight off her shoulders. "It's fine," I mumble, waving at the floor. "She's more bothered about the carpet staining." My words are dry, and I don't miss the way a hint of surprise and mischief dances in Wren's eyes as Vito glances between us.

"The carpet staining?" His words are said slowly as his brows knit in confusion.

"The what now?" Enzo's voice is higher pitched than usual as he tries to wrap his head around my statement.

"My thoughts exactly," I reply, making his jaw slack even more as he realizes I'm telling the truth.

Without missing a single beat, he cuts the distance between him and Wren, wrapping her in his arms as he pins her to his chest. She doesn't lift her arms at first, frozen in place, before she slowly lifts her palms to his waist.

It almost makes me want to stab myself in the heart, the way it gallops at seeing her in this state. It's like nothing I've ever felt before in my life, and I don't fucking like it.

Watching my brother run his hands down her sides as he gets up close and personal with her drives me insane. For the first time in my life, I think I'm... jealous? I need a distraction from this. Now.

"Are you bleeding anywhere?"

Wren shakes her head at Enzo's question. "Nowhere. It's all his."

Thank god for that.

I force my gaze to my left, looking at Vito, who is still staring aimlessly at Wren and Enzo in the center of the room, and I have to clear my throat to get his attention. When his eyes cut to mine, I can tell he's mad that I've drawn his attention away, but I don't give a shit.

"Call in the cleanup crew, Vito. They can take care of this."

He offers a single nod in response as Wren's voice cuts through the air. "I can take care of it."

I know my brothers are glaring at her just as hard as I am as I shake my head tersely.

"Like fuck you are," I grunt, folding my arms over my chest as she steps out of Enzo's hold. Her gaze ping-pongs between the three of us.

"What are you even doing here?" Her question catches me by surprise at first.

"Uhh..." Enzo's hesitation washes over me as I find his gaze aimed in my direction too, and I understand. She's trying to distract us instead of dealing with the situation in front of us, and just this once, I'm willing to allow it.

"You recommended we shouldn't go," I murmur, attempting to be as soft as possible.

Wren's nose scrunches up in confusion as she flicks her eyes over the three of us. "And?"

"And we didn't go," Vito explains with a shrug, his gruff voice bouncing off the walls around us as she pinches the bridge of her nose.

I can't decide if she's pissed or not, but thankfully, Enzo takes the lead, reaching out to squeeze her arm gently as he speaks. "We may be assholes, *Bella*, but we can have a civilized conversation between us. We know we need to lean on you right now, just like you need to lean on us." His gaze drifts down to Teto, likely wanting to avoid the knowing look in her eyes, but it doesn't come. If anything, there's only more confusion there.

I purse my lips as I look at the lifeless body on the floor. Teto was never our favorite part of the family; he was here solely to please a friendship my father once had. An agreement we no longer need to honor.

One thing is for certain though, there is more to Wren than meets the eye.

"Do you need something to calm you down? Some sugar to take away the shock? A shower to wash away all of the blood?" My eyes squint a little in Enzo's direction as he fires questions at Wren, taking a far better approach than I am as I stand here like a fool.

"What shock?" Wren frowns at Enzo, and I scoff at her ability to remain so casual.

"I don't know, the shock of fucking killing someone, *Bella*, or whatever you want to call this," Enzo replies, a little bewildered too as she dramatically rolls her eyes at us and shakes out of his hold.

"Honestly, I think the three of you need to catch up here. Your brains are seemingly still stuck on thinking I'm sweet and innocent Ava, and that's far from the truth. It never has been and it never will be. I'm Wren Dietrichson, and I told you what I did back in New York, the entire reason I'm here, but it doesn't seem to be registering in your brains."

Absorbing the truth in her words is quite tough. Not only that, but she has proven she knows how these fucking Russians operate too. The only people underestimating her ability is us, even while we're standing here with a dead man at her feet.

"You're right." Surprised, she cuts her eyes at me.

"I've killed before, Matteo, and I'll likely kill again." Her eyes remain fixed on mine until I nod, and only then does she seem to relax her shoulders and sigh. "I could do with something to take the edge off. Like, eat a steak sandwich or some shit. I'm starving."

"A steak sandwich?" Vito repeats, saying exactly what I'm thinking. Who the fuck is this woman standing before me? And why does she become more addicting with every passing moment?

The sound of a door slamming shut in the distance breaks the atmosphere between the four of us as footsteps make their way down the hallway. I'm hopeful it's the cleanup crew, but I hear Nonna's voice a moment later, and Wren gasps.

"If that's Nonna, I don't want her to see what I've done

here." The panic in her eyes matches the tone of her voice as she begins bouncing from foot to foot, glancing down at Teto.

"Why?"

Her hands clench at her sides as she glares at me like I should already know the answer. "Because…"

"Because what?" I push when she doesn't expand, only for her to fluster under the gaze of my brothers and I.

"Because she seems to like me." Her words surprise me, the rawness present in her tone as she twiddles with her fingers.

A soft chuckle breaks past my lips as I shake my head dismissively at her. "*Stellina*, if anything, this is only going to make her like you more." My chest warms with the truth as Wren tilts her head at me in confusion.

"What?"

Both Enzo and Vito chuckle at her response, just as the footsteps stop and a gasp can be heard from behind me. I don't turn to look though, too focused on Wren's reaction to tear my gaze away.

"I never liked that boy," Nonna states, a smile threatening the corner of my mouth at her admission. I'm quite sure she expressed her distaste for him daily, so I know she means every word.

What I don't expect, however, is the voice that follows after her.

"What the fuck is actually going on here? Please do not tell me that my awful brothers left the woman to take out the trash." I whip my head around to see the most elegant and beautiful De Luca there is.

A bundle of trouble and a heaping of sass, there's a reason this girl was never allowed near the family business. She would have been used as our weakness, like she didn't have the mental capacity to destroy us with the snap of her fingers.

"Crazy one, meet crazy two. Wren, this is Valentina. Valentina, this is the beauty I've been telling you about."

REDEMPTION

TWENTY THREE

Wren

Why on God's green earth is there another fucking person here right now? I'm used to killing and exiting as swiftly as possible and this is turning into a fucking mother's meeting. Although, by the looks on everyone's faces, no one is mad.

I shake my hands out, trying to loosen up my body and the resting bitch expression I'm sure has taken over my face, but that's easier said than done. I really need a fucking minute, but I know I'm not going to get one.

My skin has tightened due to the blood, and I cringe as I lift my eyes back to Nonna. It seems she was tracking my line of sight because confusion etches across her face as she takes a step toward me.

"Wren, please tell me that's Teto's blood and not yours because I swear on all that is holy, I will bring the motherfucker back to life, only to kill him all over again." Her chest heaves with each word, catching me by surprise with how much she means everything she's saying.

Someone scoffs, but my focus is set on her as I shake my head subtly. "Please, Nonna, you know me. Even when he thought he had control, it was only because I was intrigued at what he might do, but his actions were just as shitty as his threats." I shrug, hoping to play it off and get out of the room, but nobody seems to move.

"I can see why Nonna thinks you're so fabulous, Wren." Valentina's eyes flicker over me in my blood-drenched tank top, shorts, and messy hair.

I don't attempt to apologize, and she doesn't look all that taken aback as she steps toward me and reaches her hand out for me to shake.

"Pleasure," I mutter as I place my hand in hers, unsure of how I'm supposed to react to her, but she smiles as she drops her arm back to her side. She's not bothered about the blood, or that it could now be on her. Hmm.

At first glance, you would think she was a billionaire's wife, with a long cream coat draped over her shoulders, brown linen trousers, and a cashmere sweater tucked in. She looks far too elegant to even be in this room. Her brown hair is swept back into a chignon at the back of her head and her make-up is beyond perfection.

"Shall we move into the kitchen so the cleanup crew can get in? They will be here any second," Vito announces, and I'm moving before I even realize it, dodging between everyone as I head for the door.

The second I'm through the doorway, a weight lifts off my shoulders and my body finally relaxes. The others move behind me, but I'm hoping I'm far enough in front that I can slip into my bedroom without any issues and get some peace.

My hopes are temporary as an arm drapes over my shoulders and pulls me along the extra steps to the kitchen. Glancing to my right, I'm not surprised to find it's Enzo beside me, looking down at me with a mixture of awe and worry flashing in his eyes.

He leans in closer, his nose ghosting over my ear before he presses his lips to the skin. "I can't let you out of my sight, Wren. I'm now in protective mode and you're going to have to deal with it for a minute," he mutters, sending a zing down my spine.

This isn't the norm for me, not one bit, but as he leans back and makes eye contact with me once more, I get the feeling this isn't the usual for him either.

Enzo leads me to the fridge, the others piling into the room behind us, but I opt to avoid their gazes for an extra second. He hands me a sweet fizzy drink, encouraging me to take a sip, and I oblige, even though I really don't need the sugar to take the edge off.

Turning on the spot, I find Matteo and Vito watching my every move, while Nonna and Valentina are muttering between themselves by the table.

This is awkward.

I've killed someone, one of their men, and it's a family gathering.

With a flourish, Valentina spins on the spot, her long coat dancing around her as she settles her gaze on me. I have no idea what is about to fall out of her mouth, but I get the feeling I won't have a choice either.

"Wren, I think it looks like you could use a minute to decompress."

I practically sag at her words. Yes. That's exactly what

I want and need to do. Preferably with a steak sandwich too. "I do. If you don't mind, I'm just going to—"

She waves her hand around, edging toward me as she interrupts my escape speech. "No, not here. You're *never* going to get a second to even breathe without these three crowding you and making everything worse."

"Fuck off, Valentina," Matteo grumbles, yet not one of the De Luca brothers actually disagrees with what she's saying. The way Enzo's arm tightens around me only confirms it too.

With a dramatic eye roll, Valentina switches her gaze from her brother to me with a pointed stare. "I have the best plan… Well, Nonna agrees, too. It's exactly what you need."

"And what is that?"

She cuts the distance between us without a hint of hesitation, grabbing my hand before I can stop her and pulling me from Enzo's hold. He mutters something under his breath, but I'm too focused on whatever plan Valentina and Nonna seem to have.

"We're going to the spa." Her eyes light up with excitement as she continues to hustle me toward the door, taking the can of soda from my other hand and placing it down on the kitchen island as we move.

My steps slow as I frown at her, glancing down the length of my body as I shake my head in disbelief. "I'm literally covered in blood. I can't go anywhere right now."

She turns to look at me with a grin still playing on her lips as she leans into my side and winks. "That's why we're going to *my* spa. This mafia princess can do whatever she pleases. If you didn't know that already, I think you're about to find out."

Never, and I mean *ever* in my life, have I stabbed a man to death and taken a trip to the spa straight after. Nope. That's not how this shit works, but apparently in Italy, things are done differently.

I would be hiding away for a good few days, weeks sometimes, but none of that seems to be the norm here. Instead, I am whisked away from the family home and led to the outskirts of town where the *Valentina* Spa is. It looks high-end before I even step inside. Attached to its own private vineyard and draped out with expensive decor, it's like a slice of heaven.

It was obvious as soon as we entered that the entire

place had been cleared out. There wasn't a single client or member of staff anywhere I could see as I was led into the ladies changing rooms.

Valentina ushered me into a hot shower and gave me a navy blue designer swimsuit to put on after I was done, leaving me to relish in the burn of the water. I stepped out of the stall to find them waiting for me, and then I was led to a large space where the swimming pool and four jacuzzis were situated.

Making a beeline for one with the perfect view over the vineyard, I sank into the water, and I haven't moved since. Every bubble melts away my worries, seeping into my skin and making me whole again.

Soft music plays in the background as I duck my head under the water, soaking my hair. I might be rid of the blood that was staining my skin, but my mind hasn't healed from it yet.

Lifting my head out of the water, I push my hair back off my face before my hands start rubbing against my shins. I can't help but do this every time I get blood on me, especially when it's someone else's. But as the years go by and I continue to do this, the process slowly shortens.

The first time I killed someone, I was scrubbing at my

raw skin for weeks, and now, it's merely a few hours. It's relieving to get over it so much quicker but also depressing that I've become so accustomed to it that it's not as painful to handle anymore.

"You're going to make your skin raw if you keep doing that," Valentina says from my left, perched on the edge of the hot tub when I turn to look in her direction with a quirked brow.

Her swimsuit has a red floral pattern, complementing her olive skin perfectly as she assesses me. Her brown eyes are just the same as her brothers', somehow combining the three of them altogether. There's a hint of Enzo's mischief, a shimmer of Vito's curiosity, and a whole heaping of Matteo's judgment.

"It's my usual ritual," I reply with a shrug, relaxing into the bubbles as she looks on across the room. I follow her line of sight, only to find Nonna relaxing on a lounge chair with a book in her hand, and I smile at the sight of her.

It seems like we've made a little vacation out of me needing to decompress, and I'm more than willing to admit that I like it.

Valentina clears her throat, drawing my attention back

to her as she looks me square in the eyes. "Dare I ask how you ended up at my brothers' home?"

I consider my answer before I adjust my position so I can see her better. "You know them better than I do, so what do you think happened?"

She cocks her head as she shrugs. "Honestly, I can't figure it out. Nonna said you're there under surveillance, and no one is *ever* there under surveillance. But she insisted that I come to meet you and stake a claim on you so they wouldn't end your life if it came to it."

My eyes widen at her admission, before I glance at the woman enjoying whatever book she's reading. "That won't be necessary," I state, turning back to face her once more, and she chuckles.

"Oh, I know. You can definitely handle yourself, but you intrigue me too. So there is no way in hell my brothers are going to hurt a single hair on your head." The determination in her tone surprises me, but I don't say a word in response, which leads to her explaining herself. "Crazy is my middle name, well, given to me by Nonna, so if she labels someone else as crazy too, I know they're on my level. Besides, it's definitely a first for me, to meet someone for the first time, especially a woman, covered in blood with a dead man at their feet, and I think it's fantastic." Her grin widens, and I'm sure she's close to clapping too, but she manages to hold herself back.

"I can't say I've ever met anyone under those circumstances either, but I really don't need you to pity me."

"Girl, please. There's not a single ounce of pity here. I'm in fucking awe of you and if I wasn't trying to help you decompress right now, I would be begging you to come out and have some fun with me." She's talking a mile a minute, and I struggle to keep up with her, nodding along the best I can as my nose scrunches in confusion.

"Fun?" A simple three letter word and I have no idea what it fucking means.

She pats my arm lightly as she shakes her head in disbelief at me. "Yeah, like going out dancing, getting drunk, and stumbling home to piss my brothers off. Any of it. *All* of it. I like your vibe. Sure you might be a bit closed off, but shit, with my past, I am too."

A part of me is eager to do all of those things and just be… free. Even if it is for the briefest of moments. But now isn't the best time for that. Not just that; I know the shit the brothers are dealing with, and something tells me they wouldn't let us out of their sight anyway.

An invisible connection thrums between us, an understanding that comes so naturally, it's confusing. Whatever it is, it has me leaning closer as I stare deep into her brown eyes.

"How much do you know about the De Luca business?" She doesn't shy away from my question as she seems to assess me too.

"Everything." One word said with such ease and confidence that I know she's telling the truth, but I still want to hear a little more from her first. Quirking my eyebrow at her, I don't say anything as she playfully rolls her eyes at me. "For real. I knew nothing when my father was alive, kept as a privileged princess in my tall tower with nothing to do but make myself look pretty." She rolls her eyes again, but this time, there's no playfulness to the action. "Then when he passed, Matteo decided that he didn't like how vulnerable being kept in the dark made me. Now I have my own businesses, my own life, and I know everything. I've never felt more a part of my family than I do now."

My chest warms at her words, my heart and soul begging to feel anything even remotely close to that, but the reality is, I'm my own family now. There's no one else here but me.

Clearing my throat, I pull myself from my thoughts as I ask her another question. "Do you know why they went to New York?"

"To meet with the Russians about the death of Totem and everything he promised them," she says with a nod, making my heart rate kick up. I have no idea what I'm fucking saying right now, but I can't seem to stop it.

"How do you feel about that?" I ask with a gulp, my hands flexing in my lap under the water as I wait for her to reply.

"About what?" Her lips purse as she tries to understand what I'm asking.

"What do you think about everything Totem promised them?" I think I might be sick, but the verbal diarrhea just isn't stopping.

"I thought it was utter bullshit, all of it." A bubble of laughter bursts past my lips, and I quickly slam my mouth shut to stop anything else escaping. "What? I did."

I shake my head, a smile teasing my lips. "And how do you feel about the vengeance they declared on his killer?"

If she has any idea of where I'm heading with this,

it doesn't show on her face as she scoffs. "Please, that man was no good. No. Fucking. Good. If he was, then my brothers wouldn't have gone to such lengths to keep me as far away from him as possible."

A sharp pain tugs at my chest, not because of who he was to me, but the fact that he had this impact on so many people. Someone should have ended him before it came down to me. Shit, before I even existed.

When I don't say anything in response, my eyes downcast as I track my hands floating in the water, I sense Valentina stepping into the jacuzzi and taking a seat beside me. "Why do you ask?"

Her question is so soft, I almost don't hear it, but I turn to her with a tender smile and a hint of sadness I know is visible in my eyes. "To see if you were worthy of knowing why I was here."

"Which is…"

Before I can think anymore of it, I release a deep breath. "Because Totem was my father, and I killed him."

Silence falls over us as she gapes at me in surprise, her eyes wide for what feels like an eternity before she claps her hands together.

"Holy fucking shit. I *knew* I liked you. I knew it.

Now I'm definitely glad that I've arranged for some steak sandwiches to be delivered because you deserve it, girl. You deserve whatever slice of peace life can offer you, and I'm all for it."

REDEMPTION

TWENTY FOUR
Matteo

I lean back in my leather seat, surrounded by my brothers and our men in the separate building on-site at our home, completely at the end of my tether with the bullshit we're dealing with. The Russians haven't made any other moves, and we can't seem to pinpoint what the next may be, which only pisses me off further.

My fingers flex in my lap as Enzo leads the discussion on the nightclub incident and the collateral damage as a result of the attack. Looking up, I meet my brother's gaze. "How is Torres's family?"

The room remains quiet as everyone waits solemnly

for a response, and my brother shakes his head gently. "As best as they can be." His pain is evident as he hangs his head for a brief moment, before he looks around the room again. "His funeral is being held in two days' time," he adds, sending a wave of murmurs around the room.

Everything becomes more real when the funeral is confirmed. We're going to spend the next forty-eight hours wishing it was over with, while simultaneously praying for it to never come.

It's a finality to the anguish we're all feeling at the loss of our most trusted man and friend.

"Make whatever arrangements are necessary," I state, nodding at my brother who offers a tight smile in return.

It's something none of us wish to be dealing with, but the reality of life is so fickle, so delicate, that it has a crazy way of sweeping the rug from under us.

The sound of someone clearing their throat interrupts the silent communication between Enzo and I, drawing both of our gazes, along with Vito's, to Gio, one of our newer recruits.

He glances around the room, searching between each of my brothers as well as the men beside him before he speaks. "Has anyone seen or heard from Teto? He sent me a text message earlier, asking for my help with something, but I haven't had any contact with him since."

I can tell by the furrow between Gio's brows that he really is curious and concerned, but he's about to be caught up to speed with everyone else here. My fists tighten and my spine stiffens as I try to keep my anger at bay, but it's Vito who takes the lead by responding first.

"No one will be seeing or hearing from him because that *putana* is dead." There's a pin-drop silence as widened eyes and raised brows stare in our direction, hoping for more of an explanation. "We have rules and orders and he didn't follow them," Vito continues, his gruff voice getting darker and edgier with every word. "This is the De Luca family business, not the *every man for himself* brigade." His nostrils flare as his hands clench at his sides, making the whites of his scars shine brighter.

I know he's as angry as I am. Once Wren left with Valentina and Nonna, the three of us rushed to search the surveillance cameras we have set up in the gym. We watched everything unfold, watched every move he made, and listened to every word he uttered. He's fucking lucky he only had Wren's wrath to deal with and not ours as well.

"Does anybody else have an objection to that?" I

interject, meeting the eyes of every single one of the men at the table, one at a time, until I've gone full circle.

"No, sir," Gio finally verbalizes, nodding sharply as he falls in line.

We need to find a replacement for Torres, someone who can handle this shit going forward so we don't have to. Could it be Gio? I'm not sure, there's something holding me back, but realistically, I know I won't get the answers I want right now. My mind isn't here. I need to take a step back to refocus.

"Go." Nobody misses a beat as they rise from their seats and exit the building. I feel my cell phone vibrating in my pocket just before the last two men leave through the door, but I don't take it out until it's only myself, Vito, and Enzo remaining.

"Have you heard anything from the women yet? I want eyes on Wren," Enzo mutters under his breath as he takes a sip of water, adjusting his position in his seat as he looks from Vito to me, and we shake our heads.

Pulling my cell phone from my pocket, I hope to see one of their names, but to my surprise, it's a private number, and I know who it belongs to immediately. It's been calling incessantly, and I've never considered answering until now, until today.

Pressing the green button, I hit the speakerphone button so my brothers can listen. "You're being quite persistent, Mrs. Steele."

Enzo's eyes widen as Vito leans back in his chair, loosening his tie as he glares at the phone.

"And you've been avoiding me." Her voice sounds surprised that I've answered this time, but I can't deny that I'm just as caught off guard with the move too.

"I don't answer to you or Featherstone. If I don't want to take your call, then I won't take it."

Silence greets me for a moment before Luna sighs down the line. "That's very true, Matteo, but we're both dealing with the same enemy right now, and a conversation could be beneficial to both of us."

My gaze flicks to Vito and Enzo for a brief moment before I respond, "What makes you say that?"

"I heard about what happened at your nightclub. Classic Dmitri move if you ask me."

My heart rate spikes, thumping in my chest as I inch closer to the cell phone. "Who did you hear that from?"

Fuck. Fuck. Fuck. Fuck. Fuck.

If she says Wren's name right now, I'll explode with

rage.

"Matteo, let's be real. Dmitri is more than happy to parade this information around New York City. I'm not sure if he thinks it's a tactic that may scare me, but I get the feeling he doesn't quite understand how Featherstone operates here in the States. How *I* operate." Relief rushes through my veins.

My head rolls forward for a second as I try to calm my breathing. I was certain it was going to be Wren. I did leave her with her phone after all.

"What's the reason for your call, Luna?" Vito asks, thankfully taking control as I take a moment.

"I want to bring you back to the table again. For the two of us to work together. We have the same enemy right now, and I'm done with this going on longer than it needs to. I want to bring them down, and I want to do it now." The determination in her voice is firm through the phone line and I'm almost impressed.

"What's in it for you?" I ask, lacing my fingers together as I brace my arms on the table.

"Wren's safety. Her freedom." She doesn't miss a beat, attempting to conjure up some bullshit. But of all the things I expected her to say, that wasn't one of them.

"And..."

"And nothing. I don't know what is going on with the four of you, but she showed her loyalty to me, to Featherstone, before you left New York. She can tell me a thousand times she doesn't want my help and that she's happy where she is, but I want to prove to her that I am worthy of the redemption she pursued. She's a survivor, like me, and I won't let you hurt her."

I process every word she says, saving them all for later as I hum in response. "Hmm, and what is it you want from us?"

"Your men, your intel, your strategy. Then once they're out of the way, we can discuss whatever it is you had going on with Totem."

Enzo taps his fingers on the table, his eyes wide as he nods to her words.

"I'll consider your offer," I murmur, before stretching my hand forward and ending the call. Silence blankets us as we process everything we just heard.

Hurt her? Hurt Wren? Fuck, even if I'm not ready to admit it yet, she holds way more power over me than I do over her, and I'm sure the same goes for my brothers.

We shouldn't be in this position. She should be dead

and I should be focused on spilling Russian blood, but here we are.

"She's home."

My heart clenches at Vito's words, and I'm up and out of my seat before I even realize it. My brothers are hot on my heels, but when I step out onto the driveway, the SUV is already moving away again.

She's inside.

I reach the front door, but turn to face my brothers before I step inside. I don't get a chance to open my mouth and plead my case when Vito nods at me. "Go."

Enzo pouts instantly, clearly wanting another taste of the woman he was lost in last night, but I don't wait around. That one word from Vito is all I need.

The moment I step inside, I make a beeline for Wren's door. As I come to a stop, the door slightly ajar, I hear my brothers interacting with Nonna in the kitchen, and I know I have her to myself.

Using the tip of my finger, I nudge her door open a little further so I can get a peek inside. She's sitting at the edge of the bed, palms flat against her knees with her head tilted back. She inhales slowly, holding her breath, before she exhales.

She repeats the motion a few times then opens her eyes. She must notice my shadow out of the corner of her vision because she turns to look at me. There's no jolt to her movement, no surprise at my presence, just a soft smile touching the corners of her lips.

"How are you, *Stellina*?" The nickname I gave her back in New York feels natural on my tongue again. The second she revealed herself as Wren and not Ava, I avoided it at all costs, but it's impossible now. Today's events have changed everything, even if I can't explain why.

I enjoy the way her eyes move over me from head to toe, before settling on mine. "I'm actually okay." My eyebrows raise as I take a step into the room. She doesn't show any signs of wanting me to leave, so I don't stop until I'm standing right in front of her.

"Some people struggle after killing someone."

She rubs her lips together as she nods ever so slightly at me. "Fortunately for me, I'm no stranger to killing. Especially, when they're as worthy of death as he was." It's my turn to nod this time. We're far more similar than I care to admit.

Reaching forward, I stroke my finger down her cheek, then tilt her chin to make her look at me better. Yet she takes it one step further and rises to her feet so we're chest to chest.

I have no idea how to describe the emotions running through me at the moment, allowing myself to feel something other than pain for the first time since we enjoyed Ava at the club. And it was a hell of a long time before then.

Tucking a loose tendril of hair behind her ear, my lips move, my filter broken as I murmur against her lips, "I'm sorry we left this morning."

Wren's eyebrows pinch as she looks up at me, her hands rising to my arms as she shakes her head. "Don't apologize for running your business how you see fit. I was just—"

I can't take it anymore, I can't take her understanding, her toughness, her strength. Even though I need it all. I need it all for myself. Without wasting another second, I cut off her words with a kiss.

It's brutal, it's devouring, it's frenzied. But most of all, it's intoxicating.

I feel the press of her fingertips at my biceps as she clings to me, and it only drives me more insane. When I can no longer breathe, I tear my lips from hers, resting my forehead and nose against hers.

"You should be dead, not working your way beneath my skin," I bite, but there's no malice or venom in my tone. Nothing but raw desire.

Wren scoffs in response as if I just said the most ridiculous joke. "Please, you and your brothers are driving me to insanity," she breathes, before pressing her lips to mine in the sweetest fucking kiss I've ever felt.

Fuck.

I can't contain my need any longer. I can't.

Bending at the knees, I grab the back of her thighs and lift her into the air effortlessly. She gasps in surprise, all husky and needy, and it makes me pin her body to mine even tighter. Without a single word, I turn on the spot and exit her room, glancing over her shoulder to navigate toward the stairs before taking them two at a time to reach the top.

I almost sag in relief when I see my bedroom door, and I charge toward it, flinging it open before kicking it shut behind me. My pulse pounds as I get lost in her blue pools of desire.

Our chests heave with every breath as we engage into short, harsh kisses, seeing who will take it to the next level first. She's teasing and encouraging as she grins, running her tongue over her bottom lip, and I'm even more of a goner.

"How strong are you, Wren?" I ask, before cutting the distance to my huge bed and tossing her down on it. She bounces a few times, her mouth parting as she quirks her brow at me.

"Strong enough for whatever you're thinking of," she replies, her voice raspy, and I have to grab at my dick through my pants to contain myself.

"Oh, I doubt that very much." I loosen my tie and kick off my shoes, but instead of taking me at my word, she tilts her head to the side with a grin on her lips.

"Try me, big man."

I pause in place, my tie hanging loose in my hands as I discard it. She has no idea what she's getting herself into, but if she's willing to try, I'm willing to test it out.

Shaking out of my blazer, I let the navy material fall to the floor as I reach for the top button of my shirt. Her eyes track my every move as I undo each button, before her tongue sweeps across her bottom lip as she feasts on my chest and abs.

It's only when I'm reaching for the button of my

pants that she rises to her knees on the bed and pulls off the oversized sweater she's acquired since leaving earlier. The red lace bra underneath encases her tits perfectly. She looks like every fantasy I've ever imagined all in one.

The pair of us strip, not uttering a word as we take each other in, until we're both standing completely naked.

"Wait here." I reach out my hand to run my finger over the soft skin between her breasts before I head for the closet. It only takes me a moment to find what I'm looking for, and when I step back into the room, I find her exactly where I left her.

Her eyes flick from me to the spreader bar in my hands, and a spark of excitement flashes through her blue orbs. My cock juts with need at her expression, and I catch a shiver running down her spine as she clenches her thighs together.

"Come."

I'm desperate to lay her out bare on the bed and take exactly what I want, but I want to continue the intensity that is floating between us.

I head for the bathroom, flicking on the light switch as I enter before turning on the shower. I can sense her behind me, taking the room in, but I know she's watching me specifically when I place the spreader bar on the high hooks in the large shower space. I give it a little jiggle to make sure it's secure, then I turn to meet her gaze.

Steam starts to frost the glass of the shower and the mirror above the vanity, but it doesn't shield my view of her exquisite body. Her nipples pebble under my gaze, her chest rising and falling harshly with every breath as she pushes her hair back off her face.

It's on the tip of my tongue to beckon her closer, but she moves of her own accord, slipping past me with a needy smirk on her face as she comes to a stop right beneath the bar.

"Are you going to fasten me in, or am I?"

Her words are like a prayer as some of the spray from the shower touches her skin. A droplet of water trails from her collarbone all the way down to her core, and my feet move me closer to her before I even realize it.

"You are quite possibly the strongest, most independent, and damn crazy woman I have ever met in my life. I know why I didn't kill you when I would have slayed anyone else on the spot, but I'm not ready to admit that yet." I'm revealing truths in time with my acknowledging them, and I can't stop it. "That being said, in here, you're mine. Not even my brothers get to hook you up to anything or restrain you in any way. Not like me, not like I did when we were at the club."

The memory flashes in my mind as I step closer, pressing my lips to her ear as I coast my fingers down her sides.

"Please."

Fuck, if I wasn't addicted to her already, then hearing her beg for me definitely finalized it.

I circle her left wrist, slowly lifting it above her head before securing it in the first loop. Repeating the motion with her right arm, I take a step back when she's strapped in on both sides.

"Perfection."

She preens under my praise, before giving me another one of her raised eyebrows. "Perfection would be you stretching me out on your cock right now." Her gaze slips to my dick at the same time as she speaks.

She's like a beacon for my dick, but instead of a lighthouse warning me of danger, she brings me closer like a siren to her prey.

My siren.

I press a kiss against her jaw, trailing slowly down her

neck, across her collarbone, and over the swell of her tits before I suck sharply on her taut nipples.

"Fuck."

Her grunt makes me grin, but I don't continue to tease. If she spent last night with Enzo, then I have a feeling those pretty pink pebbles are still a little sore. When they're this much like perfection, everyone is going to be a breast man.

Continuing down the valley between her breasts, I circle my tongue around her belly button. Dropping to my knees, I inch closer, nipping slightly at her skin as I get nearer and nearer to her core.

I tilt my head, looking up the length of Wren's body until my eyes rest on hers, the need bleeding from every inch of her as her fists hold on tightly to the bar above her.

"Please."

That's exactly what I wanted to hear.

Without breaking eye contact, I run the pad of my tongue from her entrance to her clit, gliding through her folds as she groans with pleasure, making me repeat the process again and again, just so I can elicit that same noise from her lips.

When her hips start to buck against me, I bring two fingers to her core, feeling her damp entrance with a smile on my lips before I thrust them deep inside of her.

"Yes," she cries, head flung back as water continues to spray over us.

Swirling my fingers deep inside of her, I rake my teeth over her clit before sucking it into my mouth, making her moans and cries get louder. My god, she was made for me. I've never been more positive of anything in my life. The way her back arches, her body clenches, and her groans fill my ears…

She's mine.

"I… I-I'm…"

She trails off before she can even begin her sentence, and in the next breath, her pussy clenches tightly around my fingers and she explodes. I don't stop circling her pussy as I lap at her clit, wringing her dry of her climax, before I slowly pull my fingers from her body and stand.

I taste her on my tongue as I tease the tips of my fingers over my lips, and she gasps, her chest heaving as she pants for a breath.

"Please."

That one word was made for her, for her to mutter to me in times when we both know the outcome.

"Only because you asked me so nicely, *Stellina*."

I grab her thighs again, like I did downstairs, and she wraps her legs around my waist as my cock finds her entrance without guidance. "Tell me I can fuck you like this, Wren." Her eyes search mine, understanding flashing in her bright blue pools. "Please," I add, using the special word back at her, and she nods immediately.

I thrust forward, her pussy gripping me tightly as I continue inch after inch until I'm fully seated inside of her. She's heaven. Fucking heaven. I pause for the briefest moment, giving us both a second to adjust, but my cock twitches repeatedly inside of her, desperate for more.

There's no more denying either of us.

Pulling her back off the wall, her arms raised above her head as I tilt her hips in my direction, I look over the length of her. Her eyes are half-mast in delight and her back is arched even in this position.

She likes being hooked up like this, but not as much as I do.

I pull out until only the tip remains, before slamming into her hard and fast, repeating the motion as my body takes over.

Our breaths mingle together.

Our moans are like a symphony.

Our bodies collide until we're merely one.

"Matteo."

My name on her lips has me inching closer, my mouth only a breath away from hers until she surprises the hell out of me and cuts the remaining distance between us, running her tongue over the scar that marks the right side of my mouth.

I can't stop my fingers from digging deeper into her thighs as my orgasm begins to ebb through me, starting at my toes before ripping through every inch of my body.

Her pussy clamps down tightly around my cock as I explode, falling over the cliff with me as my nose presses into her neck.

It takes us both a moment to regain our focus, and I lift my head up to look at her, only to find a grin tainting her pretty lips.

"I told you I was strong." Her voice is raspier than ever, and it makes my cock flex in her pussy once more as I shake my head at her with a grin.

"You're also cute for thinking I'm even close to being done with you."

TWENTY FIVE

Wren

My heart races in my chest, my hand clenched tightly to the pistol in my hand as I try my best to stick to the shadows. I can hear my father and Luna talking, but to get a better visual, I will need to inch closer to the balcony before me.

I release a breath as I pin my back to the pillar on my left and peer over the ledge to get a better view. I know there are more people down there, but I don't register anyone but Luna and Totem. His demand from earlier repeats in my mind.

"Be prepared, oh daughter of mine, your time has

finally come to bring Luna Steele to her end. You'll know when to take the shot."

The pair of them argue back and forth, but it all dissolves into the background as I lift my gun and aim it down below. My target is in sight, my finger itching to pull the trigger, and as I release one final breath, I do just that. Only instead of shooting Luna, I aim for him.

My father.

Bang.

I bolt upright in bed, my palm flat against my chest as I gulp back a few breaths, cataloging my mind as I come to realize it was just a dream. It's been a hot minute since I've had one, but I get the feeling they'll continue to live with me for the rest of my life.

It's not a nightmare, it's a dark and twisted reminder of the exact moment I changed my future. For better or for worse, I stand by my choice.

Grabbing the sheet to cover my naked body with one hand, I push my hair back off my face with the other, taking in the foreign room around me. I didn't really get a chance to glance at it last night in the sex haze Matteo had me in, but now I have a moment to look over it properly.

It feels strange being upstairs, let alone in one of their bedrooms. The white sheets that are draped over me match three out of the four walls in the room, the other being a deep forest green with matching curtains and a rug to go with it. The furniture is oak, the color balancing the contrasts in the room, and I'm certainly impressed with his choices.

With a hint of uncertainty, I cling to the sheet a little tighter as I consider whether I should stay here or make an escape. Was yesterday a moment of complete insanity? The aftermath of the craziness of the day overwhelming the both of us?

I hope not, but the decisions weren't mine alone, and I stand by them. My chest clenches, my heart pounding as the reality washes over me. *I'm falling for them.*

I don't know how, I don't know exactly when, but I sure as fuck know why. Admitting it, however, is not something I'm up to facing today, and sitting around here isn't going to make me feel any better about the unknown hanging over my head.

Rolling my shoulders back, I drop the sheet from my body and swing my legs over the side of the bed. The instant ache between my thighs has me stifling a groan as my body tingles, remembering exactly where he touched me and the pleasure he brought along with it.

As I stand from the bed, I search around the room for my discarded clothes, but come up empty. There's nothing at all except for a folded white shirt on the desk in the left corner of the room.

I might be confident in my skin, but I'm not leaving this room naked, so I reach for the crisp material before I slip my arms into the sleeves and slowly fasten each button. When there's only the final two at the top left to do, I start moving toward the door, but startle when the adjoining bathroom door swings out, catching me off guard.

"Holy fuck," I gasp, my spine stiffening as I watch steam billow from the room, followed moments later by Matteo with only a towel wrapped around his waist.

Fuck.

How did I not hear the shower running? This man has me lost in my head, combined with the dream that woke me, I was clearly more distracted than I would like to be.

Running my eyes over him, I don't miss the small grin teasing the corner of his mouth as he appreciates me ogling him. I want to cut the distance between us and run my tongue over the scar down the right side of his mouth again, but I refrain as he interrupts my thoughts.

"I was supposed to be wearing that shirt today, *Stellina*."

My thighs clench at the nickname that rolls off his tongue as I bite down on my bottom lip and look up at him through my lashes. "Do you want it back?" I offer, beginning to unbutton it again, but he shakes his head, his eyes heating despite his action.

"I can't say it would look any better on me if you did." A grin takes over my lips as he takes a step toward me. I feel awkward, unprepared for what his intentions are as he stops right in front of me, placing his hands on my hips until our chests are flush against one another. "Besides, we have a busy day ahead of us."

"We do?" My hands lift to his chest, his skin still damp from the shower as he nods in response. "Are we going anywhere fun or exciting?"

There's a hint of teasing in my tone because I know the likeliness is slim with the craziness going on around us, but the shrug he offers leaves me intrigued. "That depends on what we're calling fun and exciting."

Now I'm even more intrigued. "Enlighten me."

With bated breath, I wait for him to respond. He hooks a loose tendril of hair behind my ear before cupping my chin and tilting my head back. "I want you to get dressed and eat, then I want you to show my brothers and I what it is you're capable of."

I stand frozen in place, completely surprised by his words, and apprehension tingles down my spine. "What I'm capable of?" I repeat, needing clarification as he nods.

"Yes."

Fuck. I love nothing more than proving I'm worthy, that I'm skilled, and that I know how to handle myself. If this was a date, I would be inclined to confirm this is my idea of fun, but he doesn't need to know that.

No.

He just needs to know I was born to do this.

"Lead the way."

Standing in the gym with Enzo to my left and Vito on my right, I take in the space that consumed me yesterday. There's no dead body, not a drop of blood or anything out of the ordinary. They have a good cleanup crew, that's for sure.

I watch as Matteo walks over to the window, peering outside before he turns to face me with his arms folded over his chest. Each one of the De Luca brothers is dressed in a fitted black tee and a pair of black shorts. Gone are the suits and in their place are some hot-ass outfits that make them appear just as delectable.

Shaking my head, wanting to remain focused on what we're doing here, I pat my hands on my legs as I speak. "So, what are we doing in here?"

Enzo runs his hand down my spine at the same time Vito clears his throat. My gaze drifts to his, and I hate that I can't guess what he's thinking. Things have changed a little with Matteo and Enzo, but Vito still has a wall placed between us, a wall I fucking hate and have no idea how to knock down.

"We're not doing anything in here," he states, making my eyebrows furrow.

"Why are we in here, then?"

Three breaths. It takes three breaths for Vito to exchange a look with Matteo, before cutting his eyes at me, still giving nothing away. "To see how you react to being in here again."

My eyebrows go from being knitted to almost reaching my hairline as I gape at him in surprise. How ridiculous. Taking a deep breath, I step out of my spot between Vito and Enzo, placing a stride or two between us as I turn on the spot and pin my gaze on them.

"My mother and father once left me home alone for the evening. Unbeknown to me, they had arranged a hitman, a trained killer to attack me in the middle of the night to see how I would handle it. To see if I was as prepared as they hoped." My hands clench at my sides as I continue spinning slowly in a circle, making sure to catch their gazes each time. "I slayed that motherfucker on my goddamn bed. His eyeballs bleeding, his gut bleeding from the stab wounds at his stomach, and the gaping hole in his head staining my pillow." My nostrils flare despite me trying to contain my emotions. "I rolled him to the floor, proceeded to change my sheets and laid in complete darkness as I stared up at the ceiling." Enzo's eyes widen as I scoff, shaking my head in disbelief as I add in the punchline, "I was eleven."

"Fuck." The raspy tone tells me that it was Vito, but when I turn to him, he's swiping a hand down his face.

"So, if this is test number one, I think we're good. Shall we proceed?" I can't keep the sharp tone from my voice, but I'm pissed off. It's not their fault they don't know my past or believe the craziness that was my childhood, but they need to catch up, and fast.

"This scar on my face is from my father," Matteo announces, his voice lower than normal as I turn my attention to him. "I know what an unstable household looks like, probably not as much as you, but you have to understand, *Stellina*, it's not normal for us to find someone else like us. Someone who has been through as much as we have and survive. Someone who has perfected their armor and wears it with honor."

My chest heaves with every word he speaks as I slowly nod in understanding. I know it's different for me. Growing up within Featherstone, especially going through everything at the academy, you know everyone there is dealing with similar shit to you.

No matter what anyone says, it causes trauma, trauma we can't escape or shy away from, so I choose to be at one with it instead of giving it a chance to consume me.

Relaxing my shoulders, I offer a tight smile to each of them as I head toward the open doorway. "I understand what you're saying, and I understand it's like that for most people. But Featherstone is made up of crazy-as-fuck families trying to survive. Everyone there has their own shit to handle, their own walls around themselves, and their own desires to chase. This lifestyle, though, yours and mine, it's not one of choice, and it's not for the faint-hearted. It's destined for us, for our bloodlines, and once you see me as an equal in that way, you'll understand that."

I leave the room, giving them a moment to soak in what I just said. It's weird for me to unload like that and feel lighter at the end of it, but I roll with it. I don't actually have a clue where I'm going, so I head toward the front door, and just as I reach for the handle, I feel an arm band around my waist.

Enzo.

He's gazing at me with a soft smile on his lips and something I haven't seen before flashing in his eyes.

"You just might be the death of me, woman," he mutters, pressing a kiss on my temple as he reaches for the door and escorts me outside.

I don't respond, not really knowing what to say, but I'm also too distracted by what I'm seeing. There must be twenty men over to the left on the perfectly cut lawn, all dressed like the brothers.

Enzo moves me toward them without a word as I try to decipher what is actually going on. I notice two large circles, outlined with rope, in the middle of the grass, and what look like targets at the far perimeter of the trees that shield the property line.

Vito and Matteo are right behind us, both observing me with a sense of newfound appreciation as Matteo plants his hands on his hips.

"We've got three rounds set up, but something tells me this is no longer necessary," he starts, and I lift my hand immediately, shaking my head before he can continue.

"You would be correct, but we're here now so…"

He tilts his head to the side slightly, a smile teasing his lips knowingly before he nods. "I thought you might say that."

I roll my eyes at him as he waves his hand toward the men lined up at the sideline like spectators, and the two that are standing in each one of the circles. "We're going to do unarmed combat, armed combat, and see how you are with the firing range," he explains, sending adrenaline coursing through my veins faster as excitement buzzes through me.

If anything, that little trip down memory lane in there has only fueled me more.

"Which one of you will I be going against at each stage?" I quirk a brow as I step out of Enzo's hold, and he laughs.

"None." I glance over my shoulder at him as he frames his face with his hands. "I can't be messing this pretty face up, *Bella*, that would be ridiculous," he says with a wink, tempting me to roll my eyes at him again, but I shake my head instead.

"Of course not. Is there anything else I need to know?" I ask, walking backward to the first circle as Vito's eyes run over me from head to toe.

"I don't think so," he replies when his eyes meet mine, and I nod.

"Am I killing them or simply injuring?"

Vito's eyes widen in surprise, the first reaction I've had out of him, which almost makes me laugh as he waves his hand around.

"No killing, *Bellisima*, no killing," he repeats as I hold back a smile, butterflies fluttering in my belly. "Injuries aren't even required, just a clear winner," he adds, his raspy voice washing over me like a prayer as I give one final nod and turn to face the men I'm against.

I crack my neck from side to side as they assess me, underestimate me, while any hint of humor is long gone from my face.

"Can we place bets?" someone hollers from the small

crowd to my right. I don't pay them any mind, but that doesn't stop Matteo from responding.

"Fuck off." The grunt gets complete silence in response, and it impresses me. The power he holds, the leader that he is, fuck, I'm wishing I didn't have an overwhelming need to prove myself so I could go back upstairs and recreate last night.

Maybe this time with two other participants, but that's definitely wishful thinking.

The second I step my foot over the rope, the guy inside starts circling. He's at least five foot ten and stocky, with his dark hair cropped short. He's definitely one of the De Luca musclemen, that's obvious, especially given the way he carries himself and watches my every move.

Healthy competition, I hope. This is going to be fun.

We dance around the edge of the circle three times, my steps controlled and my eyes sharp. If he's waiting for me to make the first move, he's truly mistaken. That's not how this works. I've got all day to wait.

As if sensing my thoughts, he drops his right shoulder a little deeper as his steps widen further, and I know he's getting ready to pounce. With the sun beating gently down on my back, the spectators fizzle into the background as I lock my attention on him.

I spot his tell instantly, the left corner of his mouth lifting ever so slightly, like he's already fucking pleased with his accomplishments, before he charges toward me. Time slows around me, my moves well trained and practiced as he comes for my waist, lifting me off the ground.

His shoulder hits my stomach, threatening to knock the air out of me, but I was anticipating the move so it doesn't catch me by surprise. Feeling him spin on the spot, wanting to keep us inside of the circle, I use the opportunity to wrap my arms around his neck, getting him in a deathly grip as he grunts.

As expected, his fight kicks in, and I feel us falling to the floor in the next breath. I gasp for air as my back takes the brunt of the fall, the wind escaping my lungs in a whoosh. I don't have time to worry or relish in the pain though, not when he so predictably releases his hold around my middle, giving me the advantage I need as I continue to keep my arms banded tight around his head.

Using his weight against him, I thrust my knee into his thigh, knocking him off balance, before rolling with him. I don't use the motion to place myself on top of him though, no, I make us do a full three hundred and sixty degree roll. In the process, I manage to lift my legs, trapping one of his arms in my hold as my thighs tighten around his neck.

"Holy fuck."

The two words filter in from the otherwise blurred surroundings, but they only make me double down my efforts as I move my arms to start pounding my fists into his face. I only manage to get two punches in before I feel his palm slapping against my thigh, and in the next moment, someone is tearing me from him.

It takes a moment for my limbs to unlock, but when I see it's Vito with his hands on me, I let go, moving willingly into his arms as he places me on my feet.

My opponent coughs and splutters on the floor beside me as the rest of the noise from the spectators registers into my brain.

"Who the fuck is she?"

"What just happened?"

"I definitely want bets now."

I don't take my eyes off Vito's as he looks down at me. My fingers itch to run over the scarring at his neck, but I know that would only make him hate me more. I want to apologize to him since I hurt him the most. He literally fucked me against the door in New York, and within thirty minutes, I had ruined everything.

It's on the tip of my tongue, but if he can sense it, he doesn't want to hear it because he places me on my feet a moment later and walks away.

Running my hands over my shorts, I sigh, masking the pain I'm sure is there, before someone claps their hands.

"Are you ready, *Stellina*?"

Undeniable pride shines in Matteo's eyes, and it's almost too much for me to handle so I turn my attention to the next ring instead.

"Do I get to choose my own weapon?" I ask, approaching the table set up next to the circle. It's filled with everything one can imagine — blades, nunchucks, bats, brass knuckles, and throwing blades.

It's like I'm back in the vault at Featherstone Academy, looking at my family heirlooms that come in the form of violence. My fingers glide over them, before slowing on the throwing blades. I've used them before, enjoyed them even.

"You do," Enzo states, pulling me from my thoughts. I offer him a small smile before turning to see what my opponent will use against me.

A blade.

He twirls it between his fingers, dancing it over his skin. He knows exactly what he's doing with it.

Excellent.

"How much blood is enough, Matteo?" I keep my eyes trained on my opponent, sizing him up as I continue to graze my fingers over the throwing blades on the table.

My opponent scoffs, shaking his head dismissively as he looks to the other men for encouragement. "I think you will find, *little girl*, that I'll get as much blood as I want. Not the other way around. This is a man's world, a man's business, and it will serve you well to know your fucking place."

Blind rage burns up my spine as I wrap my fingers around one of the throwing blades and toss it in a split second, but it's soothed by the sweet sound of this motherfucker crying out in pain as the blade hits his thigh. I don't waste a second, not wanting him to have a chance to throw his blade my way, so I grab another throwing blade, identical to the previous, and send it in the same direction. This one hits him straight in his right shoulder. His grip on the dagger in his hand loosens and the metal drops to the floor.

He falls to his knees next, grunting with anger as he almost begins frothing at the mouth, and I take that as my cue to approach him. I get within five feet of him before I crouch down and offer him a sickly-sweet smile.

"I don't know who you are and I really don't care. I couldn't give a fuck if I was inside of the circle and whether the challenge had started or not. No asshole gets to say shit like that to me. But please, continue, I do love seeing you bleed."

My chest heaves with each breath, my fury slowly ebbing as he sneers at me, but before he can say a single word in response, I feel a presence behind me.

"Please, someone explain to me how she manages to get hotter and hotter? I can't take it."

I don't want to take my eyes off the man in front of me, but I can't stop myself from glancing over my shoulder to find Enzo standing behind me with his arms folded over his chest and a wicked grin on his face.

Rising to my feet, I squash down the tension rippling through my body and turn my back on my opponent. "Flattery will get you everywhere, Enzo, but if you actually want your man to survive, you might want to call in a medic asap because I don't know if I hit one of those teeny tiny important arteries," I state, showing him how *teeny tiny* I mean with my thumb and forefinger.

Matteo scoffs as he comes to stand beside his brother, a true look of disdain on his face as he glares down at his man on the floor. "This fucker can roll around in the dirt for a bit, think about his actions, and that goddamn mouth of his that makes me want to kill him with my bare hands."

Fuck, I know what Enzo means about getting hotter and hotter. This is too much.

Shrugging, I head toward the gun range at the bottom of the garden, knowing every single man is following behind me. The brothers because they seem to be as magnetized to me as I am to them, and the rest because they're enjoying the show.

"Gio, you're up," Enzo calls out as I turn and stop at the table to the far left set up with two assault rifles. Gio walks toward me, his body relaxed and his smile seemingly genuine as he approaches.

"Nice to meet you," he mutters, brushing his arm against mine as he comes to a stop beside me, but I don't take him on.

Instead, I turn my attention to Vito who hovers quietly to my right. "Please tell me this is your best shooter who

I'm going to be comparing shots with and not someone you actually want me to aim at."

The corner of his mouth tilts up, surprising me as he nods. "You would be correct, *Bellisima*," he breathes, before pointing at the table before me. "Assault rifles, handguns, shotguns, and finally, snipers." His hand moves with each item, pointing at each table and the targets laid out before them.

"Are you sure you can handle this?" Gio interrupts, and it pisses me off, but I force a smile to my lips as I turn to face him.

"The assaults, the shotguns, and the snipers are my preferred. Handguns remind me of tiny dicks, and I was just built to take more, you know?"

Someone laughs behind me as I reach for the assault rifle, going through my practiced motions as I bring it up to my face and knock the safety off. In the next breath, the shots ring out around me as the paper target in the distance flaps in the wind, revealing all six holes dead center on the head.

Placing the gun back down on the table, I don't wait to see what he can do before I repeat the exact same motion with the handguns, shotguns, and finally, the snipers. When

I take the last shot, I sneak a peek to find Gio looking at me with awe in his eyes.

"Fuck, those were some nice shots." He runs his tongue over his bottom lip, hinting that this whole thing is turning him on.

"Thanks."

I move to take a step back at the same time he reaches out a hand, grabbing my upper arm to regain my attention. I'm ready to knock this fucker to the ground, but the thunderous bite from Vito does the work for me.

"Get the fuck away from her, Gio." My heart races faster in my chest at his tone, but Gio's fingers only relax a little, not actually letting go of me. "Let go of her arm or you lose your trigger finger." I didn't think it was possible for his voice to get lower, but I was wrong.

Gio releases me in the next breath, while I discreetly rub my thighs together in appreciation. I'm a sucker for these men, there's no doubt about it. I turn back to look at Vito, wanting to portray my thanks without words, but I'm distracted by the vision of a woman in pale pink marching toward us.

"Holy. Fucking. Shit. Am I going to continue showing up here with a trail of injured bodies leading me to Wren or is this another one-off occasion?"

Valentina.

I grin at her as she slows, gaining the attention of every man here as they gape at her with lust flashing in their eyes. I don't get a say in the matter as she throws her arms around me, shaking her head in disbelief at what she's saying.

When she releases her hold on me, turning to give her brothers a stern look, I grin.

"Valentina, this is fun for me. Bringing men down feeds my soul." Her smile matches mine as she wraps her arm around my shoulder and starts leading me inside as she hollers loud enough for everyone to hear.

"It's official. We're definitely keeping her."

REDEMPTION

TWENTY SIX

Wren

With Valentina's arm still around my shoulders, we step into the kitchen to find Nonna cooking away. There's a knowing smile on her face as she glances at us out of the corner of her eye.

"Sit," Valentina says, releasing her hold on me to flick her long hair over her shoulder. Since she's hovering over my spot, I sit in the next chair along as she shakes her head in disbelief. "What the fucking hell were my brothers thinking? Don't you worry though, I'm going to take care of all this bullshit. You're coming home with me."

My eyebrows pinch in confusion as I glance at her.

"I'm good where I am, Valentina. I—"

"Call me V," she interrupts, and it takes me a second to process what the fuck she's saying. We go from one subject to another in a split second and it makes my head spin. No wonder I fucking like her.

"Okay, *V*, but if we're being real with each other, I live for this shit. If anything, today was a good bit of exercise," I admit as she gives me a pointed glare, one that I match with my own, and after a moment, her face relaxes and she sighs with a soft smile.

"You really are meant to be here, Wren. Only a fucking De Luca would say something as crazy as that. Am I right, Nonna?" Nonna chuckles and nods.

These two are a force to be reckoned with. I would deem them more of a handful than the damn brothers themselves.

"I agree, but let's get the girl some coffee before you start going on a tirade."

Valentina tosses her head back with a laugh as her hand falls to my shoulder. "Nonna, please, she needs something far stronger than coffee."

Nonna rears her head back, gaping at Valentina like she just stole her last piece of chocolate from under her nose. "Nothing takes the edge off quite like my coffee, Valentina, don't try me," she grumbles, before turning her back to us and starting up the coffee machine.

Valentina doesn't utter a word in response as she smirks at me before taking the seat to my left. The peace that settles over the room has me relaxing back in my seat, my head lulling slightly as I take my time to regulate my breathing.

Fuck, that was fun.

I don't know what I enjoyed more though, proving the spectators wrong, making the asshole in the weapons circle bleed, or having the brothers be somewhat protective over me. The latter is definitely making my heart beat a little faster, and I like it.

"Did you see what she did out there, Nonna? From the aftermath of a man bleeding out in the grass and another looking red and swollen in the face, I would say she had fun putting those grown-ass men in their place." Valentina eyes me as she recounts what she saw, and I can't wipe the smile from my face.

"I was watching. It was a lot more fun than the aftermath even gives her credit for," Nonna responds, and when I tilt my head further back to look at her upside down, she winks at me.

"Was this one of my brother's tests?" Valentina asks, turning her attention to me as I sit upright once more, but before I can offer a single word in response, the De Luca brothers step into the room.

I don't turn to look, but holy fuck, I know it's them without a shadow of a doubt. I have their footsteps mastered, their presence is palpable around me in a way I've never felt or understood before. I just know it's them.

Matteo appears in my line of sight first, his hair swept back off his face as he takes his usual spot at the head of the table. My tongue peeks out, running slowly over my bottom lip as I look him over from head to toe.

There's a lightness to him today, a sense I haven't felt coming from him before, not even on that night at the club, and it's like he's a different person. Gone are his dark and serious eyes and the tension that radiates from his body when he assumes his role as head of the family, and in his place stands a brother, a man, a son.

My attention is drawn to the right when Enzo takes his seat to the left of Matteo, wearing nothing but his shorts and abs. My mouth dries up with need as my gaze meets his. The smirk on his lips tells me he's well aware of the impact he has on me. An impact he fucking loves, craves, needs.

Shit, I'm so screwed.

My heart races in my chest at the sound of a third chair dragging along the floor. Partly because I know it's Vito, the man laying claim to me even though he's barely uttered a word to me since we arrived here, but more so because he's not pulling out the chair beside Enzo that he usually takes. No. It's the one next to me.

A weird tingling swirls in my stomach, possibly like butterflies fluttering their wings against my insides, or maybe it's hundreds of bees assaulting me with their stings all at once. Either way, it's worth enduring for this moment of peace that settles over me.

I don't look to Matteo or Enzo to see their responses to Vito's move as I draw my attention to the man himself. His eyes are already aimed my way, his left hand resting on the back of my seat as he relaxes in his. My gaze is pulled to the bobbing of his Adam's apple, and my fingers plead to reach out and run over the scarred skin at his neck to feel the motion for myself.

I'm so engrossed in checking him out that I miss the smile that spreads across his face before he opens his mouth. "Your eyes are feasting on me so hard you're practically panting, Wren."

I almost gasp at the sound of my real name on his tongue, my body buzzing with excitement as I scramble to think of a response, but I don't have a single one.

He's right, and I don't even care to try to deny it.

My eyes are locked on his, my voice frozen in my throat as Nonna's arm cuts between the two of us and breaks the moment. She places a mug of coffee down in front of me, the smell reaching my nose as my eyes remain locked on Vito's.

"Oh. My. God. All four of you are menaces. That's you three assholes and you, Wren, just to clarify. Total. Fucking. Menaces. I told you years ago you better find one woman who can cope with the three of you because there is never going to be three of them in this world," Valentina declares, amusement clear in her tone as I rub my lips together and opt to grab my mug before I say something stupid. If only I could get my tongue to work.

"Shut up, Valentina," Matteo grumbles, no real bite behind his tone as his sister chuckles at him.

"Not until you admit I was right." Her retort breaks my eye contact with Vito as I glance at my mug instead.

Is this what feeling embarrassed is like?

Am I embarrassed though? No, not really, but this level of attention on the matter when there's never been even a hint of a conversation between any of us has my face heating all the same.

"Unfortunately, Valentina, we have more important things to discuss," Vito interjects, his hand moving from the back of my chair to the top of my thigh as I fail to strangle the gasp that slips from my lips. "Discussions that are business related, so if you want to stick around…" His words fade off, insinuating that if she wants to stay, she needs to quiet down, and surprisingly, she does just that.

"Fine, business first, me saying I told you so second, got it."

I grin into my coffee at her antics. She definitely does have an impact on the people around her in a far too much fun kind of way.

Placing my mug back on the table, acutely aware of Vito's fingers against my bare skin beneath the material of my shorts, I clear my throat and focus on what he said moments ago.

"What business do you need to discuss with me?" My gaze wanders from one De Luca brother to the other until I settle on Matteo with a slightly raised brow. I'm very aware that business conversations don't require my opinion, or he said some shit along those lines previously, so now I'm intrigued.

"All of it."

My eyes widen and I wait for him to continue. After a few moments though, it's clear he's not going to utter another word until I acknowledge what he said.

"All of what?"

He shrugs, leaning back in his seat as he opens his hands in front of him. "We want your help."

"You want *my* help?" I repeat slowly, glancing at Enzo and Vito for confirmation, and I find them nodding eagerly in response.

What the fuck is this alternate universe?

I lean forward in my seat, bracing my elbows on the table as I bite back the smirk on my face. "So, to use the words of a De Luca, business first and my I told you so second?" Valentina bursts into laughter beside me as I let my grin free on my face. Vito rubs his hand over his mouth to hide his, while Enzo openly chuckles with his sister, leaving Matteo to weakly glare at me in annoyance. After basking in the moment, I roll my shoulders back and drop the grin from my lips. "Okay, whatever you need, I'm here."

The table quiets once more at my words and the glare from Matteo softens as he nods.

"We need a plan. We need to bring these motherfucking Russians down for what they did and they need to pay for the unnecessary lives they took." Enzo's jaw tightens as he talks, anger burning beneath the surface as he speaks.

"Plans are for amateurs. Let's just fuck it all to hell, go in guns blazing and watch them bleed," I offer as I sit tall in my seat, ready to fucking go, but the look on everyone else's face tells me that's not going to happen.

"It was literally you telling us *not* to do that yesterday," Vito states, his gruff voice matching the calloused fingertips grazing over my skin.

"Yeah, but that was before you had me out there drawing blood. Now I'm hungry for it," I admit with a hint of humor, an understanding that Vito seems familiar with as his eyes gloss over. "But for real, I'm in. When do you want to leave? We can plan on the way."

Enzo smiles as he stretches his arms over his head. "Excellent. Hopefully we can fly out tonight, have it all done by the end of tomorrow so we will be back in time for Torres's funeral."

I try to hide the fact I hadn't considered his funeral, but it makes my body stiffen. I've never been to a funeral before. I've never mourned someone's death, but I nod anyway.

"Let me shower and I'm ready to go," I reply, rising from my seat with reluctance as Vito squeezes my thigh before removing his touch, and I feel the loss of it. Moving toward the door, I pause, turning on the spot, only to find all four De Lucas watching me leave. "Featherstone… are we using them or going at this alone?"

Matteo assesses me for a hot minute before shrugging. "Alone first. If the time comes that we need more people and you trust them, then we'll make that call."

It makes total sense.

Clearing my throat, I lace my fingers as I try to relay the thoughts that have been running through my head since I woke up this morning. I was too worried to actually accept them, but I feel like I need to voice them now, so here goes nothing.

"I just… on a serious note, the respect and appreciation between everyone here is overwhelming yet life changing for me. Despite who my father was, I was a soldier first.

My opinion didn't count, even when I had all of the facts and insights, so you sitting there and accepting my voice for what it is means more than I would really care to admit." Valentina's eyes gloss over slightly as she offers a soft smile my way, while the brothers stare at me silently. Thank god, I don't want a full conversation right now. I just needed to air those words of truth. "But more than anything, back in New York, I'm sorry my deceit cost us so much, and I'm not even sure I achieved redemption."

TWENTY SEVEN

Vito

My fingers flex on my armrest, every hair on my body standing on end as the plane rumbles beneath me. I can't focus or concentrate on a single thing other than *her*.

I know exactly where she is without looking. My body is acutely aware of her presence, and it's driving me insane. I've been on edge since I saw her step into the gym this morning, then watching her literally slay our men before our very eyes only made my dick harder.

The clouds drift by, but my mind isn't satisfied with the view. Not when she's so close.

Fuck.

Despite my efforts, my gaze turns back to her, just like it has for the past two hours we've been traveling. I'm seated at the table of four, the plush leather seats surrounding me, while she's lying across two chairs on the other side of the aisle as she sleeps.

I'm drawn to the way her eyelashes lie perfectly still against her pale skin, her chest rising and falling slowly with each breath she takes as a serene air floats around her. She's such a mystery yet raw and real with her heart on her sleeve.

No one should be this complex and intoxicating all at once.

Crossing my legs at the ankle, I turn away, looking at the rows further back where Matteo is sitting, going over everything with our men in New York waiting for our arrival. Enzo is across the aisle from him, making sure Italy will continue to run smoothly in our absence. It doesn't help that there's no Torres, no one in charge, but he came to New York with us last time and we entrusted Gio to take care of things at Torres recommendation. Let's hope this doesn't bite us in the ass.

Sighing, I mentally roll my eyes at myself as my gaze falls back to Wren. Stretching my legs out in front of me,

I adjust my semi that's making itself known in my pants. Thankfully, everyone is either busy on their cell phones or sleeping, so they can't call me out on it. Instead giving me the opportunity to let my thoughts of Wren consume me.

I'm as obsessed with her now as I was when we first met her in New York. If not, more. I should have known she was under my skin in a way I've never experienced when I left that meeting to check on her. Then *insisting* she come to another meeting because I couldn't bear to have her out of my sight.

Closing my eyes, I take a deep breath. I've worked so hard on keeping my distance from her, barely talking to her at all. Not because I feel betrayed or enraged at what went down shortly after I fucked her against the hotel room door.

No.

It's because I didn't feel any of those things that I'm supposed to.

I blink my eyes open, shaking my head slightly at myself as a realization washes over me. This woman could tear my heart from my chest, throw it to the ground, and stomp all over it before tossing it in the trash, and I still wouldn't give a shit. I would rather come back for more.

I've kept every thought and feeling completely to myself, locked away in a small part of my brain, refusing to let the words even play in my mind, but there's no stopping it now.

Not now that I've observed my brothers melting around her too. I don't know what it is about her that has us magnetized despite our efforts, but I'm done fighting it. It's not worth the effort, not when I *want* to win the fucking prize at the end.

Wren Dietrichson was mine before I even knew who she truly was, and she's mine just as much now. We didn't choose this, and I don't think she did either, but it is the most honest, raw, and real thing I've ever felt in my life.

I see the way she looks at me when she thinks I'm not looking. She ogles my scars time and time again, but there's never a hint of fear or disgust in her stunning blue eyes, only intrigue with a hint of desire.

Fuck.

Wiping a hand down my face, I try to calm myself, but now I've opened the door in my mind, there's no stopping it.

"I can feel your brain turning from over here."

I freeze at her voice filtering through the air and making

my cock jerk as I turn my attention back to her. She runs her hands over her loose white tank top, before wiping invisible lint off her leggings as she remains lying down, eyes fixed on mine.

"It's where I'm the loudest, *Bellissima*," I admit, aware that I prefer to be a man of few words.

A knowing smile graces her lips and my hands grip the ends of the armrests as I try to restrain myself from barreling over and laying claim to her like my dick, soul, and goddamn fucking heart want to.

No one should be this phenomenal. It shouldn't be possible. Not with a history like hers that only makes her even more of a survivor. A warrior.

I'm in awe of her.

Shit, I wear my scars with pride, there's no other option for me. Scars I gained at the hands of one of my father's challenges he liked to organize to *strengthen* us. But while mine are visible, hers are hidden away amid layers and layers of trauma she doesn't deserve. Trauma I want to wipe away, save her the pain and heartache, yet it makes her exactly who she is.

My cock juts in my pants, all too eager to show her just how much I respect her and her strengths.

Wren tilts her head to the side, assessing me as she slowly sits up, running her fingers through her hair. She looks behind her to find both Matteo and Enzo deep in quiet conversations before turning her attention back to me.

Her tongue sweeps out, tracing over her bottom lip as her eyes burn into mine. "What are you thinking about?"

It's not even a question that needs consideration. The truth spills easily from my lips.

"You."

Her eyes widen slightly, like she's pleased to hear that as she inches forward a little in her seat. "What about me?"

The corner of my mouth tilts up as I quirk a brow at her. "Do you really want to know?"

I can lay it all out there, but I don't know if she's ready to hear it. If she'll *ever* be.

"I wouldn't ask if I didn't," she retorts with a shrug, her eyes shimmering with a hint of teasing.

The slight tilt to my mouth turns into a full smirk as I shake my head at her. "Bullshit, Wren. Bull. Shit," I state, leaning back in my seat as she eyes me. "Don't lie, *Bellissima*, not when we both know my gruff voice has your thighs rubbing together. You could be just setting me up to talk about shit you don't care about so you can get yourself off later."

Her jaw falls slack for the briefest of seconds, confirming I've caught her off guard, but it's quickly squashed as she rises from her seat. "I mean, I was hoping I could convince you to let me come on your dick instead, but beggars can't be choosers. Can they, Vito? At least this way, I know exactly what I need to get the job done."

Her shoulders roll back and she moves toward the toilet as my heart thunders in my chest.

"Like fuck you are."

The words are out of my mouth before I even realize it, and I stand to grab her by the waist, pulling her toward me as I fall into my seat, bringing her with me. Her thighs fall to either side of mine, her hands clutching my shoulders as I grip her waist.

We stare at each other for what feels like an eternity, before I finally find my tongue. "How are you even real, *Bellissima*?"

"I could ask you the same thing," she breathes back in response without missing a beat, and silence consumes us as we stare deep into each other's eyes.

The hum of the airplane engine is amplified in my

ears, until I watch her gaze cut from mine, glancing down between us before she looks back up at me with a pained glint in her blue pools.

"Vito, I'm so sorry for what I—"

I slam my pointer finger against her lips, cutting her off from finishing her sentence as I shake my head at her. "There's nothing to apologize for, Wren, so I really don't want to hear it." Her eyebrows furrow as her lips move against my finger, but no words come out. "I'm not mad at you for what happened in New York, Wren. If anything, I'm fucking impressed and I'm *never* impressed." My hands flex on her waist, trying to silently convey the truth in my words.

"So you're saying that being a bitch turns you on? Noted."

I roll my eyes at her as my grip tightens. "No, you being *you* turns me on," I state, grinding my now rock-hard cock exactly where it wants to be as she stifles a groan.

"It definitely does," she mutters, her hands lifting to my shoulders, and in the next breath, her lips are on mine. Or are mine on hers? Either way, we're melting into each other effortlessly.

Bringing my hands to her back, I pin her chest to mine

as I devour her lips, teasing her plump mouth with my tongue, before the heat of hers touches mine.

Fuck.

I want more, I need more, I have to have more.

Blindly gripping the hem of her tank top as I continue to consume her lips, I pull at the material until I hear the telltale sound of it tearing. I pull back just in time to watch as the final threads pull apart, revealing her breasts beneath them.

No bra.

Hot. As. Fuck.

It's like she knew I was going to feast on them.

Without uttering a word, she lifts up on her knees, bringing her pretty pink nipples to my mouth as her hands run over my cropped hair, encouraging me closer. I don't need her to tell me twice as I suck on her taut peaks gently at first, before intensifying my suction until she groans. Her head falls back with a sigh. My brothers grunt and curse, but that only encourages me to feast on her more.

Skimming my hands over her skin to find the waistband of her leggings, I tug the material, groaning at the noise as it echoes in my ears. When I can't get the leggings to rip any further, I release her nipple to let her lean back against the table behind her.

Her heated gaze remains on mine as I reach for her panties, slowly dragging them down her thighs to meet the torn fabric of her leggings until she's bare before me. Running my tongue over my bottom lip, I feel my heartbeat start to gallop in my chest as I yearn for something I've never considered before.

Without further ado, I grab her hand in mine and bring it to my throat. Her eyes widen in surprise as she falls back into my lap, eager to do exactly what I'm offering.

The scarred skin doesn't have the same sensations as the rest of my body, not usually, but under her touch, it feels like I'm on fire because I feel every inch of her fingertips against me.

"Vito," she whispers. I reach down for the hem of my black tee and pull it over my head, revealing the scars that thin out over my chest and abdomen and become harsher again around my wrists and hands.

Since I broke contact when I took my top off, Wren waits patiently for me to nod at her before she brings her hands down on me again.

Oh. My. Fucking. God.

I hiss through my teeth, my skin beyond sensitive

to her touch as my eyes feast on her naked body. She's so confident in her own skin, and I want to feel like that with her too. Since we brought her to Italy, all we have done is take from her, and now it's time to turn the tables around and let her see a rawness in me no one else has the opportunity to view.

I'm sure she'll have questions, but they're for another day, not now. Not when I'm so close to feeling her again.

Her fingers slowly run over my abs, making my muscles clench and my cock beg for attention, and I'm sure I almost sob when her fingers tease the button of my pants.

"Do it, Wren. Take me out," I mutter as she undoes the button and slowly pulls down the zipper. I lift up ever so slightly to pull my gun from my holster at my hip, placing it on the table behind Wren just in time for her to free my solid cock from my boxers.

My dick throbs as she runs her fingertip over my burning skin, teasing me with the briefest of touches, and I grab her wrist as I halt her movements before she does anything else.

"Don't touch me, Wren. I'm going to explode," I grunt, testing my grip at her wrist as she looks at me with a hint of pride in her eyes. "I don't want to feel anything but your pussy stretching around my cock, clenching and clenching for more as I take what's mine." Her pupils dilate at my words.

"Fuck," she gasps, moving her hands to my shoulders as I grab my cock to line it up with her sweet entrance.

"You guys better knock it the fuck off," Matteo growls, interrupting our moment as we both glance in his direction to find him standing in front of his seat with a glare aimed our way.

Never.

"Sorry, Matteo, but that's not going to happen," Wren declares, eyes glaring at my brother as she slowly drops down on my dick.

Holy. Fucking. Shit.

Inch after inch, she takes me, drowning my cock in her sweet pussy as she clenches around me. She angles her body to face me again. Matteo grunts something, but it's not audible over the ringing of pleasure in my ears.

Wren remains seated on my cock for a moment, adjusting, as we both attempt and fail to catch our breath. I want to be panting, I want to be sweating, and I want to be exhausted, all because of her.

Flexing her hips, Wren keeps her eyes fixed on mine as she lifts up, until only the tip remains inside her before she falls down on my cock once more, only faster this time.

"God," I grunt, my teeth grinding as I bite back the need to climax already.

I place my hands on her hips, flexing my fingers against her skin as she shivers against me. Looking up at her, I wait until her half-mast eyes are opened a little before I reach my tongue out and flick it over her right nipple first, before repeating the same process to her left.

It's fucking hot how she rakes her nails over the nape of my neck, encouraging me, until the sound of a door opening from behind me startles us both. Before I even have a chance to process anything, Wren's right hand leaves my skin and metal is scraped over the table.

"Get the fuck out. Now."

Her hips don't stop moving, her body still taking from mine, demanding pleasure, but as I look up at her, I find her pointing my gun at someone behind me. Tilting my head further back, I realize it's the stewardess assisting us on this flight. Not the same as the last one, not after Wren showed her distaste for her, but now this girl hasn't helped either. Especially when she doesn't move a step and continues to gape at Wren who is naked as hell, her tits bouncing as she fucks me, all while pointing a gun at the unsuspecting woman.

"Are you fucking stupid?" Wren bites as I hear the sound of the safety being taken off the gun, and in the next moment, the woman is gone.

Thank fuck for that, I wasn't stopping to clean up blood anyway.

"I don't know how you have the ability to get hotter and hotter, Wren, but you fucking do." I thrust up into her, driving home my point as she brings the gun down, resting it against the seat beside my head as she grins, slamming down on me with more force as she groans.

"Fuck, Gio, I'm going to have to call you back." Enzo sounds panicked, but I know he's far from it. He's likely unable to control himself after watching Wren just now.

I'm very aware of the gun beside my head with the safety off as I tighten my grip on her hips, holding her in place as I thrust hard into her core for extra measure as she gasps for breath. I love how her skin turns pink along her chest and neck, need and desire painting my girl before my eyes.

Running my tongue over my bottom lip, I loosen my

hold as I let her take the reins again. When her eyes meet mine, I nod over her shoulder indicating for her to follow my line of sight.

"Look what you've done now, Wren."

"Fuck," she whispers as she turns to find both Matteo and Enzo with their cocks out, jerking off to the mere sight of her as she rides me.

I don't know what I did to get this lucky, but like hell am I ever letting go. Living life on the edge comes naturally with being a part of this world, and she just might be the craziest but most perfect risk we've ever taken.

My orgasm crests inside of me, turning my blood to lava as every inch of my body comes alive. But there's one more thing I want before I fill her with my cum. I don't speak a word as I reach for her right wrist and tilt her position so the barrel of the gun presses into the side of my head.

Her face turns to me, eyes wide as her movements slow, but I quickly bring my hands back to her hips again to encourage her to continue.

"Vito…"

"Whatever you do, *Bellissima*, don't pull the trigger," I breathe as the metal presses further into my skin, igniting the volcano inside of me and sending the lava racing through my veins as my climax bubbles to the surface.

"Fuck, Vito. Fuck." Wren's pussy clenches around my cock as I flex inside of her, wave after wave of pleasure tumbling through me as she keeps the gun pressed against my head. Just when I think I'm close to being done, her core burns around me as she explodes, sending me over the edge once more.

I can't stop myself from edging forward and sinking my teeth into her nipple, making her back arch as she cries out in ecstasy, letting every motherfucker on this plane know she's filled with pleasure.

Moments later, I feel the pressure at my temple alleviate before the thump of the gun falls at my side. My breath hitches, waiting for the sound of a bullet leaving the chamber, but nothing comes as I sag with relief.

"Fuck, Wren, how are we ever going to survive you, huh?" Enzo's question goes unanswered as I cling to her.

Banding my arms around her waist, I rest my forehead against Wren's stomach as she curls her arms around my neck, clinging to me just as I am to her.

She's everything. It's not a worthy word to describe her, but nothing else even comes close. She was made for us, for me, and I know that without a shadow of a doubt. I can let my craziness free, encourage her to aim a gun at me as I climax inside of her, and she's right there with me.

Fuck.

Now we need to get this bullshit sorted in New York, bring justice to the De Luca family business, before we can get right back on this plane and go again.

And again, and again, and again.

TWENTY EIGHT

Wren

I reach the bottom of the airplane steps and take a deep breath. How does US soil feel so foreign when I've only been gone for such a short period of time? Clearly being fucked so hard by my Italians is morphing me into someone else entirely.

Someone tolerable? The world would be so lucky.

Matteo is a few steps ahead, talking with the driver of the SUV parked beside him, and I don't miss the way his gaze keeps drifting back to me. Vito brushes past me, his hand running across my butt as he goes, glancing back over his shoulder with a wink as my thighs clench together.

These men are going to ruin me in the best way possible, and I'm going to enjoy every minute of it.

"Come on, *Bella*, let's get this show on the road," Enzo mutters as he reaches the bottom of the steps, tossing his arm around my shoulders as he guides me toward the SUV.

I fall into step with him as I wrap my arms around my waist, pinning the hoodie I'm now wearing tighter to my skin. Even with one of their t-shirts on underneath, it's nowhere near as warm in New York as it was in Italy, and I'm feeling the temperature dip on every inch of my skin.

Vito climbs into the SUV first as Matteo finishes talking with the driver, patting him on the shoulder before he follows suit. Enzo bows dramatically at the open door, waving his hand for me to go first, and I shake my head at his antics as I do just that.

Getting comfortable in the leather seat, with Vito to my right and Enzo taking the empty seat to my left as he shuts the door, my gaze latches on to Matteo's, who sits directly facing me with his elbows braced on his knees.

He looks every inch the businessman that he is. Not one of them are wearing casual clothing, all draped in designer navy suits, buttoned-up shirts, and matching ties. The way he moves in it, it's like a second skin, while you can tell Vito and Enzo would rather be wearing something else. Or at least, I can tell that.

"Tell me the plan, *Stellina*." Matteo quirks a brow at me as he waits for me to respond, just as the SUV starts to move.

Not this again. He must have asked me the same question fifteen times since we went over everything on the plane.

"You already know the plan, Matteo, you came up with it. I'm not repeating this again." I give him a challenging look of my own, but he doesn't falter under my gaze.

"I know I did, but I want to confirm you know the plan as well as you claim to. The more you repeat it, the more you remember it."

With a dramatic eye roll, I fold my arms over my chest before tilting my head back, closing my eyes as I repeat the plan word for word to him.

"We're going to head straight to your stock warehouse here in New York, where you keep your weapons for shipping and trading. After we've met with your men there and confirmed all the finer details, we'll head to the hotel. All while keeping off the radar, I might add. So, backstreet detours, long routes, and everything in between to avoid the Russians knowing we're here. Which will make it all the better when we hit up *their* nightclub tonight and let the retaliation commence."

With every word that falls from my mouth, the pitch of my voice gets higher and higher, a smirk forming on my lips as I open my eyes and look at Matteo once more.

His head is tilted to the left slightly, which somehow manages to enhance the depth of the scar down the right side of his mouth. "Are you always this excited?" he asks.

"Always." I wink in his direction as he shakes his head at me in disbelief, at the same time as Vito and Enzo chuckle on either side of me.

We head around the outskirts of New York in silence then. I'm ready to get the meet over and done with. I'm ready to freshen up at the hotel, but most of all, I'm ready to have some Russian blood on my hands.

I tentatively rest my head on Enzo's shoulder, watching the world go by outside the window as Vito places his hand on my thigh, and Matteo stretches his legs out so they're tangled around mine.

Maybe what I'm most ready for is to have the three of them all to myself without any interruption, but I guess that's going to have to wait as the vehicle rolls to a stop outside a large warehouse building.

It's not discreet or derelict, or even remotely hideous enough to seem like it's an inconsequential building. No, it looks completely brand new. Fresh gray walls cover the entire site, with shiny steel doors offering the only entrance.

A dozen or so vehicles are parked in the small adjoining lot, indicating their men are here already. Hopefully, this could be over quicker than I expected, and that feels like a win.

Enzo steps out of the SUV first, turning on the spot and offering his hand out to me, earning him a scoff and an eye roll from his brothers, but I take it nonetheless. Letting him pull me against his chest, he throws my arms over his shoulders as he grabs my waist, before spinning us around and placing my feet on the ground.

I look up at him with a grin, obsessed with this side of him as he leans down and presses a whisper of a kiss at the corner of my mouth. "Put her down, asshole, we have a job to do, and we can't have any distractions or show weakness, no matter who is around," Vito grumbles as he steps past us, but stops a few feet in front, waiting for the four of us to go in together.

Taking a step back, I run my fingers over the spare pair

of leggings I packed, looking down at the ground as I take a deep breath and focus. Vito is right, now isn't the time for any of that, no matter how much I fucking want it.

The SUV door is shut, and it draws my attention toward Matteo as he straightens his blazer and glances toward the door.

"Shall we?" His words are void of emotion and almost clipped as he nods in the direction of the warehouse.

I hold back a moment, my eyebrows knitting as I feel the hairs on the back of my neck stand on end.

"Something doesn't feel right," I breathe the words without second thought as I glance up at the building before me. A building I've never been to before, didn't even know existed, yet I get the sense that not all is as it should be.

"What do you mean?"

The question comes from Vito, but when I flick my gaze to his, I struggle to find the right way to describe it. So instead, I explain how my body feels.

"I don't know, I just know my spine is stiff as fuck and I have zero clue why, but it's not the norm for me. My instincts are kicking in." I purse my lips, flexing my fingers at my sides as I look up at the building again.

Every window is blacked out, offering no insight inside,

which is great for security purposes, but does nothing to help me right now when I'm the one on the outside.

"It's all good, *Bella*, it's just—"

I wave my hand to stop him from finishing whatever he's going to say to pacify me, before striding past them. "I don't know what it is, and I really don't want to go inside, but there's no other option. So… everyone, get inside… now." I don't waste a second to turn and check that they're following, instead I keep placing one foot in front of the other until my hand wraps around the door handle.

Their presence is noticeable behind me, my body aware of their whereabouts without looking, but their shadows also loom above me in the late evening sun, confirming they're right with me.

We're drenched in complete silence as the four of us step through the doorway. Vito takes the handle from me once he's inside, shutting it quietly behind us as we're met with a dark entry hall.

I can barely see anything except for the flickering of a security camera in the top left corner of the room, and a hint of a light filtering under the doorway directly ahead. While the two other doors offer no clue what's on the other side.

"How many men are supposed to be here?" I ask, running my tongue over my bottom lip as I focus on my hearing.

"If we're being precise, forty-six," Matteo replies just as quietly as I asked, making me shake my head even though none of them can see me.

"It's far too quiet in here for there to be forty-six men waiting on our arrival, Matteo." Adrenaline pumps through my body.

Not one of them offers me a verbal response, instead, I hear the telltale sound of them each drawing their guns, and I do the same, reaching for the one Vito gave me earlier.

"Vito, take the lead," Matteo mutters, keeping his orders low and straight to the point. "Enzo, watch our backs. Wren, stay with me."

I nod, fully aware that he can't fucking see me, taking two steps forward as I try to move with him despite being unable to see. I can handle myself in these kinds of situations, so staying with him wouldn't be my usual move, but it's not a bad plan, so I do as he asks without hesitation.

Squinting, I see the outline of Vito's chiseled jaw as he steps right up to the door with the light creeping through underneath. But after a breath or two, I frown, noticing the light dimming. Not because it's been turned off or anything, but because there's something seeping through the gap under the door.

"Wait," I whisper, taking the final few steps to stop at his side. I crouch down, assessing whatever the hell it is as I run my finger over the top. The tips of my fingertips are tainted red, the only kind of red you get from one thing, and one thing only.

Blood.

Vito's jaw tightens in fury as he sees the red on my skin, before glancing over his shoulder at his brothers. They must hold a silent conversation between them because by the time I rise to my feet, I'm being given a new set of orders from Vito.

"Spread out, Matteo with me, Enzo and Wren take the door to the left and cover the back corridor into the main room of the warehouse."

Enzo laces his fingers with mine as I grasp my gun in the other hand, letting him lead me toward the door Vito mentioned. Enzo releases my hand when he's at the door, slowly pushing it open before entering, and I follow after him.

Remembering to hold the door so it closes quietly behind us, I almost jump out of my skin when Enzo flicks the light switch on and the corridor comes into view. I sigh in relief, pleased to have my vision to work with again, but no sooner than we take two steps does the sound of gunshots ring out from behind us.

Fuck.

I lift my gun instantly, spinning on the spot to point it at the door we just stepped through, ready to take down whichever motherfucker steps through next.

"Let's cover the other side of the warehouse, *Bella*."

I purse my lips, keeping my gaze set dead ahead for another few moments, before I reluctantly turn back to him. "You better be right, Enzo," I mumble, flicking my raised gun toward the other end of the corridor, and he takes the hint, leading the way.

One shot. Two shots. Three.

That's how many more ring out by the time we get to the other end of the hallway, spiking my blood with fury as I pray to fucking god that Matteo and Vito are okay and it's their gunshots I can hear and no one else's.

"Through this door we turn right, and the next door on the right again will lead to the main room where they are,"

Enzo explains as he glances back at me over his shoulder for a brief moment, before he opens the door and inspects the area.

Once he's happy it's empty, he waves for me to follow him, and I stay hot on his heels until he brings us to a stop at the next door. Just as he presses the palm of his hand against the wood, another shot rings out, followed quickly by two more in short bursts, making my heart thunder in my chest as my pulse rings in my ears.

"Come out, come out wherever you are, De Luca. Watch me set fire to your empire and burn it down." I'm not familiar with the voice as humor ripples through every word.

We're dealing with a psycho on the other side of the door, it seems, and I don't have time to waste on whoever the hell it is.

"What is the likelihood of them seeing us as soon as we open this door?" I ask, keeping my voice as low as possible.

Enzo's brows knit as his jaw tightens before he gives me an answer. "Not likely, but also not one hundred percent."

Fuck.

Of course it's not going to be easy, Wren. Nothing ever

is in this life.

Taking a deep breath, I exhale slowly, tightening my grip on my gun as I nod at the door. "Open it a bit."

Enzo wraps his knuckles around the handle as he steps to the side and opens it ever so slightly.

I wish he fucking hadn't.

I don't need a bigger gap to see any more of the horrors playing out on the other side. I can't see Matteo and Vito, the priorities my eyes are searching for, but what I can see burns my fucking soul.

There must be seven or eight men in total, but the man at the center of them all holds my attention as he waves around a lit match while one of the others doses the fucking *pile* of dead bodies that stands tall beside them.

"I said come out. Since I'm unable to attend the other funeral on our agenda this week, I thought it would be fun to hold one of my own," the man with the lit match grinds out, clearly not appreciating his first demand being ignored. He turns, seemingly in search of the 'De Lucas' he's after, and I hope that means he hasn't managed to hurt Vito and Matteo.

His accent tells me he's Russian, the lilt and sharp bite in his broken English clear as I watch his nostrils flare. His hair falls loosely around his shoulders as he glances from left to right looking for his targets.

"Have it your way, then." With a wave of his hand, he tosses the match onto the heap of dead men, and they ignite all at once.

"Fuck," Enzo grunts, tilting his head so he can get a glimpse of the view that has me locked in position.

Two shots ring out simultaneously from across the room, knocking two of the Russian men to the floor. I know without a shadow of a doubt that it's Vito and Matteo and it fuels my anger even more knowing that they're still here to fight alongside, to fight *for*.

"Take them out."

At the order from the other side of the door, two full rounds of gun shots fire off, and with each bullet that leaves the chamber, I see the rage engulfing Enzo's face.

Those are his brothers, and our next move is his call, but I don't expect him to shove me backward out of the way before charging through the door. I fall to the floor with a thud, hissing through clenched teeth at the pain shooting up my spine, but none of that matters. Not when I feel my soul leave my body as fear consumes me.

Scrambling to my feet, I grip my gun as I move toward

the door, taking the same strides as Enzo did. I see him up ahead, coming out from behind the crates we were obscured by, to come face to face with the Russian giving the orders.

He's so focused on him as his target, so enraged by the slaughtering that has happened here today, that he doesn't spot the other guy coming around from the back of the burning pile of people.

I pull my trigger without hesitation, but not quickly enough that this fucker doesn't release a bullet from his barrel too. Pain ricochets through me as Enzo drops to the floor, his gun falling carelessly from his grip as he staggers backward. His hands cup his stomach, before he glances down at the crimson blood staining his hands.

Hysteria consumes me, pain and agony rip through me, but it's too much. I'm not someone who cares, who feels hurt or pain, fuck. I feel nothing. I fear nothing. I have always been nothing more than a pawn to be moved around, but now… this is different.

I'm moving before I realize it, my feet carrying me toward the carnage that awaits as gunshots ring through the air, only this time… they're mine.

The man who injured Enzo is already down, two more

follow swiftly after him as I continue to charge toward them. The flames are growing bigger, replicating hell before me as the man who seems to be the leader of these fuckers turns toward me with a sneer.

He lifts a shotgun in my direction, running his tongue over his dry, cracked lips as he readies to take his shot, but there is no fucking chance in hell that I'm going to die at the hands of this man today.

Never.

Before he can even pull the lever back, I pull my trigger again and again until there are no rounds left. I don't need anymore though, not as I look down at the asshole who did all of this as he bleeds out all over the floor.

It's a fucking blessing when he sways backward in slow motion, falling into the fire he created as the embers and smoke consume his cries of pain.

My chest heaves with every breath as I stand frozen in place watching him burn before me. More gunshots go off around me, pulling me to my senses, but not to protect myself. My focus turns to Enzo as I spin on the spot, finding him still on the floor with one hand pressed against his wound, while the other is gripping his gun, before it clatters to the floor.

Silence echoes around the room as I rush to his side, fear gripping me tightly as I panic over what to do.

"Fuck, Enzo, are you okay?" I internally groan at the fucking ridiculous question that falls from my mouth. He's quite clearly *not* okay, but he tries to smile up at me despite the circumstances.

"Of course I am with a pretty view like you, Wren," he breathes, his voice raspier than usual, and not because he's drenched with desire and need, but because he's in so much pain.

Fuck.

Footsteps approach us as I pull my hoodie off and press it against his wound, making him hiss, but he doesn't stop me from helping.

"Enzo, fuck," Vito bites as he drops to his knees beside me, squeezing his brother's shoulder as he grimaces.

"We can't take him to a hospital, he'll be an open target," Matteo states, crouching down on my other side, and I can only assume that there's no one else here alive because my sense of surroundings is diminished as I sit consumed by the state of Enzo.

Wetting my dry lips, I tuck my hair behind my ear as I look at Matteo. "Do you trust me?"

One breath, two breaths… "Yes."

"Then call Luna and tell her we need Ethan or someone of that level to meet us at the airport. Now."

His brows furrow in confusion as he glances down at his brother before coming back to me. "At the airport? We're not fucking leaving." The bite to his tone isn't aimed at me, but it still riles me up all the same.

"Yes, we are. We need to get home, not only to keep Enzo safe and protected, but because Dmitri and the others aren't here. I know it. Since they're not making progress with Featherstone, with the Ring, they're channeling all their efforts toward you in a show of strength."

Vito scoffs bitterly as he shakes his head at the mere thought of the Russians thinking they can outdo him, his family, his business. "How do you know they're not here?"

I glance to the remains of the burned Russian guy as I sigh heavily. "There was something he said earlier, that he was sad not to be attending the other funeral, so he was making one for himself."

My gaze drifts from Matteo to Vito, before settling on Enzo, as realization washes over them.

"Fuck." The curse comes from Matteo who hangs his head low, hiding the emotions I'm sure are consuming him, but we don't have time for that, not when Enzo is bleeding out like this. "Call her, Matteo. The sooner, the better," I state, before reaching into Vito's blazer pocket to retrieve my cell phone I gave him earlier.

"W-who a-are you c-calling?" Enzo stutters out, still just as nosey when he's bleeding out, but I don't get a chance to respond as the call is answered.

"If it isn't my new favorite person. Please don't tell me my brothers have fucked up and you're injured or something ridiculous like that because I will literally skin them alive."

Valentina.

"I-I'm down, Valentina. Wren battles better than us," Enzo states, and my chest squeezes with worry at the mention of him being injured.

Matteo rises to his feet, stepping toward the exit as I wave my hand at Vito for him to get Enzo, and he does just that. We don't have more than a few minutes left to get out of here before something blows or we start choking on the smoke.

"I never doubted my girl for a second," she replies with pride, making me shake my head in disbelief. "Are you going to be okay, E?" she adds, finally getting to the important part, and he half chuckles, half scoffs in response.

"He'll be good, Valentina, I won't accept anything less," I interject, rushing a few steps ahead of Vito to hold the door open for him, before racing toward the SUV that's still waiting idly for us. The driver's eyes widen in shock as Matteo points toward us, but I turn my attention away from him as I focus on the cell in my hands. "What matters now, Valentina, is how we move next."

"Shit, hit me with it."

A tight smile graces my lips at her willingness as I step back to let Vito climb into the SUV with Enzo in his arms, placing him down across a row of seats as he grunts in agony.

"They knew we were coming, V, from what I can tell, they wanted us to," I explain as Matteo climbs into the vehicle and slams the door shut behind him, nodding at me in confirmation that he did as I said.

I relax a little in my seat, hopeful that we're going to get the help Enzo needs in time.

"Why?"

"Because it looks like they got wind of Torres's funeral and they're going to hit that too, in an attempt to bring down the De Luca empire." I pinch the bridge of my nose in anger as Vito curses and Matteo slams his fist into the door beside him.

"Over my dead fucking body," Valentina bites out, anger evident in every word.

"Let's hope it doesn't come to that. But I'm going to need you to listen very closely to everything I say because you'll have to get the ball rolling before we even get back on the fucking plane," I state, my brain going a mile a minute as I try to piece together all the information we have.

"Yes, boss. You tell me what to do and I'll do it."

My gaze falls to Enzo as he groans on his spot, and I drop to my knees on the floorboard and shuffle toward him as the SUV takes off toward the airport.

His heart races against my palm as I speak to Valentina. I just need him to not bleed out on me, not when we're this close, not when I care this much.

Every step we take now is for the De Luca family, and that means all of them have to be fucking alive.

Including him.

REDEMPTION

TWENTY NINE

Enzo

Fuck.

Every inch of my body hurts like a bitch. I've never felt pain like this, and I've been through some shit. Closing my eyes, I groan, attempting to calm my breathing as I continue to put pressure on the hoodie that's covering my wound. The leather of the SUV seats offer me little support or comfort as I fail to release any tension from my body.

I'm very aware I'm losing a lot of blood, but I'm helpless to it.

Grinding my teeth, I take another deep breath before

blinking my eyes open. I need to see her again, if this is how I go, if this is how I end, then I'm willing to accept it as long as my last vision is of Wren.

I settle my gaze on her, not missing the pain and worry that flashes in her eyes, before she suddenly drops to her knees before me. I don't utter a word, letting her come closer. She places her palm against my chest as she runs her eyes over me from head to toe.

I'm in awe of her.

She saved me from taking any more shots. She saved us all with every stride she took toward the enemy, releasing bullet after bullet.

Without a shadow of a doubt, she was made for us.

This world, our lifestyle, isn't for most, but fuck, when she's in action, it's like she's the one who created it all.

She walks with confidence, she aims with precision, and she slays like it's her birthright.

She runs her tongue over her bottom lip and shuffles closer. "I know it's the worst question, but are you okay? Is there anything I can get you?" she asks, lifting her hand from my chest and running her fingers lazily through the ends of my hair as I smile up at her.

"I'm fine now that you're here," I murmur, hissing

at the pain vibrating through me as the SUV jolts on the uneven road beneath us.

Fucker.

"Talk real with me, Enzo. I'm worried about you."

Does she think I would just say that for the sake of it? Like I wouldn't mean it?

"I don't think you're ready for my real," I manage to respond, my body slowly getting weaker as I try to fight off the bullet lodged in my gut.

"Try me."

Two words. Just two, and she has no idea what she's unleashed. But with the pain I'm in and the uncertainty that surrounds me like a storm, I give her what she wants.

"I'm obsessed with you," I admit, reaching for her hand with my free one, and lacing our fingers together.

She doesn't miss a beat as she leans closer, looking down at me with a small grin on her lips. "I'm obsessed with you too."

My heart stutters in my chest, not the best reaction when I'm in such a state, but I have no control over my body.

"You're messing with me," I grumble, wincing with the pain I'm in as she shakes her head at me.

"You have the ability to crush me, an ability I've never given anyone else the chance to do, but the three of you… fuck, I wouldn't have a choice even if you did." Her words are like a forbidden truth as they tear from her lips, her eyes shifting down to where our hands are joined as I process the truth behind every word.

"Crushing you isn't on my agenda, *Bella*, and I get the feeling it's not something either of my brothers are interested in either." If I weren't in so much pain right now, I would show her just how much I crave her.

"I think what Enzo is trying to say is that we can't quite figure out how you got under our skin so seamlessly, so effortlessly, but we're not sad that you're there. If anything, we need it more than the air we breathe." I glance to Matteo who sits across from me, his forearms braced on his knees as his gaze remains latched on Wren's.

I couldn't have said it better myself.

Wren doesn't get a chance to respond as the SUV rolls to a stop, making me cringe once more as my body stiffens and the pain vibrating through me accelerates.

"Please fucking tell me we're there. I'm struggling to keep my eyes open," I mumble, the pressure on the hoodie slacking as I look at Wren.

"We're here." I can't tell if she's disappointed or relieved by the interruption, but I can't push her to find out because the door opens a moment later and a guy I'm not familiar with sticks his head in.

"Ethan, hey, I know I asked for you, but we're nowhere near Richmond. I thought Luna would send someone else," Wren says, clearly aware of who *Ethan* is, but she doesn't cut the distance between them, wrap her arms around him or even smile for that matter.

My brows furrow, as do both Vito's and Matteo's as we watch them interact, despite the blood coating my skin.

"I was in Manhattan when Luna called, so I made a dash for it. Luckily, I was on my motorcycle so I was able to get through the traffic a bit quicker."

I can't decide if I like this guy or not.

It could be completely nothing, but the familiarity he has with Wren pisses me off more than I care to admit, even if he is here to save my fucking life.

"Well, thank you, I know Enzo will be in good hands." She turns her eyes to mine, a soft smile on her lips as she squeezes my hand one last time before edging back. "I promise you, I wouldn't trust you in anyone else's hands half as much as I do this guy, and believe me, I need you more than my next breath."

Her words consume my mind. The understanding in both of our eyes as she refers to what Matteo said moments earlier.

Swallowing past the lump in my throat, I nod. "I trust your judgment."

"Let's get the patient out of the vehicle and onto the stretcher. I was told we are doing this in the air, is that right?" Ethan asks as Matteo and Vito climb out via the other door, while Wren stays right at my side.

"Correct," I respond as his gaze drifts down to mine, and he offers a wide grin in return.

"I've never been to Italy before," he remarks, sliding the stretcher half into the SUV before helping me get down from where I'm lying on the seats.

Once I'm secured on the stretcher as best as possible, he follows after my brothers through the door near my head, before appearing outside at my feet. I grind my teeth in agony as he pulls the plastic I'm lying on toward a metal frame, securing me to the unit, before wasting no time in heading toward the aircraft.

I tilt my head back to set my eyes on Wren who falls into step between my brothers, and I breathe a slight breath of relief knowing she's close by, before turning my attention to the doctor beside me.

"So, how do you know Wren?"

I attempt and fail to raise my eyebrows at him in question. My muscles tense in my face from the pain I'm in as I try to get past it.

Ethan glances down at me for a second before focusing straight ahead once again. "I'm the licensed doctor at the on-site medical center at Featherstone Academy."

"What the fuck actually goes on there for them to require a fully-trained doctor?" The question falls from my lips before I can stop the eagerness in me, but the scoff from Ethan tells me it bewilders him just as much.

"You would be surprised. I was actually trained as a student there."

My eyes widen in surprise at his words, but something else intrigues me more. "Why do I get the feeling there is more than that between you and Wren?"

"Not of the romantic kind if that's what you're hinting at," Ethan states as he comes to a stop by the steps of the aircraft, turning his full attention to me. "But yes, it did seem to me that I saw more of her than the other students."

That's the most cryptic of cryptic answers I've ever

heard.

"You'll need to elaborate for me," I grumble as he waves his hand for someone to come over and help him. It's on the tip of my tongue that I'll get myself up the damn steps, but when I attempt to sit up, pain ricochets through me from head to toe.

I'm not going anywhere whether I like it or not.

"I'm not telling you anything."

My jaw tightens with annoyance at his response, not that I don't respect him a little for it, protecting her privacy, but it's not his to keep. I'm not pushing him though, I'll go directly to the source.

"Wren," I holler the best I can, glancing back to see her at my side a moment later, worry evident in her glistening blue eyes. "How do you and Ethan know each other so well? He won't tell me."

I likely sound like a bratty kid, but I'm beyond caring at this stage.

She smirks at me as she rolls her eyes dramatically, but before she can respond, Vito appears at my head, lifting the stretcher beneath me at the same time Ethan grabs the bottom, and I'm hoisted into the air.

If I fucking fall, someone else will be dying with me,

I'll make sure of it.

To my relief, we reach the cabin without a hitch, and a moment later, Wren reappears at my side. Ethan doesn't wait for her to explain though, he gets straight to work removing the hoodie from my stomach, before tearing into my clothes to get to the root cause of the pain.

Wren doesn't flinch at the blood or cringe at the wound. If anything, she almost looks bored by it all, that is until her eyes reach mine and I see them looking a lot more glossy than they did moments ago.

With a shake of her head, she wets her lips before finally speaking. "I met Ethan on my second day at Featherstone Academy. Not because my mom, who was the head, gave me a tour of the facility, or because I was assigned to learn about medicine, but because I was beaten so badly I couldn't tend to all the wounds myself."

I must be dead because my heart is lodged in my throat as horror washes over me.

"Who?" The venom in my tone is palpable as anger courses through my veins.

She gives me a pointed look, but my brain is working slower than usual, and it takes Vito's response for her to continue.

"It was Totem, wasn't it?"

"It was, and it wasn't the last time I was there either."

I glance down at Ethan, but he doesn't even look away from his job. An unusual sense of pride and respect for him squeezes my chest tightly as I turn my gaze back to Wren. I clearly appreciate his actions, more than I care to admit, but—

"Before anyone fucking says it, I didn't bury the motherfucker like I wanted to because this woman's wrath is a force to be reckoned with. Something tells me you guys know what I'm talking about," Ethan explains, interrupting my thoughts on the matter, and I snort at his assessment of her wrath.

"I don't know what you're talking about," Wren grumbles, making even Matteo splutter in surprise.

"Well, you told me you had it handled the first time, the fifth you admitted it was at the hands of your father, the ninth visit I learned who your father was, and I was willing to take that name to the grave, his fucking body along with it, but a tenth visit never came. Wren, I've never been more relieved not to see someone again." The smirk on his face eases the tension in the air as she smiles back, pride in her posture as she sits tall.

"The *only* person putting that man in a grave was me."

"And to think I wanted to kill you for it," Matteo muses, making Ethan gape in horror at him, but Wren laughs, breaking any tension before it rises fully. The pair of them make me chuckle, which causes me to wince in pain.

"Shit, this is a great story time and all, but your man here needs my full attention if we plan to have him still with us by the time we land in Italy," Ethan interjects, a solemn air drifting over us.

Nothing kills the room quite like a shot man dying out with nowhere to escape.

"Take care of him," Wren murmurs, blindly finding my hand as she pleads with Ethan. "I need him in one piece."

THIRTY

Wren

No organs were hit by the bullet. He's extremely lucky.

I could have cried with relief at Ethan's words as he explained the situation. The medical facilities he was able to provide onboard the flight were astounding, and I will be eternally grateful to him and Featherstone for saving Enzo's life.

Ethan was able to remove the bullet, clean the wound, and bandage him up before we landed, plying him with enough morphine to help him rest and numb the pain. Matteo didn't hesitate in asking Ethan to stick around for a bit to provide Enzo with the care he needs at home, and that's where we're heading now.

Home.

Leaning into Enzo's side, I rest my head on his shoulder, feeling his warmth against my body as he sleeps beside me in the SUV. When we landed at the airport, there were three SUVs waiting for us, a precautionary measure Vito ordered their men to take before we landed.

If I'm right, which I truly believe I am, then the Russians are here and there's a battle to be had. So despite how tired I am, how drained and exhausted my aching bones are, all of that will have to wait. Especially with everything I asked Valentina to organize.

At this stage, I'll sleep when I'm dead.

I glance out of the window and spy the iron gates that offer entry to the De Luca family home, and I sit up straight, stretching out my muscles as the SUV takes the gravel driveway up to the house. Placing my hand on Enzo's arm, I rub gently as I murmur his name.

His eyelashes flutter as he slowly wakes, and when he opens one eye to see me beside him, a smile graces his lips as a soft sigh escapes him.

"I love you, Wren."

My heart practically stops before kicking into overdrive at those words on his tongue. My veins are filled with shock and confusion, making adrenaline course through my body. It's like he's triggered my fight or flight, but I remain as calm as possible.

"Tell me that again when you're not drugged up on morphine, Enzo." I force a tight smile to my face, struggling with my internal thoughts so much that my features react of their own accord.

I don't know whether I'm elated or panicking; I've never been in this situation, but it feels like my heart is swelling inside my chest and it's going to explode with a feeling I've never felt before.

Enzo's hand lands on my thigh, squeezing until I turn my gaze to his, and when I do, I find him wide-eyed and looking at me with determination.

"I. Love. You. Wren."

He repeats the words slowly, rawness and vulnerability flashing in his eyes as I gape at him, my heart skipping another beat as the SUV rolls to a stop outside the house.

"I can't believe I'm saying this, but I think I love you too, Enzo." My pulse rings in my ears, my body tingling as I speak those three words I've never spoken before.

"You only think?" He quirks his brow at me as his lips curve up teasingly, and I shake my head at him as I feel my cheeks heat.

Fuck.

"Well, I've never felt love before, or been told those words, or learned to describe the feelings swarming my body right now. So I can only assume it's..." My words trail off as Enzo lifts his hand from my thigh and cups my cheek. I lean into his hold as he strokes his thumb across my skin, lulling me into a sense of peace despite the storm I feel like I'm in.

"I'll take that, *Bella*, I'll take whatever it is you have to offer as long as it keeps you here by our side."

I offer the smallest nod in response, my eyelids closing just as he pulls me closer and claims my lips with his. It's soft, it's raw, and it's full of the feelings we're trying to convey. Bringing my hand to his neck, I'm careful not to lean against his wound when the door beside Enzo opens and our moment is cut short.

Pulling my mouth from his, I look up to see who it is, to find Matteo glaring at the side of his brother's head.

"Stop hogging her and stealing all of her kisses just because you're injured, asshole," Matteo grumbles, before turning his attention my way with a pointed look.

I can't help but grin at the pair of them as he reluctantly offers his arm to aid his brother out of the car.

"It's not just because I'm injured, she thinks I'm the nicest too," Enzo states proudly as he stands from the vehicle and turns his head to look at me as I follow him out.

"Bullshit," Matteo retorts, shaking his head at his brother before they both turn to look at me.

"Wren, tell him it's true."

I scoff this time, waving my hand dismissively between them as I move a few steps ahead. "I'm not saying shit."

I pass Vito as he moves to help his brother, offering me a wry smile as he runs his fingers gently down my arm.

This round-trip has served a purpose in pulling us closer together. I just hate that it cost Enzo such an injury. Ethan explained to me how close it could have been, and I'm thankful for the chance we've been given, and I don't want to waste it.

Glancing back over my shoulder, I spy the brothers walking slowly together, and a sense of calmness blossoms inside of me as I step into the house.

I startle when an arm wraps around me and a small kiss

is pressed against my temple. Nonna offers me a relieved smile.

"I'm making you all something to eat, but I think Enzo would be more comfortable in his room," she states to all of us, but doesn't get a chance to say anything else as Enzo curses.

"Like fuck you're getting rid of me that easily. I might be wounded but I'm not completely fucking broken, and I'm not being kept out of the loop. I feel helpless enough as it is."

Nonna shakes her head with a knowing smirk to her lips. "I thought you would say that, so I set you up in the lounge. The young doctor you sent in is preparing your room to accommodate the medical supplies you're going to need." She turns on the spot and heads to the kitchen without another word as I let the guys lead the way to the lounge.

Stepping through the door across from the gym, I'm surprised to find a cozy space with a large sofa and a huge television on the wall. The different tones of blue and gray scream man cave, but you can also tell it had Nonna's or Valentina's touch with the cushions, drapes, and plush carpet.

Matteo and Vito get Enzo comfortable on one of the sofas, propping his legs up so he can rest just as Ethan steps into the room.

"Why do I get the feeling you're going to be the biggest handful of a patient I've ever had?" He smirks at Enzo as he approaches him, pulling out the tablet he's been keeping all of his vitals documented on.

"I'm always the biggest *everything*," Enzo replies with a wink. Even as he winces with the pain he's in, he still has his humor.

I roll my eyes at him as Ethan glances back over his shoulder at me.

"He's good for you, Wren," he states, like he has a clue, but the way his eyes shine, I know he believes it to be true and so do I. "They all are," he adds, nodding toward Matteo and Vito as I nibble on my bottom lip, nodding ever so slightly in response.

"Thank you for this," I murmur, hoping to change the subject, but I'm saved by the phenomenal queen that is Valentina as she waltzes into the room.

"There you are, I've been so worried," she exclaims, throwing her arms out wide, but it's not Enzo she charges at… it's me. As she engulfs me in her arms, it takes me a second to respond, and I hug her back, surprised by how much it actually calms the tension that's been rising inside of me since we left.

When she leans back, her eyes rake over me from head to toe. "Let me check you over, are you injured in any way?" she asks, and I shake my head, unable to respond when Enzo scoffs from his spot on the sofa.

"What the fuck, V, what about me? I'm the one with a bullet hole in my gut," he grumbles, but she waves her hand at him dismissively like it's not that big of a deal.

"I can still hear you whining, fucker, so you must be okay," she retorts, turning a pointed stare in his direction, and she manages to make both Matteo and Vito grin.

The De Lucas are all crazy as fuck, and that's exactly why I feel like I belong here.

Despite the calmness in the room, I know I have to ask Valentina about everything I mentioned on the call before we left New York. Turning my attention back to her, I clear my throat. "Did you manage to get everything in order like I asked?"

She whips her head around with a smile as she nods eagerly. "I did, and I have to say, it was much more fun getting demands from you instead of my brother for a change."

Matteo rolls his eyes at his sister's comment, and I grin. "It was the politeness, wasn't it?" I reply with a chuckle as the house phone rings in the distance.

"I'll get it," Nonna hollers from the other room, and I take the moment to approach Enzo, wanting to be as close to my injured soldier as possible. I get two steps away from him before Vito grabs my waist and pulls me down into his lap.

I gasp as I fall into his hold, but when he wraps his arms around me, I sink further into him as Ethan checks over Enzo's bandages methodically.

Nonna clears her throat from the doorway, and we all look to her in question.

"That was Luna on the phone," she starts, glancing at Matteo before turning her full attention to me.

"And what did she say?" I ask, a hint of uncertainty washing over me as Nonna smiles.

"She asked me to tell you she's about twenty minutes out, they're trying every coffee shop on the way to find something called a caramel frappuccino because, and I quote, it's as hot as a bitch in heat right now." That definitely sounds like something Luna would say.

Relief washes over me. There's a chance this is all going to fall into place, there's a chance for vengeance. But one wrong move, and my whole house of cards will fall, and I refuse to let that happen. So I have to swallow my pride and do the one thing I never thought I would do, and that's ask for help.

But not just anyone's help.

Featherstone's help.

Luna's help.

It's with great reluctance, I admit I can't handle the situation on my own, but here we are. I'm willing to do whatever it takes to bring down the Russians to protect my guys.

REDEMPTION

THIRTY ONE

Wren

I slowly wake from the darkness, unsure when I even closed my eyes, when I feel the heat of someone pressed against my back, engulfing me in their arms as my chest rises and falls rhythmically. This is something I could definitely get used to.

Blinking open my eyes, I release a heavy breath, noting I'm in my room at the De Luca estate. I don't recall much after everyone left last night, but in my jet lag induced haze, I seem to have made it back to my room. Although, something tells me that the body pressed behind me had a hand in helping me.

When Luna arrived, I expected the boys to be with her, and all four of them were, Kai, Roman, Oscar, and Parker. Unexpectedly, Jess, West, Aiden, and Maverick were there too, along with Rafe and Bryce, Luna's fathers, making an appearance to help.

The meeting was brief and to the point, and not held in the main house. Matteo refused, but they nodded along with our plan and agreed to play their part. It's not for me, I'm aware of that, it's for Featherstone, for their greater good, but if it allows me to help the men consuming my body, mind, and soul, then I'll take it.

I blindly run my hands over the arms banded around my waist, and as I reach their wrists, I know instantly who it is. Only one De Luca has scarring like that.

Vito.

I nestle further into his hold as the reality of today washes over me and the sunlight begins to peek through the closed curtains in my room.

Today is the day we either triumph against the Russians or become another bug they've squashed beneath their feet.

Fuck.

No pressure then.

I'm not nervous about what I've set in motion, I never

am, but this is the first time that my plans will directly impact others around me. I want this to go right. I *need* this to go right, but more than anything, I feel like *this* is my redemption for the De Lucas.

Then I'm done with all of this.

I can't offer another fucking soul redemption, except myself.

For the bitch I was, for the things I put Luna through, shit, everyone at Featherstone through; I can't right every wrong. Especially the wrongs of my father.

A squeak falls from my mouth as the arms at my waist move quickly, allowing Vito to spin me so I'm facing him. My head is encased into the crook of his arm as I look up at him with tired eyes. His own are just as blotchy as he offers me a tired smile and squeezes me to his side.

"And you call me a loud thinker, Wren. You have me spinning, you're that deep in thought right now."

I roll my eyes at him as I trail my hand over his abs and chest, coming to a stop just before the scars that crisscross over his body. He let me touch them yesterday, or however many fucking hours ago it was, but that doesn't mean I get the same freedom again today.

I'm not sure whether he catches the hesitation in my

eyes, but in the next breath, he's wrapping his fingers around my wrist and placing my palms on the raised skin.

Neither of us speak a word as I slowly trail my fingers across his skin, idly caressing him as he strokes his fingertips up and down my spine.

It feels like heaven. Serenity has never been a luxury of mine, but lying here as if we don't have a care in the world, just the two of us basking in each other's presence... It's a gift.

Vito clears his throat after a while, making me tilt my head back once more to meet his deep brown eyes. "Imagine if this is how we could wake up every day? This sense of calmness and contentment, shared with another. I've never felt anything like it."

His words make my heart lurch in my chest, my throat clogging up as I fail to find the perfect words to agree with him. But when I finally get my damn tongue moving, all I can come up with feels dismal.

"That would be a dream."

"I hope that one day it's our reality."

Holy. Fucking. Shit.

What is it with these fucking De Lucas lately? Hitting me in the feels and leaving me speechless. I don't do speechless, not ever. Yet here I am, captured by him so completely that I have nothing to say.

The more I gape up at him, the wider Vito's grin gets. This fucker knows exactly what he's doing to me, and I'm soon glaring at him.

"I was going to say me too, but now you're pissing me off," I grumble, lacking any hint of true anger or irritation in my tone, and he knows it.

"Wren Dietrichson, the De Luca family is a force to be reckoned with. Every day, without question. We were raised to be resilient, unforgiving, and vengeful. Yet you manage to carry the same energy, leaving dead bodies in your wake all on your own. I don't know how you do it, survive everything life has thrown at you already, but I have to admit, I'm in awe of you."

My heart thunders in my chest as I lean up on my elbow, my eyes scanning his as I let the words wash over me. "You seem to bring out a better version of me," I admit, knowing very well that I was the biggest cunt that existed before I met them.

"No, you do that to yourself, *Bellissima*. Now you're no longer under your father's rule, you're paving your own path, and I'm fucking proud of you."

Hearing someone say they are proud of me is just as foreign as hearing I love you. Both knock me off my feet just the same.

Vito lifts his hand, stroking my hair behind my ear as he looks up at me lovingly.

Fucking. Lovingly.

I feel so damn soft in his hold, delicate in his palms, and angelic in his presence.

I don't want this feeling to ever end.

"You make my heart soar, just like when Enzo said he loved me yesterday. This feels like that," I murmur despite not wanting to actually share what's going on in my head, but it seems my heart has other ideas.

He doesn't flinch at the mention of Enzo saying those three magical words to me yesterday. Rather, he relaxes on the bed with a wider smile on his face.

"This is exactly like that, Wren."

I attempt to bottle the rest of my emotions up as I cup his cheek. There are no words to describe this whirlwind we're going through together, but it's a ride I'm not willing to get off.

Rolling further into him, I press my lips against his. When his palm rides up my spine beneath my tank top, goosebumps pebble on my skin as he holds me close to him.

"Get the fuck up. Now." The order comes from the door, tearing our mouths apart as we glare at the intrusion. Matteo has no cares as he stands in the doorway with his hands planted on his hips giving us a pointed stare. "I'm about to kill this asshole with my bare hands if you don't get out here and help me."

"Who?" Vito asks, his voice extra raspy, just how I like it.

"Who do you think?" Matteo bites back, dropping his hands from his hips before quickly lifting them to the lapels of his blazer, straightening himself up.

"You better not be in there talking about me." Enzo's voice drifts into the room, and understanding washes over my features as I glance down at Vito.

"Rain check?"

Vito smiles softly at my words, running his fingers through my hair as he nods in response. "As long as it means we get to do this again, *Bellissima*, I'm all in."

"I still can't believe you're leaving without me," Enzo

grumbles, folding his arms gently over his chest as he pouts. I don't even entertain an eye roll in his direction, he doesn't deserve it, not when we've been over this so many times already. We all get it, no one wants to be left here when shit's going down, but he nearly died. He's lucky we're not forcing him to stay in bed at this stage.

Vito sighs beside me, pinching the bridge of his nose as he tries to keep himself calm. "You're more of a hindrance than an aid in this state, Enzo. I can't keep repeating myself."

His words go unheard as Enzo continues to grumble. When he realizes no one is going to give in, he turns his attention to me. "Fine, if you're all going to be fuckers, then at least come and give me a kiss, Wren. Make me feel better."

I almost push for him to give me a please, but that would only delay the inevitable, and we really should have left five minutes ago. Running my hands down my black leggings, I take a step toward him, feeling his eyes rake over me as I go. With a black tank top and matching blazer completing my look, it makes my blonde hair stand out even more.

Valentina tried to get me to wear a pair of black designer

heels, but I nipped that in the bud and opted for combat boots instead. I know what I'm comfortable in when I need to be focused, and heels aren't an option.

Leaning forward, I brace my hands on either side of Enzo's head as I press my lips to his, deepening the kiss when his hands trail up the back of my thighs. I'm ready to ask for five more minutes when I feel hands at my waist, lifting me into the air without a grunt, before carrying me toward the door.

Vito is hovering by his brother, which tells me I'm in Matteo's hands. I can't say I'm against it.

"Say goodbye to Enzo, Wren," Matteo orders, bringing his palm down swiftly and sharply on my ass, making me yelp.

"Goodbye, Enzo."

"Bring my woman back in one piece," he hollers back in response as Matteo steps into the hallway before moving to the front door.

Despite my circumstances, I grin at the sound of him referring to me as his woman, and when Matteo finally places me on my feet, I can tell he senses it because he shakes his head, a hint of a smile on his lips too.

Turning on the spot, I find a dozen or so SUVs parked

and ready to go and when Matteo laces his fingers through mine, pulling me toward the blacked-out vehicle toward the left, I go with him willingly.

Each of them is filled with men dressed in black like us.

Respect comes in many ways, and the fact that we mourn those we loved and cared about by wearing black always baffles me. I don't know why, but my mind just can't comprehend that my clothing matches my somber mood and aching heart.

Matteo steps back, waving for me to climb in first, and he's right behind me before Vito appears at the door too. Once the three of us are secured, someone closes the door and the driver takes off, joining the convoy as we slowly make our way through the grounds.

I relax back into my seat, sitting opposite both the brothers who sit by each door with their guns in hand.

"Are you ready for this?" Matteo asks as we drive through the wrought-iron gates and head down the hillside.

"For a funeral? Sure," I reply, shrugging my shoulders. I probably sound disrespectful, but that's really not my intent. I just don't have a clue what I'm supposed to do at one.

"You know what I mean, Wren," he retorts with his eyebrows raised at me. Ah, he means the Russians. Fuck, I think I'm more worried about the damn funeral.

"I do, but questioning whether we're ready or not only gives the feeling of doubt the opportunity to slip into our minds, and I refuse to allow it." Confidence oozes from every word, the mantra I've said to myself so many times leaving my lips.

"You are something else entirely, you know that?" Matteo finally murmurs in response as he stretches his legs out in front of him, and I bite back the smile threatening to appear.

"I do now," I reply with a wink.

Silence usually comes with eggshells and fear, but I'm learning with them, it's one of the most comforting settings.

I watch the world go by, the afternoon sun casting the perfect light over the trees that line the roads, before we finally slow to a stop. My nerves kick in despite my attempts at taking a deep breath.

Matteo opens his door first, offering me his hand to join him, which I accept willingly before Vito follows after us. My hands are clammy, but if Matteo notices, he doesn't comment. Instead, he focuses on leading me toward the crowd that has already gathered around the six foot deep grave.

As the De Luca brothers approach, many nod their heads in respect, murmuring their thanks for coming, and ultimately step out of the way for them to stand as close to the front as possible.

My fingers tighten around Matteo's as I notice the dark mahogany coffin nestled in the dirt, and my heart clenches. I have no idea who Torres really was, but with the sobs coming from the women standing on the other side, and the memory of how hurt Enzo was, my heart aches all the same.

A man clears his throat, drawing everyone's attention to him before he begins the service. I half listen, half zone out, completely overwhelmed by the entire thing as the sobs get louder and sadness swirls in the air around us.

It's clear we're mourning a truly loved and respected fallen soldier today. A loss undeserving and far before his time, but it doesn't change the reality. Just like avenging him won't bring him back. Pain is a powerful feeling, and we're all tainted by it, just in different shapes and forms.

It's not until someone drops a rose on top of the coffin

that I pay full attention again as both Vito and Matteo join them. Watching them take a moment at the foot of the grave, I wish Enzo was here, saying goodbye to his friend, and I can only hope Matteo and Vito do him justice.

"Hey."

I turn at the whispered word to find Valentina beside me with a tight smile on her face. Wetting my lips, I make sure no one can hear us when I lean in closer to mumble in her ear.

"Is everything in place?"

"Yes."

I sag a little with relief, but only for the briefest of moments before I'm back to being on high alert. We came back to Italy in a rush for this funeral, a move that was both a risk and a statement all at once.

"Perfect," I reply, squeezing her hand as I sense someone approaching and stand tall once more.

"Valentina, thank you so much for being here." I turn to the lady speaking to see her wiping at the tears still trailing down her face. "And you too. Matteo said your name was Wren?" she clarifies, and I nod in response. "I'm Torres's mother."

The crinkle in her sad smile has me choking up as I

manage to find my tongue. "I'm so sorry for your loss." It doesn't mean enough, it doesn't make her pain go away, but she pats my hand before going to speak to other people in attendance.

"It seems the funeral was unscathed," Matteo states as he comes to a stop beside me, hands tucked into the pockets of his pants as he glances around the cemetery.

"Thank goodness." I pull my sunglasses from my blazer pocket, covering my eyes so I can focus on what is going on around us without people actually seeing where my eyes are aimed. But I needn't have bothered, because not even five seconds pass before the sound of an explosion can be heard in the far distance.

A few people around us squeal in surprise, but most of us don't react at all.

"Oh my gosh, what was that?" a woman shouts with a gasp, pointing in the distance toward the billowing smoke in the sky.

"That was right on time," I mutter so only Matteo, Vito, and Valentina can hear me.

"That sounds like we need to move. Now," Matteo states, swirling his hand in the air to signal his men to get back in the SUVs parked behind us.

"What was that, sir?" Gio asks, approaching the four of us, and I don't miss the way his eyes linger on Valentina for a split second longer than everyone else, but I opt to tuck that information away for later. That little tidbit isn't going to get us what we want right now. Not when the explosion is a beacon for our next move.

As I start moving toward the SUV, I don't miss Vito's response that sends a thrill of excitement down my spine.

"That was the sound of the Russians setting off explosives at the *wrong* funeral. Now let's move, revenge is waiting."

THIRTY TWO

Wren

Vito holds the door open for Valentina and I to climb in, but when I expect both him and Matteo to follow after us, I'm surprised by the door slamming shut and the pair of them climbing into the front of the SUV.

Matteo's foot hits the accelerator without a moment's pause, and seconds later, he's driving like a mad man toward the explosion. The smoke can still be seen in the sky, casting a gloom over the town, and with every inch closer we get, the more exhilarated I feel.

We are barely half a mile away from where the Russians believe Torres's funeral took place, but to Matteo, that's still too far as he continues at full speed toward the chaos. Weaving through traffic, gone is the man that laid his friend to rest, and in his place sits the man who earned the right to lead the De Luca mafia.

There's finally going to be an outlet for all of his rage; he just has to hold on for a few more minutes.

Needing a distraction until we get there, I quickly pull my cell phone from my pocket and hit the speed dial on Enzo's number. It barely rings once before his voice filters through the line.

"Hey, *Bella*."

"Did you see everything?" I ask, cutting straight to the chase as he hums through the line.

"Valentina made sure I saw it all and I said a prayer for my brother. Thank you for ensuring that happened, Wren, it means a lot to me, my family, and our men," he says.

"Don't thank me yet, Enzo. Not until the Russians are no longer an issue. Only then can we discuss how awesome I am," I try to lighten the mood in an effort to distract myself from the raw emotions he elicits within me.

"Come home to me, *Bella*," he murmurs before ending the call, and I quickly tuck my phone away as I turn my focus to the gun in my other pocket.

Matteo turns off the main road, cutting across a field as the explosion site nears. When he pulls the vehicle to a stop, it looks like pure chaos on the other side of the tree line before us, and without a hint of hesitation, we all leap from the SUV and run toward the carnage.

I take the safety off my gun as I hear the others do the same. Even Valentina is locked and loaded.

As we approach the flames, gunshots ring out from the other side, but my view's obstructed by the damn smoke. I wave my hand for the others to follow as I stick to the tree line, making my way around the edge of the cemetery, when a man steps out of nowhere with his gun aimed in my direction.

I clasp the bottom of my weapon, ready to take my shot in an instant, but before I even pull the trigger, I hear the sound of a bullet slicing through the air. My worry is short-lived as the man aiming his gun at me falls to the ground with a thump.

Glancing around, I can't truly sense where the bullet came from, but my gut tells me it was a sniper, and there's only one sniper known to be that good that I'm aware of.

"West."

Edging toward the dead man on the ground, I find the

bullet lodged perfectly between his eyes, and I know it's him. I silently thank him before glancing to Valentina, who is gaping at the lifeless body on the ground.

Fuck. Is she not familiar with this side of the business?

Before I can ask, Vito wraps his arm around her shoulder as he continues to move her along. "That shot was amazing as hell," she whispers in disbelief, before a bubble of manic laughter bursts from her lips, leaving me to be the one gaping at her.

Well, shit.

"Wren, over here." I follow the sound of a voice I'm familiar with, to find Luna sticking her head out from behind a mausoleum. Her brown hair is swept back off her face as she wears a similar outfit to me, dressed head to toe in black, but as I step closer, I notice the splattering of blood covering her.

"Is everyone okay?" I ask, concern getting the better of me as I quickly round the back of the mausoleum to find Jess, Kai, and Maverick there too.

Each of them is fully loaded with guns and ammunition, and likely a blade hiding in a place or two as well. Jess side-eyes me, which is less than I expect, but I don't let myself get hung up on it as I turn my attention back to

Luna.

"Everyone is okay. This is the remains of a Russian," she explains, waving her hand down her clothes, and I sigh in relief.

"Tell me where we're needed." Matteo comes to a stop beside me, barely keeping his gaze fixed on anyone as he continues to assess our surroundings.

"I could use you with me," Maverick explains, nodding for him to follow his path, and Matteo takes off without a backward glance, while Vito points at Kai.

"Show me where Dmitri is."

Kai doesn't respond right away, stepping toward Luna to press a kiss on her forehead, before finally waving for Vito to follow him.

If this was anyone else, you would assume the men are leaving the women here while they handle the situation. Only, the four of us aren't your usual women.

"Tell me where the other cunt is that we're aiming for." Valentina moves to stand beside Jess just as shots fly by us, and I quickly press my back into the stone of the mausoleum with my gun poised.

"Dmitri is hiding behind the caretaker's building, that's where Kai is taking Vito, and I think Maverick is likely leading Matteo toward Aleksi, Dmitri's brother. If we can bring those two down, the rest will crumble. But it's them that we need to get through since they have them spread out so wide," Luna explains, just before a loud grunt to our right captures our attention.

Roman fucking Rivera pounds his fists into the flesh of a guy again and again and again, until his weapon drops from his hand, leaving him even more vulnerable to the Featherstone trained assassin. Once he's sure the fucker is no longer breathing, he drops him to the floor like he's nothing before turning to glance at Luna.

"Let's go before she starts dry-humping him for being all manly and shit," Jess announces, eye rolling her friend as Luna scoffs in response.

"Please, I fucking wouldn't and you know it."

"Uh-huh, just like you wouldn't fuck him in the gym at Ace block," Jess retorts, making my eyes widen as I bite back a grin, watching as Luna gapes at her, but the fun and games are quickly interrupted by a bullet lodging into the stone right beside Valentina's head.

"We need to move. Now," I state, heading for the trees where the bullet must have come from.

Everything else drifts into the background as I catch a

flash of hair floating in the breeze from behind a tree, and I take aim. I keep moving one foot in front of the other, only slowing slightly now as I push all of my attention to the target.

Exhaling once more, I pause just as they spin back out from behind the tree with their gun pointed in my direction, but it's already too late. I pulled the trigger one thousandth of a second after I noticed a hint of movement on their end, and my bullet hits them square in the chest, bringing them to their knees before they ultimately fall flat on their face.

I roll my shoulders, spinning on the spot to hunt for any more targets, when I hear Jess call out my name. "Wren, watch out."

She's pointing over my shoulder, and I turn and duck just in time as the air whooshes above me from a bat swinging in the air.

Holy fuck.

"Don't you fucking dare," Valentina yells in an almost battle cry, before two bullets leave her chamber, and the splatter of the fucker's blood hits me across the face. My pulse rings in my ears as I smear the blood on my cheeks, turning to glance over my shoulder just as Valentina rushes toward me. "Are you okay?" she asks, lifting my chin up to inspect me.

"Who knew friends could be just as crazy as us," I mumble, watching as Luna glances toward Jess before turning back to me with a look of understanding taking over her face.

"We can't live with them, and we would *never* live without them."

No truer words have ever been said.

Turning my attention back to Valentina as she steps back, I reach out and squeeze her arm. "Thank you," I breathe, before cringing as I shove her to the side and shoot at a man ready to take aim from back beside the mausoleum.

"What the... Oh, I would say thanks, but you dirtied my cute pants," Valentina mutters as she rises to her feet, brushing the dirt off like I'm not standing here covered in blood in the middle of a goddamn shootout.

"Arghhh!"

The angry growl echoes around us, making the four of us pause as we all quickly exchange a look before running toward the sound.

This is really fucking happening. I'm working with them. On what seems to be the right side for a change?

Fuck knows, all I know is they're not getting all the blood on their hands today, not after what happened to my Enzo.

We slow our steps as we move from one mausoleum to another, hearing the same cry of anger as we press our backs to the final stone structure.

Glancing around the corner, I spot Matteo in the distance, and before I can think better of it, I start heading in his direction, my gut telling me to get closer to him. But the second I get to the other side of the mausoleum, I'm dragged sideways, knocked off balance and pinned against a chest. I almost sob when my gun drops from my hold at the exact same time I feel the metal end of another firearm press against my temple.

Motherfucker.

Everything moves in slow motion as Dmitri calls out Matteo's name.

"Come out, come out wherever you are, Matteo. I have something sweet that I believe belongs to you." I can hear the excitement in his tone, but I don't falter with the pistol aimed at my skull. Instead, I use the opportunity to take everything in around me.

Oscar is standing a few meters away, his gun aimed at Dmitri as he eyes the situation, while Parker and Roman pause the beatings they're laying onto the men at their feet. I haven't seen Rafe and Bryce yet, but I can only assume they're here somewhere.

Running my tongue over my bottom lip, I stay still in his hold as I pray that Matteo doesn't come out. I don't pray hard enough, because a moment later, he steps out from around the flames that continue to flicker in the middle of the fucking graveyard with his gun aimed in my direction.

"Ah, there you are. I show up here to offer my condolences and this is how you greet me?" Dmitri hisses, jabbing the gun harder into the side of my head, but I don't move an inch, not even blinking back the pain. Instead, I continue to focus on Matteo's every move.

"Fuck your condolences, Dmitri, and fuck you," Matteo bites, which only makes the crazed man behind me scoff in response.

"Lower your gun or I put a bullet in her skull right now."

I offer the subtlest shake to my head, watching as Matteo keeps his eyes trained on me, and in slow motion, he lets his gun hang loose on his finger, before dropping it to the floor.

Idiot.

He shouldn't have fucking done that.

"Where's Aleksi?" Dmitri shouts, making my ears ring with discomfort.

"I don't know, Dmitri. Now, let go of her," Matteo grunts, his jaw so tense it could cut through fucking steel at this stage.

"You lured us out here, you played your games, and now I want to know where my fucking brother is." Dmitri sounds more crazed with every word that passes his lips, and I know he's not going to ease off.

"Someone, take the shot," I shout, before Dmitri smacks the gun into the side of my head, making me hiss with the pain, but it doesn't change my mind. "Take. The. Shot," I repeat, hoping like hell someone who isn't a De Luca is willing to make that call, but before I can find out, I hear the raspy tone of Vito's voice in the distance.

"Did you say you wanted Aleksi?"

I follow the sound of his voice to find him walking side by side with Kai, who has a limp body tossed over his shoulder, while Vito seems to be carrying something in his hand. They're both smeared with blood, far more than I am, and as they draw nearer, I gape in utter surprise at what it is exactly that they're carrying.

They come to a stop beside Matteo and Kai drops the lifeless body to the ground with a thump, making my spine stiffen as I watch it clatter to the ground without a head.

There's no head, because it's hanging by the hair from Vito's hand.

"What have you done to my brother?" Dmitri yells, his body vibrating behind me as Vito shrugs.

"Let her fucking go before I do the same to you," he bites, wiping his hands in front of him, completely weaponless and defenseless, and I start to panic.

This crazy man can kill me, lay me dead in an instant. I'm not bothered, but like hell will he bring any more pain to another one of the men I'm obsessed with.

Never.

"No, *I'm* the fucking boss around here, I call the shots," Dmitri growls, jabbing the gun even harsher into my temple as I flex my hands at my sides. "You fuckers all better start listening to *me*," he continues, pulling the firearm from my head to wave it around at everyone, before quickly placing it on my skull again. "I was promised everything from Totem. E.V.E.R.Y.T.H.I.N.G. Just like Matteo was. I thought we could work together, but you deceived us, deceived me, and you all deserve the death bestowed on you today." He swings the gun around once more, and I immediately move into action.

Dropping my body to the ground, I purposely throw myself backward in the process, knocking him off his feet so he topples down with me. I can't see anything, and I can barely hear anything over the adrenaline rushing through my system, except for the sound of gunshots firing around me.

I pause in a state of panic as soon as my ass hits the ground, fearful of where the gunshots came from and where they were aimed, but as I let the outside world filter back in, I notice a hand being offered to me at my left.

Blinking, I see Jess with a tight smile on her lips, but despite the animosity between us, and rightfully so, I take her offering. She pulls me to my feet with more strength than I expect, to find both Luna and Valentina hovering over Dmitri, their guns aimed at him where two bullet holes now reside in his face.

Yup, I'm definitely covered in far too much blood.

"Is everyone else okay?" I ask, glancing around as the members of Featherstone slowly assemble.

"Fuck everyone else, *Stellina*, are you okay?" I hear Matteo before I see him, and he's lifting me off the ground before I can even answer, but I quickly spin in his arms so I can wrap my arms around his neck.

"I'm okay, but we're going to have to fucking talk about the fact that you disarmed yourself. You shouldn't have done that," I whisper in his ear, but he only holds me tighter.

"What the fuck was that, V?" Vito's voice has me leaning back to see him approach us with his finger pointed in his sister's direction. "You could have killed her," he adds, anger flashing in his eyes as I gape at him in surprise.

"But I didn't, so a thank you will suffice," she retorts, coming to stand beside me with her hand on my back in a silent show of support, and I can't help but grin at her.

She definitely *is* crazy as hell.

Matteo slowly places me on my feet, moving me just out of Valentina's reach as he grabs my chin and tilts my head back. "I have never been more scared in my entire life, *Stellina*, and I literally watched my brother almost bleed to death." I don't know what to say to that, but he doesn't give me a chance anyway as he inches closer until our noses are touching. "I fucking love you, Wren. I will disarm myself each and every time you're in harm's way, because let's face it, this won't be the last time. You're my vulnerability, and I don't give a fuck if that makes me predictable when it comes to your safety. None of that matters, not when I feel like this."

My breath is lodged in my throat, making it hard for me to breathe, let alone find the words to respond to a speech like that. It takes almost a dozen attempts at a deep breath before I finally manage to reply, but it's only four words. I can't muster any more than that.

"I love you too."

"Does that mean you're going to stay with us forever?" Vito asks from beside me.

"When did I ever say I was going anywhere?"

I can sense eyes on us, but I can't bring myself to care that we're having such a private conversation in front of everybody.

Vito's response doesn't come in the form of words, instead he crushes his lips to mine, knocking Matteo out of the way.

"Woohoo! Yes, brother, you get some," Valentina cheers, making me grin against his lips before he takes a step back, throwing a mocking glare in her direction.

As he moves out of my immediate space, I find Luna and her men hovering to my right, with Jess and her three guys with them. When my eyes fall to West, I can't stop myself from asking.

"Was that sniper shot from you?" I blindly point over my shoulder to the location I'm talking about, and he nods with a grin on his lips. One that I match with awe on my face. "That was an amazing fucking shot," I blurt, very aware that I'm being almost nice to these people, but it catches me off guard even more when he steps toward me with his palm raised in the air.

Without thinking, I slap mine to his as Aiden cheers. "High-five!"

My grin spreads at the ease that rolls through my body, but I falter when West grabs my right wrist before it falls back to my side. "I do believe that the greatest shot that was ever taken was done so with this hand."

I know what he's referring to instantly.

Totem.

My father.

The death that changed my life for the better.

I nod slightly in response, taking his praise before Luna comes to a stop beside him. "Thank you for this, for all of this, to all of you. I wouldn't have been able to pull it off without you."

She smiles at me and I feel like a different person standing before her. I'm not the same girl that I was when we met at Featherstone Academy, and I'm not even the same girl who arrived in New York to pay back my debt. I'm someone else entirely, and the way her eyes shimmer knowingly, she can see it too.

"Not a problem, it's the least we could do after everything else that has happened." She pushes a loose tendril of hair back off her face as she turns to look at Matteo. "What did Totem promise you?"

I follow her line of sight, as does everyone else present, waiting to hear his response. He looks between Luna and me for a few moments, before shrugging. "He promised a war I no longer have any interest in. I want none of my operations running on US soil, not one. Not when we have Wren. Nothing else matters. Our business is thriving here, even despite the setbacks from the Russians. If you stay out of Italy, I will do the same in return."

Vito nods in agreement beside him as I gape at the pair of them. Is it possible to give up something so easily? From the outside looking in? Maybe not, but after I spent my entire life following the plan my parents forced on me, only to shoot them and step away, I know the true answer.

Maybe we're designed for this world, but not every aspect of this world is for us.

Roman steps forward to murmur in Luna's ear, and I watch as she nods along at what he's saying, before clearing her throat.

"Every bloodline in the Featherstone hierarchy has a role to play, no exceptions, not even Wren," she starts as my heart rate increases.

"What the fuck does that mean?" Valentina interrupts, moving to stand at my side.

"The Ring believes that the right course of action is to end Totem's bloodline within the structure of our business, along with the Dietrichsons."

"I feel like we're talking in riddles. What does that mean?" Matteo grunts, edging closer toward me as relief falls from my shoulders in waves.

"Without being able to think of a better word right now, it means I'm banished from Featherstone," I state, looking at the other members of the Ring standing behind Roman and Luna, who nod.

I feel like I could drop to my knees and cry, my eyes welling despite my efforts to contain my emotions, but she just gave me Easter, Christmas, and Thanksgiving all at once.

"You deserve this, Wren. What you have here, it's untainted, undeniable, and unbelievably possible. It's a fresh start. Rafe asked me to tell you that if you ever need anything at all, you could reach out to him for aid from my father's security company. That way, you'll still be separate from Featherstone no matter what," Luna murmurs, digging her hand into a pocket and revealing a card a moment later. "He said to ask for Ryan." She smiles one last time, before turning in Roman's arms and walking off with the rest of the Featherstone members. I hear orders being called for cleanups around me, but I can't really piece anything together.

I fall to the ground in a heap and a small sob slips past my lips. I barely stay there for a second or two before I'm lifted into Vito's arms. Looking up into his eyes, I speak the words that warm my soul and set me free from my past.

"Take me home."

EPILOGUE

Wren

The sun beams down on me as I sit in the garden, a platter of food scattered around the table, all thanks to Nonna, as both her and Valentina continue to gang up on me.

"I'm telling you, a girly weekend at the spa with a trip or two to the vineyard is exactly what dreams are made of, Wren. Why aren't you getting that?" Valentina asks with a gasp, running her hands down her stunning yellow flowy dress before reaching for her glass of wine for emphasis.

Rolling my eyes, I shake my head at them as they both offer me a pointed look. "I just don't know if I can be away from them for that long. Besides, they've given me Torres's role to fill, and those are some big fucking boots. The De Luca family business hires crazy men that are a complete handful." My eyes widen as I point over my shoulder toward the operative building, but Nonna and Valentina still don't give in.

"Puh-lease, girl, you *know* we fucking deserve it. You definitely can survive without them for like two days."

I really don't think I can. I'm as obsessed with them as they are with me. This isn't what any of us expected to happen, but here we are. Learning this life together, learning our emotions and how to express them, but most of all, learning what makes each other happy.

"She definitely can't."

The blunt response has me glancing over my shoulder to find the De Luca brothers heading toward us. Matteo is in his shirt and pants, no blazer in sight, while Vito is in a pair of black shorts and a matching tee with sweat beading along his brow from working out in the gym. But it's Enzo who has my attention, and the pleased smile on his face tells me he knows it.

He's not wearing a top at all, but even better, there's no bandage.

"Oh my god, this is brilliant. Finally, some progress," I murmur as I rise to my feet, moving toward him, and he pins me to his chest despite still being injured as I hug him.

"No, *Bella*, the progress is for later since Ethan confirmed I'm finally ready for some extracurricular activity." No clarification is needed of course with the way he wiggles his eyebrows at me.

"You did not just say that," Valentina gasps from her seat at the table, making even Nonna chuckle as Ethan steps out of the house.

"Sadly, he did. He even asked about specific thrusting positions too. I'd like to say you're in for a good time, Wren, but…" He trails off as he nods to my crazy De Luca lover, who has zero inhibitions.

Everyone laughs at his antics, until Ethan clears his throat and steps closer to me as he lowers his voice. "Enzo is discharged from me now, but I wanted to talk to you before I left, Wren. Do you have a minute to go inside?"

I'm already shaking my head as Matteo answers for me. "No. I like you, Ethan, but just… no."

I roll my eyes at his choice of words as I take my seat at the table once more. "You can say it here, Ethan, it doesn't make a difference."

He rubs the back of his neck nervously, before taking a deep breath and exhaling slowly. "Okay, well, since the last time I saw you, something was playing on my mind, something completely crazy, and I hope you don't mind, but I did some digging into your history…"

I frown in confusion, attempting to assess him for whatever information he has, but I come up blank.

"My history?"

"Yeah." He shuffles from foot to foot, and Nonna sighs.

"Just spit it out," she grumbles, folding her arms over her chest as she purses her lips.

"When you told me about what Totem did to you, to stop…" I understand what he means, so I help him along, hoping to get to the point sooner rather than later.

"To stop me from being able to carry children."

"Yeah, it just struck me as odd. A man of his mindset, as deranged as it was, he seemed like the type who would want to continue his bloodline, but he stopped that with you."

My gut clenches at his words as I mull over. Where the hell is he fucking going with this?

"What's the point of all this?" Valentina asks, getting to the question before I can.

Ethan rubs a hand through his hair before rolling his shoulders back and staring me down. "It means two things. I found a lab in Arizona that is showing records of having some of your eggs frozen there."

"Holy fuck," I blurt, completely stunned to silence. "How the fuck did you find that out? Are you sure?"

"My main bloodline at Featherstone was medicine, but my second was tech," he explains, almost looking sheepish as Vito clears his throat.

"And thing number two?"

Ethan nods, almost to himself for a second, like he's trying to build up the courage to speak, and in the next moment, he's simply blurting it out like he's describing the weather.

"You have a brother… well, half brother, a bastard in Totem's eyes. Which I can only assume is the reason why he's never been brought into the Featherstone fold. Well, that, and the fact that his mother is of no descending bloodline and Totem isn't registered as his father…"

The world stands still as I test the foreign words on my tongue. "I have a brother?"

Ethan crouches beside me, a hint of worry flashing in his eyes as he keeps his tone as relaxed as possible. "Yes, his name is Axel and he's part of a motorcycle gang. Running in an area of the States that is completely untouched by Featherstone."

This just keeps getting crazier and crazier. One minute, I'm out here trying to explain why I don't want to be without my De Luca men, and the next, I'm learning I could have biological children, while also having a biological half brother.

Fuck me sideways, I wasn't prepared for this.

"What motorcycle gang?" I ask, as if I'm even going to know who they are, but shit, my mind wants that information, and I can't help myself.

"The Ruthless Brothers MC."

REDEMPTION

AFTERWORDS

Oh my goddddddddd! Sorry, I still need to say it again…

OH. MY. GODDDDDDDD.

Taking another trip into the world of Featherstone sets my soul on fire!

I love it too damn much.

I knew when I was drawing close to the end of Our Bloodline that Wren's story was evolving around me. I got to the scene where Totem was finally brought down and my fingers carried themselves, the story morphing into something new. I hadn't decided at that time who was going to be the one to take the shot, the outline for the chapter just said 'kill Totem' and I get the feeling that's because Wren knew it was going to be her.

I love getting to delve into the action again, getting to taste the hunger for blood so naturally, all while finding her a forever home.

Ethan was a surprise, that came completely out of nowhere, but Valentina - hell, that's all Jeni's fault haha. My alpha readers have been pleading for her to get a story, and maybe one day she will, just like Trudy, but the next steps are leading us to one place, and one place only.

THE RUTHLESS BROTHERS SERIES

Yup, At this very second, Axel is a plotted guy, along with a few others, for our new FMC in my next series. I'm not sure Wren or anyone else from the Featherstone Academy Series will make an appearance yet, I didn't decide it was her brother until about two minutes haha but never say never. Hell, none of my series were supposed to connect and yet here we are.

I can't wait to spend the year diving into the MC world that Axel belongs in.

Thank you as always for being a part of this journey with me.

You rock!

THANK YOU

Michael. Mike. Mick. Miguel. Thank you for always making me smile even when I overwhelm myself with my workload. You make it all worthwhile, and I appreciate every single thing you do for us.

My sweet children. You make my heart grow every single day. How you love and support each other as well as me and my achievements will never cease to amaze me. I love you infinity war.

Thank you to my Queen Bee's; Tanya, Nicole, and Jen. Thank you for Nonna, Thank you for Valentina, and thank you for dealing with me on the daily haha You're all superstars and I appreciate you being here with me every step of the way!

A million thank yous to my beta's; Michelle, Monica, Brianna, Kaz, Keira, Lorna, and Kerrie! Reading your comments in the group chat and in the documents gives me life! You are all total queens, and I appreciate you all dearly. Thank you.

Kirsty. Fam. Mate. You are the coolest fucking cheerleader in cxistance. I don't think I would survive without baby updates and venting with you. Thank you for being you and rocking at this life shit.

Laura, every. Damn. time. You waltz in here with those cover skills and S.L.A.Y me! Thank you for always being a star!

Cassie, thank you for working that *magic* magic you've got! I truly appreciate it.

Sloane and Sarah, imagine if you didn't help me with my shit? There would be no shit for anyone to read, haha! Thank you angel faces!

And finally, a thank you to Zainab, the newest crazy lady to join the gang! You're awesome!

ABOUT KC KEAN

KC Kean is the sassy half of a match made in heaven. Mummy to two beautiful children, Pokemon Master and Apex Legend world saving gamer.

Starting her adventure in the RH romance world after falling in love with it as a reader, who knows where this crazy train is heading. As long as there is plenty of steam she'll be there.

ALSO BY KC KEAN

Featherstone Academy

(Reverse Harem Contemporary Romance)

My Bloodline

Your Bloodline

Our Bloodline

Red

Freedom

Redemption

All-Star Series

(Reverse Harem Contemporary Romance)

Toxic Creek

Tainted Creek

Twisted Creek

(Standalone MF)

Burn to Ash

Emerson U Series

(Reverse Harem Contemporary Romance)

Watch Me Fall

Watch Me Rise

Watch Me Reign

Saints Academy

(Reverse Harem Paranormal Romance)

Reckless Souls

Damaged Souls

Vicious Souls

Fearless Souls

Heartless Souls

Printed in Great Britain
by Amazon